Rebellion

Book 3 in the Conquest Series

By

Griff Hosker

Rebellion

Published by Griff Hosker 2024

A CIP catalogue record for this title is available from the British Library.

Contents

Real people used in the novel

Duke William, The Bastard, Duke of Normandy and King of England
Richard Curthose - the son of William
Robert - the son of William
William Rufus - the third son of William
Henry - the son of William
Bishop Odo of Bayeux - King William's half-brother and Earl of Kent
Thomas of Bayeux - Archbishop of York
William de Warenne - Earl of Surrey
Agatha, widow of Edward the Confessor's nephew, Edward the Exile
Edgar Ætheling - heir to the English crown via Edward the Confessor
Margaret - Edgar's sister and future Queen of Scotland (St Margaret)
Cristina - Edgar's sister
Hereward the Wake (watchful) - an Anglo-Saxon noble and English rebel
King Sweyn of Denmark
Morcar - Earl of Northumbria
Eadwine - the Earl of Mercia, the elder brother of Morcar
Alain Le Roux - Lord of Richmond
Gospatric - Earl of Northumbria
Waltheof - cousin of Gospatric and Earl of Northampton and later Earl of Northumbria
Walcher - Bishop of Durham
Ivo de Vesci - a knight

Gilbert Tyson - Lord of Alnwick and former standard bearer of King William
King Malcolm Canmore - King of Scotland

Prologue

I am Sir Richard fitz Malet of Eisicewalt. The first rebellion in the north was over. The uprising against King William had been savagely put down. The peace that followed, however, had come at a price for many thousands were still dying, not directly as a result of war but because their animals had been slaughtered and their crops destroyed. They starved and they died. We were south of the devastated land and close to York but we still found refugees who fled south to find food and safety. The Danes had been defeated and had failed to take York but there were still bands of brigands who preyed upon the survivors.

The wounds I had suffered in the retaking of the land and the siege of Caestre had healed but I still felt them. I was often stiff and my joints ached when it rained. It was easier for me to ride than to walk. Since my return from Caestre I had been busy with my manor at Eisicewalt. I had been given property on the Tees at Norton which I had yet to visit. There were not enough hours in the day for me to do all that I wanted to. King William expected much from his lords of the manor and I had two. I had done well at Eisicewalt and made it, I believed, a happy place and a safe one but I knew I had to do more. The attack at York had been costly and constant vigilance was essential.

The manor had changed completely from the one I had inherited. Then it had been a run-down hunting lodge. It had been long abandoned to nature and bandits. I think I had been given it because it was so, apparently, worthless. I had not seen that and I had worked both with and for the people. Now there was a priest, a smithy and the farms were prosperous. People moved to the village because it was safe. We even had a fishpond. The derelict houses had been replaced with new dwellings and the village had an ordered, neat look. I was pleased, for being half English and half Norman meant I was the future of this land and what I did was a reflection on the England that would grow from our labours. King William was still Norman but he had chosen to make his home not in Normandy but in England. I was his man and I would fight for the king to make England safe.

Moray
Scone
Abernethy
Din Eidyn
Berwick
Alnwick
Otterburn
Hexham
Durham
Norton
Brougham
Persebrig
Eisicewalt
York
N
30 Miles
Peterborough
Ely
Fens
Lundenwic

Chapter 1

Ely

I now had a steward, Egbert. He had been one of the many refugees who had fled from York and along with an old man, Walter of Bootham, they ran my household. Walter had been in York when the Danes had burned the Minster and slaughtered so many. I know that Egbert could have done the job alone but I wanted the old man to end his days feeling useful. It meant Benthe could concentrate on cooking and keeping the manor clean. The management of food and the needs of a lord of the manor were too much for her. It was Egbert who told me that a visitor had arrived.

The messenger who came from the king was unknown to me, but the letter he brought had the king's seal upon it and I opened it immediately. The missive told me that I was needed once more. The summons was not for the men of my manor but specifically for me. That meant I could leave Bergil, my man at arms, to watch over my manor while I was on the king's business. I would take just three men. While Benthe, who looked after the house for me, attended to the messenger, I spoke with Bergil, Edward, Aethelstan and Alfred. It would be my squire and two pueros who would accompany me to dampen these sparks of rebellion.

"The king needs me in Ely. The Danes, it seems, have stirred up trouble there. A Saxon noble called Hereward has rebelled against the king."

Edward frowned, “Sir Richard, you almost died at Caestre. Surely the king has others who can fight for him. Ely is many leagues from here.”

I smiled, “I think that it is because I almost died at Caestre that the king needs me. I did not succumb to my wounds and the king believes that if a man survives such a test then it makes him stronger. I know you are recently married, Edward, but I would take you as well as Aethelstan and Alfred.”

Bergil said, “Not me, My Lord?”

“I do not think that the north is yet at peace. Agatha, widow of Edward the Confessor's nephew Edward the Exile, and her children, Edgar Ætheling and his sisters Margaret and Cristina, are all living at the court of King Malcolm. I fear that they may cause mischief in the north. We have done much to make our home safe and secure. It would be foolish to take all the men. The three I take will be sufficient.” I looked at Edward, “If you do not wish to come I would understand. The two pueros will suffice.”

Edward looked outraged, “My Lord, I swore an oath to you and while my brother Edgar was foresworn and fled, I have always tried to make up for his flight. Mathilde will understand. She married a warrior and I have told her my tale. She knows that but for you I might be dead. Whatever life I lead is because of you.”

I smiled, “Then all is well. We three shall represent my manor in the land of the East Angles.”

That night we learned from Henry the messenger from the king, that King Sweyn, having been thwarted in the north, had switched his support to the men of East Anglia. Another of King William’s enemies, Morcar, Earl of Northumbria had also joined him. The men who had fought and lost at Senlac Hill would now be seeking help from any who might rid the land of King William. I had English blood but I wondered if any of these rebels had thought things through. King Malcolm and King Sweyn would not simply help the rebels out of the goodness of their heart. They would want something, either a piece or all of England.

"Who is this Hereward?" I had not heard of him before.

Henry was a Norman and like many men from Normandy had a low opinion of Saxons. His tone confirmed it, "He was a lesser noble under the rule of the Confessor. He was outlawed by King Edward and he fled this land to take service with Count Baldwin of Flanders. He returned thinking to reclaim his lands when King William conquered it but his brother was a rebel and was killed. His lands were taken. He took matters into his own hands. He and his men killed fifteen of our men before fleeing to the Fens. Now that he has the backing of the Danes and the Northumbrians he is more of a threat. The king has summoned all the best of his knights to snuff out this second rebellion."

"And what of Morcar's brother Eadwine, the Earl of Mercia?"

Henry shrugged, "He disappeared. The king has men looking for him. It is believed that he might be trying to get to Scotland where the Ætheling seeks to ferment discord against us. The treacherous earl is still a rebel."

I was interested in the man sent by the king for he was not a knight and yet he wore mail, “And you, Henry, what is your story?”

He sighed, “My family lost their lands in Normandy thanks to my father’s ill-advised support for the Count of Brittany. My other brothers joined the Hautevilles in Italy. Queen Matilda took me under her wing for she knew my mother and it was she persuaded the king to let me serve him. I hope to impress him when fighting these rebels.”

I shook my head, “The road to glory is one that has many risks, Henry.”

“But I have heard that you are renowned for your courage and that you regularly take risks. You were trained by Taillefer were you not? Did I not hear that you and another knight were instrumental in the taking of Caestre? The two of you held the breach and the castle was taken.”

I nodded, “I did not hold the breach for glory. It was to help a shield brother.”

“I would be one such as you.”

“I have been lucky and I well know it.”

That night I did not sleep well. It was not the thought of service in the land of the East Angles but the worrying thought that others might see a hero in me and try to copy me. I was not a hero. I fought well because I had been trained by the best but if I never had to draw sword then I would be a happy man.

I left Parsifal with Aedgar and rode my new horse Scout. Alain, the horse master from Caux had given the stallion to me on my final visit to the place of my birth. Geoffrey would be taken as a spare. Aethelstan and Alfred led the two sumpters with our mail and weapons. Both my pueros had mail hauberks. We had taken them from Danes and they were a little too short to afford good protection. Real warriors did not care if they were wearing the right kind of mail just so long as they were protected and the hauberks, while they did not have a hood were functional. Both pueros had coifs and helmets we had taken from the enemies we had slain. Henry insisted upon wearing his Norman mail. He said it was a gift from the queen. I could not dissuade him from burdening his horse in this manner. I knew that the leather jacks we wore would be ample protection from any dangers on the road and would not tire our horses as much. The land south of York was now firmly in Norman hands. The worst we might encounter would be brigands in the forests around Ledecestre and Snotingham. We also took spare blankets. I could not guarantee that we would have beds each night although Henry had said the royal warrant he had shown allowed him to stay in monasteries and castles.

We rode south and skirted York. Had we passed through that city, busy in the middle of rebuilding, it would have added many hours to our journey. I wished to get to Ely sooner rather than later so that I could return to my home equally as fast. I was a knight but I still felt like a pueros. I had been brought up grudgingly in Normandy and it took the Battle of Senlac Hill for me to win the approval of my family. I think, as we rode south, that Henry was surprised at the closeness of me and my men. There was easy banter between us all. It had been the same with Odo and Bruno when we had been pueros. I know that it made us closer in battle. When Bruno and I had thought our end had come it was the arrival of my squire and pueros that saved us. They put their lives at risk when many knights faltered. Bonds made in blood and battle were the strongest ones. Those bonds tied us closer than blood.

It took five days to reach Oakham where the knights sent for by the king were gathering. King William was not there but William de Warenne, the Earl of Surrey was. I knew the knight well. He liked me and had been one of the few senior nobles who had shown me any kindness. It was he who had sent Henry for me. The castle at Oakham was a simple wooden motte and bailey structure. The hall was not large enough for the knights to use and so we ate and camped in the outer bailey. William de Warenne was a warrior and did not mind the discomfort. Before we dined I walked with the knight.

"This Hereward is a rebel, Richard. Worse, he is a murderer. He killed my brother-in-law Frederick." I now understood why William de Warenne was leading the assault on the rebels. He had a personal stake in it. He hesitated, "And your family has also suffered at the hands of the Danes. Your stepbrother died; did you know?"

I shook my head. No one had bothered to tell me. I knew that the loss of York had affected him badly. Perhaps his health had suffered as a result.

"I am sorry to be the bearer of such news. William was a good friend of mine. His son Robert now has the Honour of Eye."

"Is he here?"

"No, he returned to Normandy to settle his affairs in Caux. Like you and me he has chosen this land as his home. However, before we can make it our home we must rid it of Danes and rebels."

"And is King Sweyn here?"

He laughed, "What do you think? The Dane wants the crown but he sends his relatives to take it. My understanding is that he is doing what Vikings have done many times in the past. He is sending his men to rob and steal. If he can gain the crown while he makes himself richer then that is all to the good. You know that his men and this Hereward robbed Peterborough Cathedral?"

I was shocked, "The Danes robbing a church I can understand, but a Saxon and a Christian!"

"That shows you the character of the man. He desecrated the church and his soul will be in peril. We still expect more knights but within three days I intend to head to Ely where he has fortified the island and we will end his reign of terror once and for all." He paused and leaned in, "The king needs this to be over for he has heard rumours that the Scots, led by King Malcolm Canmore, intend to try to take Cumberland, Westmoreland and Northumbria. He wants the Danes gone and Morcar in chains."

"And Hereward?"

"I want him dead!" The venom in his voice told me that this was personal.

There were many new knights at the muster. These were men who had not been at Senlac or at the destruction of the northern rebels. Normandy was a little more secure and the prospect of manors and land in a newly conquered England appealed. I was still viewed as a strange beast, half Norman and half Saxon but thanks to William de Warenne my martial exploits were mentioned first and so I was accepted. Henry had been a pleasant companion on the road south but it was easier with just the four of us and, when we left for the boggy, stream riven land of the Fens it felt good to be riding together. Edward was keen to speak, now that Henry was not with us, of his plans for a family. He wanted many children and he was determined to be a good father. I asked him if he wished for spurs. While I could not knight him I had enough influence with the king to hope he would accede to a request.

Edward shook his head, "I come from common stock, My Lord. I am content to be your squire and when Bergil can no longer serve I would be your captain of the guard." He gestured behind him with his thumb, "One of these would make a good squire when you tire of me and I think they yearn for spurs."

I looked behind me at the brothers. Edward knew them better than I did and he was probably right. The granting of knighthood was a double-edged sword. It brought land but also responsibilities. The king could make demands but so could a liege lord and I was a lowly knight whose only title was Lord of Eisicewalt and Norton.

We camped just outside the land controlled by Hereward and the Danes. We had local men who reported a few Northumbrians amongst the raiders. They said that the most dangerous of the men we faced were the Danes. The boggy land suited men who liked to fight either on foot or water. Our horses would not be of much use here. For that reason, I decided to ride Geoffrey. Scout was too good a horse to risk. His strength lay in his size and his speed.

The terrain meant we had to pick our way towards Ely and the enemy knew that we were coming for we could not use the speed of our horses. They chose a piece of ground to stop us where they had a solid lump of earth upon which to stand, while we had to use low lying, boggy and stream riven land to reach them. I liked William de Warenne but his hatred for Hereward blinded him that day and he had us all mounted. He ordered us forward in a long line of horsemen except that it was not a solid line. There were gaps. It meant that horsemen could be surrounded and picked off by the Danes and Fen men. They were able to hide close to the water and in the reeds. Unwary horsemen could be picked off. The enemy had spears and axes as well as many archers.

Even as William de Warenne ordered us forward an archer, I later learned it was Hereward himself, loosed an arrow and it struck William de Warenne's horse. Our leader was thrown to the ground and his valuable war horse killed. The nature of the land meant it was a softer fall than he could have hoped but he lay there winded as the enemy, heartened by his fall, cheered and jeered. The death of his horse added to his hatred and to his blindness.

William stood and drew his sword. He roared angrily, "Dismount, we fight on foot!" Taillefer had taught me that it was better to fight cold than hot.

I dismounted. "Alfred, remain here with the horses." He looked disappointed and I said, "Next time your brother can be the horse holder and believe me there will be a next time." I knew that this day would not end well.

I drew my sword and led my two men to join what looked like a line of beaters heading for a hunt. Our long shields were perfect when riding but used on the ground they were cumbersome. The guige strap was of no use and a man had to hold his shield higher and at a slight angle. Edward and Aethelstan had smaller shields. I realised I should have used Alfred's. Other knights were having the same trouble. We had to watch the ground and make sure that the tip of the shield did not snare on the ground. The enemy arrows ensured that we needed shields. Arrows fell from the sky and we lifted our shields for protection. I heard curses as knights and men at arms found their feet sucked into the mud.

We three were luckier than many and managed to find slightly firmer ground. As we began to ascend the small mound it became easier and I said, "You two, behind me."

"Aye, My Lord."

William de Warenne was just twenty feet to my left and there were knights between us. These were his household knights and the enemy would soon find out that they faced good warriors. We were the tip of our attack. The arrows stopped as we neared their line. They had made a Danish shield wall. Their round shields were locked. Normally these would be hard to break but they had Fen men with them and they were not used to such a formation. In addition, the shields of the Fen men were smaller than those used by the Danes. I headed for one such man. He stood between two other rebels and then there were two Danes on either side of the three. Being in the front rank they held spears.

I paused beyond the range of the spear. I hoped he would panic and throw it but none of them did so. If they thought I was afraid, they were wrong. I was using what Taillefer had said was a warrior's greatest weapon, his mind. I saw that the man I had chosen to fight had his left leg forward. The Danes used their right. It was a small thing but it meant he might be a little more unbalanced as he was out of line. I took a step and his spear darted out. I angled my shield and the head slid along it. I chopped down at the haft of the spear and a large sliver of wood was carved from it. I had Edward and Aethelstan's shields protecting my side and when his two comrades in arms thrust their spears at me they did no harm. The man with the damaged spear pulled it back for another strike and this time, as I stepped forward, I put my shoulder behind my shield and held it squarely. The spear hit my shield and the damage I had wrought with my sword, wrecked his strike. The spear broke. As I punched with my shield his stance unbalanced him and he began to fall. I slashed, not at him but the man to his left. That man tried to block my blow with his spear but could not manage to turn the head in time and my blade bit into his unprotected right arm. Aethelstan's sword lunged at the Dane to the Fen man's left and managed to draw blood. With his two defenders gone and lying at my feet the man was easier to strike. I slid my sword into his throat.

When the three of us stepped into the gap we had created there was a buckle in the shield wall. A shield wall that had no integrity could be more easily broken. Other knights had done as I had done and once the solid line of the shield wall was gone then our skill and armour gave us an advantage, especially over the ones who had no armour. Some of the Danes we faced wore mail but the East Anglians did not. Even Hereward wore just a leather jack. I raised my sword and struck down at the Dane to my left. His shield was facing Edward and my blade hit his helmet. It dented and cracked. The head protector worn beneath it did little to save the man who fell to the ground.

William de Warenne sensed victory and shouted, "On, we have them!"

Had we been mounted we might, indeed, have been able to end the rebellion but we were on foot and in a land we did not know. The enemy, realising that they had failed to hold us just fled into the Fens. They disappeared like the mist and fog that hangs around such places. Some Danes stood and fought to the end. That fighting spirit was in their blood but the rebels did not relish fighting knights and they ran. When one of William de Warenne's men fell into a deep stream and had to be pulled out by his comrades the chase ended. We had the hillock and we had slain many Danes but it was not conclusive. By the time we had ensured that none remained alive and taken the mail and the arms from the dead, it was almost dark and we returned to our horses where we camped.

There was a despondent air at the camp. William de Warenne was particularly annoyed that he had lost a good warhorse. It was a lesson learned. I sat with him and his household knights. One of them was a young knight called Belsar. He was more optimistic than the rest. "Surely, My Lord, there must be a way to avoid these bogs. Let us be positive, My Lord. These men despoiled a cathedral. God will surely punish them."

"I am open to suggestions, Belsar."

"We could make bridges from wood." We all looked around. The words were spoken by Guy de Mortain. He said, "I fought in Flanders where the land is the same. There they made bridges from wood. They carried them as faggots and when there was a watery obstacle, they used the bridges to cross the water. That way we can use our horses."

It was the best suggestion that anyone had and we spent two days building small portable bridges made of bundles of wood, faggots. We knew where the island of Ely lay but finding a way to it was harder. It was not as though there was a river we could follow. There appeared to be no current in the streams and we could not tell which way the water flowed. Reeds grew high and hid the land ahead. It took days for us to move just one mile. I was filthy and the journey was doing my mail no good. It was the second night of our advance that I noticed Belsar was not with us. Had he deserted? If so I was disappointed. I had liked his enthusiasm.

The next day we resumed our advance. William de Warenne was no shirker and he worked as hard as we did. When we saw Belsar approach with a priest he frowned. "Is this your suggestion, Belsar? Bring us a priest to give us comfort."

"No, My Lord. I sought inspiration from God and it came to me that there might be priests who were unhappy that Hereward and the Danes had despoiled Peterborough Cathedral. I found one such priest and he knows of a secret causeway that leads to the stronghold."

William de Warenne's face lit up and he beamed, "Is this true, Priest? Is there a secret way?"

"It is not a secret to the men who live in this land, My Lord. It is the way we travel but you are all strangers. I can lead you and then the treasure of the church can be returned." The man was English and I could tell that he was torn. He might not have liked the Norman conquerors but he did not like men who stole from a cathedral either.

It was one thing to know the way but the attack needed to be planned. It was decided to make the attack at night. There were good reasons for this. They would feel secure in the night and we could approach unseen. It meant an attack on foot but that could not be helped. This time I took Aethelstan's shield for he watched the horses. Belsar and the priest led the way followed by William de Warenne and his knights. I followed with Edward and Alfred.

It was as though God wished us to succeed for it was a foggy night. Had we not been led by a sure-footed priest who unerringly led the way across the causeway then men would have perished in the bogs and streams that lay on both sides of us. The path was not a direct one but twisted and turned, climbed and fell but it was a dry path. We just followed, in double file, the man before us. Sounds were deadened by the fog. We had no way of knowing where Ely lay until the column stopped. The knight before me turned and whispered, "Tell the men to spread out, pass it on."

I turned and spoke to the knight behind me. The whisper slipped and slid down the line. It sounded like the hissing of a nest of serpents. I looked at the ground as I moved to my right. I was comforted that we appeared to be on solid ground. It was more like the hillock where we had first fought Hereward and the Danes. This time Alfred and Edward flanked me. We stood and waited as men filtered to our right and then filled the space behind us. There was no horn to signal the advance. William de Warenne moved and the men on either side followed. It made us into an arrow with our leader and Belsar at the fore.

I saw the wooden palisade ahead. It did not look particularly formidable. I suppose they relied on the Fens themselves to be their best protection. William de Warenne had brought men at arms with axes and when the axes began to hack at the gates then the enemy knew they were under attack. The one weakness, as I saw it, to our attack, was that there had to be more than one gate. Even as we burst through the main gates and began to slay the guards defending it the enemy were fleeing. We had caught them unawares and it was a slaughter for men were not mailed. Resistance was weak. By the time dawn broke Ely was ours and all opposition was over. The priest was disappointed. The treasure had gone and as we only found the bodies of forty Danes we had to assume that the rest had fled taking the treasure with them. Hereward and some of his oathsworn also escaped and the only tangible evidence of victory was Earl Morcar. We took him.

Two days later we learned that the Danes had returned to Denmark. Their king had failed to secure the crown but his men had taken treasure and to a Viking that was a victory in itself. William de Warenne summoned me to his side, "I must stay here and find this rebel but the king wants Earl Morcar taken to him. He has broken his oath twice now.

There will be punishment. The king is in York. I will give you ten men at arms as an escort. Return the earl to King William and then your service is done."

"Thank you, My Lord." I was relieved. The campaign had not been satisfying as we had failed to catch Hereward and the Danes had escaped with the treasure of Peterborough Cathedral. I had a bad taste in my mouth.

As we rode north I kept the earl next to me. He had surrendered and as we spoke on the way north he was confident that he would be able to persuade the king that he had learned the error of his ways. I did not trust him. I had known him and his elder brother since the time of the Confessor. He would say anything to survive. "And where is your brother, Eadwine?"

He looked shifty as he answered, "I know not. We parted many months ago."

"The king will wish to know." Again, he looked uncomfortable. "If you wish the king to be merciful then you need to be honest with him. You will have to betray your brother or…" I let my words hang and the earl knew what I meant.

It took less than five days to reach York. The king was already there for he had anticipated that the Scots would try to take advantage of the unhappiness in the north. I was there when he interviewed the earl.

He dropped to his knees before the king, "King William, I beg you for mercy. I have made mistakes and I wish to atone for them."

"I cannot trust you, Morcar. You and your brother have sworn fealty to me and then broken your word. I should have your head. Perhaps if your heads were on the spikes of York then the land would know, once and for all, who rules in England."

The Mercian's voice became tremulous and could barely be heard, "My Lord, I beg you. If we were alone I might…" He looked around at the knights who were there.

King William was not afraid of this Saxon who had never had the courage to face us in battle. "Leave us." He turned to the archbishop.

I went outside and found myself with a Breton knight. I had met him before, Alain Le Roux. He was a young man. He was not yet thirty but he had lands in Normandy, Richmont where he was a count, and had been given a manor in Cambridge. I liked him for he was brave and Taillefer had spoken well of him.

"Thank you for bringing this earl to the king. You should know, Sir Richard, that the king has given me the former manor of Earl Eadwine. I have been given the honour of Richmond." He smiled, "We have expunged its former name of Gilling and I have given it the name of my home in Brittany." I knew the manor. It lay to the west of my own manor in the rolling hills one the western side of the Vale of York.

"I am pleased to have been of service, My Lord but until we have Earl Eadwine with his brother, in captivity, then the rebels have another figurehead."

"Aye, you are right."

It seemed a short time that we chatted until the Archbishop of York, Thomas of Bayeux, came from within. "Sir Alain, Sir Richard, the king would speak with you."

When we entered I saw that Morcar could not bring himself to look at us. The king said, "This snake has decided to save his own skin. We know where Eadwine can be found. I want you two to take men and fetch him."

We both bowed and said, almost in unison, "Yes, King William."

He turned to Earl Morcar, "And you will be taken to Normandy. You will be a guest at the castle of Roger de Beaumont for the rest of your days. There you can reflect on your oath breaking." The earl shrank as he realised he had both lost his freedom and betrayed his brother. Ignoring the earl the king turned to us, "When you have Eadwine Earl of Mercia, then return with him here. I want just the earl. The rest can be killed and you may take whatever they have with them. I want the Earl of Mercia so that his threat is no more. I do not want him to join the growing number of rebels at the Scottish court. Then we shall face Malcolm Canmore. I will have my land secure."

Chapter 2

The Borders 1071

The information we had was that Earl Eadwine was on his way to Scotland to join the Ætheling. He had left Gilling West and, according to Morcar was making his way up the spine of England. He was not using the roads built by the Romans but the backways and byways. Although it seemed as though we had an impossible task both Alain and I knew that he would have to avoid any towns and that helped us. I was close enough to home so that I could have used my men but Sir Alain had twenty men at arms and household knights and we deemed it to be enough. My men could guard my home and continue to make it stronger.

We headed for Persebrig to cross the Tees. The earl had to cross the river somewhere and unless he wished to wade through the waters close to the waterfall it would have to be the Roman Bridge. There was no castle there and the earl could pass through unopposed but he would be seen. His former lands, to the south would also have influenced his decision. It was a starting point. We reached the village just before dark. The remains of the Roman fort there afforded us some shelter. I sent my men into the wood to the south of the river to seek animals and information.

They were away for longer than I had expected and the hunters' stew was bubbling when they returned. They had not found any animals but they had found information.

"We found a man who was in the forest. He was a poacher, My Lord but he bore no love for Earl Eadwine. The earl had blinded the man's brother for poaching. He told us that seven nights ago he saw the earl and his retinue pass by. There were twelve of them and they were on foot. They crossed the bridge at night and were not seen by the villagers."

Alain became excited, "Did he know where they were heading?"

"No, My Lord, they just crossed the bridge but he did say that the earl has a hunting lodge at Bellingham north of Hexham."

The Breton looked at me and I said, "Sixty miles. If they are travelling at night and hiding up by day we have a chance. We need to ride hard. We can be there in under two days. We could stay at Hexham Abbey and they might have information which we could use."

It was a chase and I was glad that I had two good horses. We reached the abbey late in the afternoon and the existence of the earl's lodge was confirmed by the prior. We had to hope that he would rest there and then cross the border to Scotland. If he hurried on then our hunt would take us over the Tweed and into the land of King Malcolm Canmore.

"What can you tell us of the lodge there?"

The prior shrugged, "I have never seen it and it has been many years since the earl visited there. I believe it is an ancient building made of wood with a turf roof. There was a caretaker once but he died when raiders crossed from Scotland." He pointed to the cemetery, "His body was brought here for burial. Bellingham has no church." He smiled, "St Cuthbert discovered the holy well there. It is said to inspire miracles. Perhaps one day they will build a church there," he sighed, "when peace returns, once more to this troubled land."

Armed with this information we left before dawn to ride the dozen miles to the lodge. There was no bridge and we had to swim the river. Luckily, it was summer and the water level was low. The water barely wet my breeks. Once on the other side we rode to the higher piece of ground that we saw. The settlement was little more than a hamlet. We reined in and saw the huddle of houses close to the North Tyne. There was only one large building and that had to be the lodge. We saw smoke rising from it. Men were there. Sir Alain took charge. He had more men than I did. He was a little younger than me but I did not mind deferring to him for he was senior in rank.

"Sir Ulric, take two men at arms and ride around the houses. Stop their escape. We will flush them."

"Yes, Sir Alain."

The Breton knight pointed to two men and they headed north.

We tied our spare horses to some trees and I tightened Scout's girth after the river crossing. We had a good vantage point and the Breton said, as he remounted, "We will wait until he is in position before we move. We have been lucky to find him here. I would not lose him this close to the border." He looked at me, "Will he fight? I believe you met him once."

"He is the elder of the two brothers and has more backbone than his brother. I think he might choose to fight."

"And the king wants him alive. We will do what we can but I will not risk the lives of any of my men for a rebel who is foresworn."

We saw Ulric and the men reach the road. His escape route north was blocked and we hefted our spears to ride towards the lodge. We rode four abreast. I had Edward to my left and Sir Alain had his squire to his right. The sound of clattering hooves on the road alerted a sentry. I saw two men look down the road and then race back within the lodge. We galloped harder. Even as we reined in the door opened and two men emerged. They were armed with bows. Stephen of Mortain stood no chance for the archer sent his arrow at him from a distance of less than ten paces. It drove through the mail links. A second arrow struck the horse of Hugh, another of Sir Alain's household knights. The door slammed and we heard the bar dropping into place. We would have to find a way through the door.

We dismounted and I said, "Alfred and Aethelstan, take the horses to safety." I did not bother with my shield but ran to follow Sir Alain. The Breton was angry for he had lost one man and the horse of another. I drew two swords and shouted, "There must be a rear entrance, Sir Alain."

He said, over his shoulder, "Take your men and find it. Roger, find an axe."

"Edward, follow me round to the back." I ran with my squire and turned around the side wall of the lodge. It looked familiar and I realised that it was a similar design to mine. There would be a rear entrance. As we turned the corner I spied the stables. They were empty. The hog bog was dry and had not seen a pig or a fowl for many years. The back door opened and Saxons tumbled out. I shouted, “Sir Alain, they are fleeing from the rear.”

The men with the earl were housecarls. These were not the same men who had caused so many deaths at Senlac Hill but they were oathsworn warriors. Seeing just two of us, four men detached themselves as Eadwine and the rest ran for the river. I wondered if they had a boat or a raft ready. It would explain much if they did.

I heard Sir Alain shout, “Sir Ulric, cut them off.”

The four housecarls thought they had an easy task. They swung their axes in long lazy loops. It was the long loops that aided us for the four men had to give each other enough room to swing. I shouted, “Edward, left!” I ran to the right. It meant that instead of facing two men we would have just one man who could use his weapon to hurt us and our horses. The two men turned a little to face us as the other two readjusted their position. At that moment Alfred, Aethelstan, Sir Alain and the rest of the men appeared. I used the slight distraction of their appearance to lunge with my left hand. Men are unused to fighting left-handed men and the housecarl was no exception. He swung his axe back handed at where the sword had been. I hacked into his knee with my right-hand sword. He dropped to his other knee and my left-hand sword slid across his neck. I was just in time to see Edward dive to the ground, beneath the swinging axe of the other housecarl and bring his sword up into the groin of the man. The housecarl gave a scream that died quickly and he fell. Sir Alain and his men had taken care of the other two but we saw Earl Eadwine and his men running across some scrubland towards the river. If they had a raft ready and waiting then they would be lost to us. It was Sir Ulric who was our only hope. He and his two men at arms were galloping to cut off the fleeing rebels. The earl and his men had to change direction. Once more four housecarls detached themselves to bravely face the horses. This time, however, the long loops of their axes had an effect. They hacked into the chest of Sir Ulric's horse and one of his men at arms' animals. The two horses fell, bringing down the third and throwing their riders.

We were now closer to the earl and the last of his bodyguards. These were not armed with axes but they had spears and shields. In an attempt to buy time for the earl they ran at us. I did not slow but used both of my swords. One sword drove up the spear while the other hacked at the head of the warrior. He brought up his shield but my weight knocked him to the ground. I tripped over his legs. I smacked my hilt into his face as I pushed myself up. Edward and Sir Alain were fighting two of the bodyguards while Sir Alain's squire struggled to contain the fourth. I know I should have ignored the squire and gone after the earl but I could not let the young warrior die. I turned and ran at the bodyguard. He had managed to knock the squire's sword from his hand and was about to spear him when my sword slid into his side. I turned to follow the earl to the river. As I reached the riverbank I saw that there was a raft and he was on it. It was then that Sir Ulric arrived at the bank. He must have made his way down the river after falling from his horse. He took his spear and hurled it at the earl.

I heard a long wail from Sir Alain, "Noooooo!" The earl fell from the raft which floated down stream. The earl was not dead and he tried to swim. The spear and the weight of his wet clothes did for him. I saw him roll over and that told me he was dead. His attempt to survive, however, had brought him close to the riverbank. We would be able to recover his body.

Sir Alain shook his head, "We wanted him alive, Sir Ulric."

"I am sorry, My Lord. I was angry and …I am sorry."

I looked around and saw the squire rise. Alfred and Aethelstan were also alive. I sheathed my swords, "We have ended the threat, My Lord. King William wanted the danger the earl represented eliminated. We have done that. The king will have to understand. Would you like me to tell him?"

"That is noble of you, Sir Richard, but it was my man who did this. I will endure the wrath of the king." He sheathed his own sword. "Give the housecarls a warrior's death. We shall put their bodies in the lodge and, when we leave, burn it." He turned to me, "We will take the body of Earl Eadwine back to York."

We shared out the treasure we found. The king had promised it to us. Sir Alain punished Sir Ulric by giving his share to the man at arms who had survived the axe attack. His comrade had been our only loss. The fall from the horse had broken his neck and that added to the arrow that had felled him were mortal. There was food in the lodge and we took that too. The chain of office would be given to the king. He could now appoint a new Earl of

Mercia. We waited until the lodge was ablaze before we left. The smoke from the fire was still visible when we were five miles from Hexham.

I did not enter York with Sir Alain. When the king came north I would simply join him. I did not know when that would be exactly but whatever time I could spend in my manor would be a bonus.

That evening, I had Bergil dine with me along with Edward and my pueros. "When we go north, Bergil, I will need you. We will have to leave Ethelred to defend the manor."

Edward chuckled, "He will love that, My Lord."

I nodded, "Bergil, how many men can we take?"

I saw him look at the ceiling as he worked it out. I was patient and eventually he said, "There are twelve of the men of the village with swords, spears, shields and helmets. We have four men who can use a bow and there are four youths who are accurate slingers."

I nodded, "Then we take twenty-five men to war."

Edward said, "What about the manor of Norton, My Lord. There might be men there who could follow your banner."

I shook my head, "Until I visit the manor I cannot know the quality of the men there. That will have to wait until we have dealt with the threat of the rebels and the Scots."

"Then tomorrow I will visit with all of them. They need to know that they will be needed sooner rather than later," Bergil stood and bowed before he left.

"And we should go too, My Lord, if you are done with us."

"Of course.."

Edward returned to his wife and my pueros to their mother and sister. I was left alone at the table. Perhaps Edward was right to refuse the offer of spurs. I had a lonely life. The burden was always there, the responsibility of the people of my manor and the demands of the king. Before I became too maudlin I consoled myself with the thought that my grandfather would be proud of me. I still thought of him. There was no one to whom I could truly speak and give my innermost thoughts expression. My grandfather and Taillefer were the only two I felt I could confide in and both were dead.

It was King Malcolm who made the first move. Perhaps the king was distracted by the failure to capture Earl Eadwine alive or the fact that Hereward was still at large. Whatever the reason, he did pre-empt the invasion of England by mustering his men and putting his army close to the Tweed. One consolation was that King William had warned his lords of the muster so that, in the middle of August, we marched north. Bergil had organised my men.

The army we joined was not a large one. The one that had destroyed the northern rebels before the end of the previous year had been twice as big. The one the king led, his household knights apart, was made up of his newly appointed knights like me and Sir Alain, and the local men, the old fyrd. The King of England was not helped by the fact that he had slain many of the men who lived north of the Tees. They might have been helpful to face the old enemy, the Scots. The north was an empty wasteland with tares and weeds growing where it should have been cereal.

We headed to Durham. The newly appointed Bishop Walcher had been the one who had sent word that the Scots were raiding the borders. Our numbers were swollen by knights from the Palatinate. The men from Durham, the old Saxons, were also hardy fighters. They were known as haliwerfolc, the defenders of St Cuthbert. They would fight the Scots as ferociously as any knight.

I did not dine with the king nor his brother but, the next day as we headed north toward the Tyne the king asked both Sir Alain and me about the land through which we would pass.

I waved a hand, "Durham is the only castle in this part of the land. The next one is Bamburgh on the coast and that stops no one, My Lord. Your castles further south are bastions against rebels but here we need bastions against those who would steal our land, our people and our animals."

"Sir Richard is right, My Lord. When we stayed in Hexham the prior there told us how the Scots still raid as they did before the Romans came. The wall that straddles the land was put there for a reason."

"Could it be manned again?"

I shook my head, "The stone has been largely robbed out. Even at Persebrig all that can be seen are the foundations. You will need, King William, castles that are like the one you are building in Lundenwic. They can guard the crossing of the river. If not then the Scots will bleed the land dry. They will take animals and slaves."

I did not add that as the king himself had killed many of the people of the north then there was little to take at the moment.

He turned to Bishop Odo who had come north with the king, "Then, Brother, we will need to build castles along the border. I have tarried long enough in the north. Normandy demands my full attention. You shall rule the south in my absence." In the king's mind he had already won. I wondered if he was being overly optimistic.

We identified, as we headed north, places where castles might be built but it was a dream for the future. The reality was that we had to stop King Malcolm. The heirs of the Confessor might think he was helping them for altruistic reasons but the reality was the Scots wanted back the lands they thought were theirs by right.

The Durham scouts found the Scottish scouts at the River Aln. The tiny hamlet that was there, Alnwick, had no defences at all and the bridge was a flimsy wooden one. The manor had been given to Sir Gilbert Tyson but he was still in Normandy settling his affairs. There was no lord of the manor as yet and certainly no hedgehog palisade. We camped on the bluffs that overlooked the river and watched the Scots do the same on the northern side. The bluffs on the south were higher but the Scots had a large forest and that hid their true numbers. I realised that it would be a good place for Sir Gilbert to build a castle. The bluffs above the river were perfect and with a ditch and rampart, not to mention the small bridge, the castle would be a hard one to take.

We had a council of war and, surprisingly, I was invited. Sir Alain was there as well as Bishop Odo and the Lord of Warwick, Robert de Veci.

The king was agitated, "I do not like to be blind. I need the numbers of the enemy to be ascertained.

How many men does he have in the woods?" He turned to me, "Sir Richard, I want you to take some of your men and get behind the enemy lines. We have a strong position here and I do not think that the Scots would be so foolish as to try to shift us but I do not want to walk into an ambush. I want you to tell me how many men we face and the defences that they have."

My training at the hands of Taillefer was the reason I was being given this task. I had not ridden in this part of the world before but as the river was not wide here and could be bridged I worked out that we might be able to swim our horses across the river upstream. I looked at the sky. It would be sunset within a couple of hours, "If I were to leave now, My Lord, I might be able to cross the river upstream and use darkness to ascertain their numbers."

"I want no guesses, fitz Malet! I want numbers."

"Yes, My Lord, and numbers you shall have but if I tried this in daylight then we would be seen and dead men cannot report can they?"

"Be careful, fitz Malet, I value your service but…"

Bishop Odo laughed, "You must expect this, Brother. He was trained by Taillefer and is as close to the character of that man as any."

"Perhaps you are right. Then go and be back by dawn."

I had all of us change from mail to our leather jacks. We did not need the jingling of mail and the mail would not enjoy a dousing in the river. For the same reason I did not wear my spurs. I also took Geoffrey rather than Scout. Geoffrey was darker. I did not take my two swords for I would be wearing a dark cloak and I used a single scabbard. I took just Aethelstan and Alfred. Part of my reasoning was that they were unmarried. Bergil and Edward now had wives and families. The other reason was that the two pueros were both quick witted and quiet.

We left the camp before the sunset. The nights were short at this time of the year and we would not have long while it was dark. The setting sun showed us a narrow part of the river. The depth did not worry me. All our horses were good swimmers and we could just hang on to our saddles. We entered the water while there was still a little golden light shimmering on the Aln. Our horses coped remarkably well with the swim and once on the other side we adjusted their girths, remounted and headed for the smell of woodsmoke and the glittering pin pricks of firelight in the woods. When we neared the woods we dismounted and I led Geoffrey towards the trees. We approached, not down the road but across the field of barley. I was looking for faces in the dark that would mark their sentries. I saw none.

As we neared the woods I heard the noises of their camp. They were to the north of the woods rather than in the trees. The Aln ran in a large loop. After the bridge it began to turn north and then almost back on itself as it headed east for a while. It protected their camp from an attack on three sides. The trees would give us the best chance of approaching and viewing their camp. I realised that this task was not as easy as the king had made out. We would have to get very close to report true numbers. The men in the camp were not mailed and it would be hard to distinguish types of men. I would need to get to the horses and count the war horses to ascertain the number of knights. I decided to do that first. I reasoned that the horses would be to the north of the camp where they would have grazing and water yet the stink of their dung would be carried north by the southerly breeze. We moved around the edge of the woods. I counted fires and horses as we moved through the woods. It was not the horse herd nor our own horses which gave us away but a mounted sentry. He was on a pony and his animal, smelling strange horses whinnied and we were seen.

"Alarm! Captain of the guard."

I whispered quietly as men appeared from the woods with pointed spears, "Keep your hands from your swords and follow my direction." Louder I said, "Thank the Lord that I have found you." I made the sign of the cross. We have come from Earl Eadwine and seek Edgar Ætheling. Is he here?"

A knight arrived. I saw his rank from his spurs and his fine mail. He had heard my words but he said to the mounted sentry, "What is it?"

The man's accent made it hard to discern his words. I had to listen carefully to do so, "I found these three sneaking around the woods. They say that they seek the Englishman." His voice was heavy with suspicion.

I laughed, "Of course we were sneaking. How else would we get past the sentries of the Bastard?"

The knight came closer, "How did you get by the army?"

I smiled, "We swam the river."

He came over and first felt Geoffrey's coat and then the hem of my cloak. He said, "Take their horses to the horse lines and bring them with me."

"Should I take their weapons?"

The knight laughed, "I think that if they were assassins they would be better at it than this. We will see what the king says."

We left the wood and entered the camp. I hoped that Aethelstan and Alfred had their wits about them and would be counting as we walked. Of course, if my story failed to convince them then we might end up as prisoners or worse. I put that unpleasant thought from my mind. Taillefer had taught me to think and never to give up. The trick at Douvres had won us the castle. I was already embellishing the story I would tell to the Ætheling and the Scottish king.

The tents of the senior nobles were the only ones in the camp. The rest, even the knights, were in hovels. If they had to break camp then they could do so quickly. The spears in our backs made us the focus of attention. I hoped that the dark and my cloak would disguise me from any who might have seen me before. I had not fought in this part of the land but there might be some in the retinue of Edgar Ætheling who would recognise me.

"Hold them here."

A spear was placed before our chests as the knight approached those who had emerged from the tent. I saw a woman amongst them. She was beautiful. That was the first time I saw the sister of Edgar Ætheling, Margaret. I wondered at her presence. Their mother, Agatha and the other child of Edward the Confessor's son, Cristina were not there. I saw that the knight spoke with a well-dressed noble and I deduced that it must be King Malcolm. The boy of about ten who stood close by had to be

Duncan, the son of the king. All of this was valuable information for King William. If he struck quickly he might not only rid himself of the rebels but also take the Scottish king and his son as prisoners. Of course, that assumed I could get the three of us out of this predicament.

The knight waved and pointed to me. A spear poked in my back and I walked towards the men. I dropped to one knee and said, "Lord Edgar, I have come from my master. Eadwine, Earl of Mercia."

Edgar Ætheling said, "Rise. I do not know you."

I nodded, "Yes, My Lord, there is no reason why you should for I am just a lowly retainer."

"You do not sound Mercian."

I smiled and said, "That is because I grew up in Wessex." Taillefer had taught me that telling a tale well meant giving little details. "My grandfather was a housecarl." That was all that I said.

King Malcolm asked, "How did you get by the Normans?"

"We swam the river, Your Majesty."

"You know who I am then?"

"I assumed that you must be the king, Your Majesty."

"And the earl, where is he?"

I pointed south, "He and his housecarls are at his hunting lodge in Bellingham, just south of the Normans."

The king suddenly pointed a finger at Alfred and snapped, "You, how many housecarls does the earl have?"

Alfred was quick witted and he said, "Twelve, My Lord."

The king turned to Edgar, "Is that right?"

Edgar shrugged, "Probably but these men are English and not Norman."

King Malcolm was clever and he had tested my men. It seemed we had passed but that did not mean we had escaped from danger.

The would-be King of England seemed to believe us, "King Malcolm, if the earl is close by then we can use his presence. We know his brother was taken and this might inspire the men of the north to rise once more and support the Earl of Mercia."

King Malcolm was still clearly suspicious, "Why did he send you and not come himself?"

"Three men could move through the land without being seen and we did not know if the heir of the Confessor was with the army. I was sent to meet with you and then to bring the earl to join you."

The king seemed satisfied. He asked, "How long before the earl could join us?"

"If we leave now we can ride through the night and reach Bellingham by dawn. If we rest our horses then we could repeat this journey tomorrow night."

The Scottish knight said, "And that would allow the men of Moray more time to join us, King Malcolm. The one thousand men they bring would swell our numbers by a third."

The knight and the king looked at Edgar Ætheling who beamed, "I spy hope, King Malcolm." He turned to me, "What is your name?"

Taillefer had trained me well. I used my grandfather's name, "I am Geoffrey son of Richard of Pevensey."

"Well, Geoffrey. When I have the crown of England upon my head you shall be rewarded."

"Thank you, My Lord, I yearn for the day an heir of Wessex sits on the throne of England."

The king turned to the knight, "Donal, escort these back to the river."

I bowed and turned. The knight led us to the horse lines. I counted just forty war horses. That told me the number of knights. The knight and two of his men mounted their horses and he said, "Lead the way, Englishman."

I did not deviate from the path we had taken to reach the camp and I saw the knight studying the muddy ground where we had left the river.

"You can safely pass the Normans?"

"They are camped by the bridge. We can ride a long loop around them. Better a sore backside rather than capture, eh, My Lord?"

"You are a brave man. Go with God."

We swam the river and headed south and west. As soon as I was able we turned and rode directly for the camp. Alfred said, "My Lord…."

I hissed, "Silence until we are back at the camp."

The king and his brother were still awake when we passed through the forewarned sentries and King William leaned forward and said, "Well…"

"The Ætheling and King Malcolm as well as Duncan, the king's son are there. They have two thousand men and forty knights. They are expecting a thousand men from Moray in the next day or so. The Scots and the rebels are camped in loop of the river. The woods are guarded and their horses are to the north of their camp. The men are using hovels."

King William beamed, "See, Odo, if you choose good men than you learn more than if you send fools and heroes. Well done, Richard. Get some rest for tomorrow we need your swords, both of them."

Chapter 3

I was so weary that all I did was to take off my wet clothes and wrap myself in my blanket. Edward covered me with a spare blanket and I slept the sleep of the dead. I knew that I had lied and that I had deliberately deceived the Ætheling and the Scottish king. I had not behaved as a knight should. My grandfather would not be happy that I had tricked the Ætheling but I consoled myself with the fact that Taillefer would have approved. The two men whom I still admired the most were a constant conflict in my head. They were the Norman and English sides of me. My destiny was tied to that of King William and Edgar Ætheling had no support in the land. The rebellion, while it lingered, would only hurt the ordinary people. The land needed peace and the threat of the Scots to be removed.

I was woken by the noise of the army being roused. My men had breakfast prepared for me. I saw Bergil and Edward speaking to my pueros. Bergil shook his head as I neared them, "My Lord, a man can expect only so much luck in his life. You are using up all that you have."

I stood and stretched, "Bergil, there was enough credibility and it enabled us to escape. It was not luck; it was like the juggling of swords. Men's eyes watch the weapons in the air and do not notice what is behind the juggler's eyes. I did the same with the tale I wove."

Bergil looked confused, "My Lord?"

"Taillefer the jongleur would juggle with swords and it was to distract the eyes. That is all I did at the Scottish camp. I counted on the fact that the only people who knew that the earl was dead were Sir Alain, his men and my men. My story sounded reasonable. If I was asked to do the same again then I would not be able to do so. I do not think the king will be able to use me as a spy in the future so you see, I shall not need that luck again. I can return to being a knight and lord of the manor. Now, I shall make water and then I need food. This day we shall whet our swords on Scottish flesh."

The king sent Sir Alain to fetch me. I had barely breakfasted and dressed when he did so.

"Alfred, saddle Scout."

All the senior lords were there. The king nodded to me as I entered. I was the last. They were dressed for war. Bishop Odo toyed with the mace he would use. The king spoke, "Thanks to Sir Richard of Eisicewalt we have the chance to not only drive the Scots from our land but also to end the rebellion and capture the Ætheling. The men of Durham, the Haliwerfolc," the old English word sounded even stranger coming from the king, "will have the honour of leading the assault over the bridge. Sir Richard has shown us that the river can be crossed by horsemen. The knights will cross that way and then the men on foot will follow the haliwerfolc over the bridge. We strike quickly and we strike hard. Enough time has been wasted already in the north. It is a troublesome thistle that I would have removed. Bishop Odo will bless the army and then we will take our positions. My horn will sound three times to signal the start of the attack."

After returning to my men, I explained to Edward and Bergil what was intended. "Bergil, you will lead the men on foot. Edward and my pueros will accompany me."

It was a simple enough plan. As my men all prepared for the attack, Bishop Odo came to bless us. He was not a particularly religious man and the title of Bishop of Bayeux was more military than religious but he knew how to use the saint. He held up the St Cuthbert Gospel, "The saint goes with us this day. I shall keep the gospel close to me so that we are blessed by the presence of the saint." The words were cleverly chosen as they inspired the men of Durham. They were the ones who would make the first attack.

We then rode our horses in a long line along the banks of the river. That was the mistake the king made. I would have hidden our movements until we reached the river. The sentries and scouts I had reported in the woods saw us and they must have warned King Malcolm for even before our horn sounded I heard the blaring of the Scottish horns. There would be no surprise attack. They would be ready for us. The king ordered our horn and we moved to the water. It is easier to cross a river by horse if there are just one or two of you. The large number of knights and men at arms, not to mention squires and pueros who splashed into the river, caused confusion. Some riders slipped from their saddles. I heard the cheer from our right and knew that the men of Durham were attacking. Would they find any left to resist them? I could not see the Scottish king standing to fight the knights we had brought.

My men and I had done this more than most and we were the ones who were first ashore and we galloped towards the camp. Alfred, Aethelstan, and I were more familiar with the layout and we galloped through the trees to the horse lines. To my dismay I saw that the Scottish horses were already being mounted. Even Margaret, the sister of Edgar, was seated on the back of a horse. I heard men closer to the bridge clashing with the haliwerfolc. Until a bridgehead could be made then the attack would have to come from the horsemen and thus far the four of us and half a dozen others, Sir Alain included, were the only ones who could do anything. The Scottish knight, Donal, was busy organising a shield wall of men at arms. He was a brave man and clearly buying time for the king and the nobles to escape.

The lances and spears we had brought would help us and I shouted, "Couch your spears and ride close to me."

There were just four of us for Sir Alain and his men were some paces behind us. Four together would have a greater impact than four individuals and if we could break this wall then we might have the chance to catch the bulk of the enemy. They would not try to cross the river but would take the route across the land and take the road that passed through Eglingham.

I reined Scout in for he was eager and more powerful than the horses ridden by my three companions. He was bigger too and I knew that the Scottish soldiers who were bracing themselves for our attack would be fearful of his snapping jaws and flailing hooves. The clash of steel and the shouts to our left told me that the men of Durham were fighting. There were also men on foot fleeing to join the horsemen. The ones who were making a stand were also buying them time. Even as I pulled back my lance I knew that King William had succeeded. We might not be able to take the Ætheling but the threat of the Scots would be ended, at least temporarily.

I rode directly at the knight who was leading the shield wall. If he could be eliminated then the rest might break. I hoped that King William and our horsemen would now be following us as quickly as they could. My helmet was open faced and I knew that the knight recognised me from his shout, "You! Treacherous dog!"

I pulled back my lance and drove it at his shield. He knew his business and he angled his shield so that the head slid along it. It speared the man at arms next to him in the side. Edward's spear had managed to hit the knight in the shoulder. Edward was still learning and the blow was not a mortal one. The man I had lanced clutched the lance as he fell and pulled it from my grasp. I drew one of my swords. The knight swung his sword at my left side. My long shield took the blow. Alfred speared a man at arms who attempted to stab my right leg.

"Richmont!" Sir Alain's war cry and the subsequent clash as his men hit the line brought me some relief. I had feared that the four of us might be surrounded and butchered.

I swung my sword down onto the helmet of the Scottish knight and he reeled. I pulled around Scout's head and he snapped at the knight. He was a brave man but even the strongest of men cannot help but pull back from such snapping jaws. I leaned from the saddle and struck him again on the helmet. He fell. Sir Alain and his men had struck the line and, as the king approached with Waltheof, the son of Siward the former Earl of Northumbria and the other knights, the faltering line of men at arms broke and they ran.

I looked down at the Scottish knight, a tendril of blood came from his mouth. He gave me a wan smile, “There was something about you, Englishman. I should have obeyed my instincts and…” he died. I know not which of the blows killed him but he died, faithful to the last.

“Alfred, take his weapons and mail and then prepare his body for burial. He deserves that.”

Waltheof shouted, “Sir Richard, secure the camp and stop it from being looted. Those are the king’s orders.” He and his cousin, Gospatric, the Earl of Northumbria, hurried after King William who was in full flight chasing the Scots.

“Edward, Aethelstan, with me.” Leaving Alfred to see to the dead knight we rode to the three tents that had housed the Scottish royal party. I dismounted and handed my reins to Aethelstan. The tents had been hurriedly vacated. The king’s crown, which I had seen the night before was gone but there was still a chest of clothes and another smaller one. There were weapons, a helmet and mail. When I opened the smaller one I saw that it contained coins. I went to the entrance and said, “Edward, guard these two chests.” There were clothes in the other two tents as well as some mail and weapons. By the time Alfred rejoined me the camp was ours. The hovels and the dead were being plundered by the men of Durham. Bergil led my men over.

"Any wounds?"

He shook his head, "The men of Durham were wild in their charge and all we had to do was to follow. I do not think that any of the men had to bloody a weapon."

"Good, we are told to guard these tents. Take over while we bury this brave knight!"

My pueros dug the grave and wrapping the knight in his cloak I laid his sword to lie the length of his body and covered his face with his shield. Bergil said, "Bow your heads."

My men obeyed and I said, "Oh, Lord, take the soul of this brave man, Sir Donal, into your tender care. He died as all knights should and was faithful to his oath. Amen."

My men intoned, "Amen."

By the time King William and the men returned the rest of the camp had been plundered and every corpse robbed. Earl Waltheof had been right to order us to guard the three tents. Had we not done so then the king would have been angry and men would have died as a result.

King William, his brother and the two earls reined in. Their tunics were bespattered with blood.

"Success, My Lord?"

The king dismounted and shook his head, "If you mean do we have the Ætheling or King Malcolm then no. We did not even manage to catch Margaret." He shook his head in disgust. "We had our chance…"

It did not do to point out that the king had ensured the failure by his attack across the river. Had

I been in command then I would have blocked his escape with my horsemen.

I pointed to the tents, "There are chests of treasure within and clothes, King William. No one touched them."

He pointed to the freshly turned earth, "And that?"

"We buried the knight I slew, Donal. He fought well and deserved a decent burial." I gestured at the rest of the camp. Butchered, naked bodies littered it. "I did not want that to be his fate."

"Nobly done." The king nodded, "We will camp here and then on the morrow I want the land scoured for signs of any survivors. My brother and I have tarried here long enough. We have a new Archbishop of Canterbury to appoint and I would have our Welsh borders made safe. Earl Gospatric, I leave you to secure the north."

As he nodded Bishop Odo said, "And I would have a castle to guard the cathedral and the bones of the saint. Have Bishop Walcher build one. He has income enough."

"Yes, Bishop Odo."

"I have tarried long enough in the north, Brother. My lands in Kent need my attention." The bishop was also the Earl of Kent and that was one of the richest parts of England. It was no wonder he wished to head back to the land where wheat grew and men ate manchet at every meal.

"We all have." The king went on, "Earl Waltheof, when the north is scoured, you shall head to Caestre and aid Hugh d'Avranches in his subjugation of the Welsh borders. Sir Alain and Sir Richard, when you are done then you can return to your manors but I want no one resting until the land of the north is free from rebels. When there is peace you may return to your manors."

Sir Alain said, "And I, too, My Lord, would build a castle."

The king nodded, "And I suppose you want one too, Sir Richard."

I smiled, "No, King William, I am content. York and its mighty walls are close enough to me and now that the Minster is to be rebuilt then I know the city will be well protected."

The king, bishop and earl left the next day as we formed up three columns to seek out survivors. We had less than eight hundred men between us. We had managed to secure ten horses and so I mounted ten of my men. We were the smallest column. The rest of my men were left to guard the camp and the bridge.

We followed the trail of discarded weapons and, twice, the bodies of hastily buried men who had died on the flight. We collected the weapons. We stopped when we reached the border at Hownam. That done we headed south and took the road to Otterburn. We would be able to head due east to the Aln and save back tracking over our journey north. The constable at Otterburn told us how he and his men had sheltered in the tower that was the refuge for that part of the land. He did, however, give me disquieting news. "The day before we saw men fleeing north we spied a warband of, perhaps, five hundred men, heading south. We have not seen them return north."

I frowned. Alfred said, "My Lord, might they not be the men from Moray?"

Aethelstan said, "There were supposed to be a thousand."

I said, "It might still be the men from Moray. Who says that they have to travel in a large warband of a thousand men? It is often better to travel in smaller numbers. Which road did they take? The one to the Aln?"

He shook his head, "No, Sir Richard, they headed due south towards Hexham and the wall."

As we rode back to the Aln I spoke with Bergil and Edward, "This sounds like the men of Moray but why did they turn south and not head east to the Aln?"

We turned east ourselves to head back to the camp. I had worked out, by the time we reached our camp on the hill overlooking the river, that the only explanation was that this warband had chosen not to go directly to the king's muster. They were simply doing what their ancestors had done for centuries and raiding Northumbria or perhaps, Cumberland, at harvest time.

The earls were back but Sir Alain was not. While my men organised their food I went to speak to the two men. They nodded at my report and Earl Gospatric said, "You may be right."

Earl Waltheof said, "The king asked me to take my men to aid Hugh d'Avranches to subdue the Welsh. I will ride with my men along the wall and then head south."

"Good and I will ensure that the river between the Aln and the Tweed is free from threat. That leaves the road south to the Tees and York for you and Sir Alain. As it is on the way home for both of you, it is convenient. The north seems at peace and if you two can eliminate this threat then the king should be satisfied."

I nodded. He was right. My men were grumbling a little. We had defeated the enemy and every day we spent away from their homes meant that their families had more work to do as a result. These were not warriors. I was used to having men like Edward and my pueros who would happily campaign for six months or more. My farmers and yeomen did so as a duty and that duty had a limited time attached to it.

Sir Alain was the last to ride in and he had encountered trouble. He had wounded men and the healers ran to them as they trudged into the camp.

"We found a warband. They were attacking the farms along the Devil's Causeway."

Earl Waltheof nodded, "The name of the old Roman Road."

"Aye, although I was confused, at first, when we were told it. My English is not as good as yours, Sir Richard, and the words sounded wrong. We were lucky that the band had split up and was raiding different farms. My men outnumbered the twenty or so we found and slew them but another band came upon us and attacked us. I lost a man. Our presence, mounted as we were, alerted the warband and I think that many of them have fled north to the Tweed. I think they thought we were the whole army." He paused, "They took animals and women. The men were all slain."

Earl Gospatric commanded for he had the bulk of the men of Northumbria as well as the men of Durham. "And you think that some were still south of us?" He nodded. "That confirms what Sir Richard discovered." He drank some of the wine we had captured. He wrinkled his nose. It was not the best quality. "I will still watch this part of the land but we will spread the net a little wider. Sir Alain, I had already asked Sir Richard to head south and clear the land on your way home. I think that this journey will be slightly longer. Clear the land of raiders and recover as many animals and captives as you can. I will use the bulk of the men of Durham and Northumbria to ensure that the main valleys are safe. You two can investigate the remote and smaller valleys of Teesdale and Weardale."

Sir Alain and I headed to our men, "I am lucky, Sir Richard, I have more men at arms and knights than you. You may struggle to do what is commanded of us."

"Aye, and unlike you I have men who need to be with their families."

My men had cooked food and Alfred brought over a bowl for me. He smiled at Sir Alain, "A bowl for you, My Lord?"

"Have you any to spare?"

I nodded, "One thing my men are good at is foraging. We may not be the richest men in the retinue but we are the best fed."

As we sat and ate we worked out a way for us to cover as much land as we could while still maintaining contact with one another. After he had returned to his men I told my men that we would be going back to Eisicewalt and that evoked smiles and a cheer, but when I said we would not be taking the most direct route then some of the smiles turned to frowns. That was the moment I decided to use some of the money I had accrued to pay for soldiers. I had no other use for my fortune and, it seemed to me, the king had given me two remote manors to ensure that I would be a protector of the land north of York and south of the Tees. York was a one of the jewels in the king's crown and he would not be happy to lose it again.

We headed south for the Wansbeck valley. The earl would ensure that Morpeth was safe and Sir Alain and I followed the trail of destruction left by the Scots. They had, as I had deduced, just raided. They were not trying to conquer. The survivors told us of large numbers of such raiders coming south. Small bands then split off and headed back to Scotland. Sir Alain had encountered one such warband. We were all depressed by what we found. Some places had been remote enough to escape the scrutiny of our enemy but others had been stripped of everything of value.

It was at Wallington, a tiny hamlet, where we found a single survivor. As we searched the burnt-out farmhouse the youth stepped from beneath a bramble bush. He had in his hand a long dagger and a bow was over his shoulder. I saw no arrows.

Bergil was ever suspicious and he held out his hand for the dagger, "What is your name, boy?"

The boy frowned. I realised that Bergil's accent had confused him. I said, "We mean you no harm, boy. We seek the men who did this."

His eyes burned fiercely, "They were Scots, My Lord, and I slew one."

Bergil grinned, "Bravely done."

"What is your name?"

"Elric, son of Eadwine."

"And your family?" I knew the answer before I asked the question but it had to be asked.

"All dead."

Alfred asked, "Even the women?"

"Even the women. My mother and my sister fought as fiercely as any man but they were still slain."

Edward said, "And yet you live."

"It is my curse that I did not die with them or help to fight. I was hunting. I am a good archer. I had returned with the pigeons and I saw them leaving. I ran after them and used my last arrow to slay one of them. I could not catch the rest…" he shook his head, "I came back to see if any were left alive. I had to hide when more of them passed through. I would have seen to the bodies otherwise. They burned the house."

"And have you any other family who can take you in?"

He shook his head. I did not know what to do with him. He said, "Let me come with you, My Lord, let me hunt these men."

"We do not seek those who did this, Elric, they will be heading back to Scotland. The Earl of Northumbria will punish them." That was not necessarily true but I wanted to give the boy some hope. "We are hunting Scots further south so that we can stop them from doing this to another."

"Then, My Lord, if you would have me, I will follow you." His hand darted into the bramble bush and he pulled out the two pigeons. "I do not come empty handed."

I liked the youth and his spirit, "Then join us, Elric."

Bergil asked, "And how many summers have you seen?"

He shrugged, “Fourteen or fifteen. I am not sure.”
“We shall kit you out a little better. Alfred, fetch out that jack we took.”

We had accumulated spare clothing during the campaign and Elric, who had taken refuge beneath the bramble bush, was ragged and tattered. His story had touched my pueros, squire and man at arms. He was taken into their company and they replaced his dead family.

It was the next day when we found some raiders. We were approaching the farms that made up Yeckham that lay a few miles north of Hexham when we heard the screams. I waved forward my mounted men. The rest would follow but I knew that every moment of delay meant it was more likely that people would die. The Scots had clearly not had their own way. As we neared the farms overlooking the branch of the Tyne, I saw two dead warriors. The men of Yeckham were fighting for their lives. That helped us for the Scots had their backs towards us and we charged into them. There were twenty of them and I led less than a dozen mounted men, but with the stout defence of the men of Yeckham it was enough. Scout raced ahead of my men and I reached the fray first. My spear plunged into the back of a warrior wielding an axe who was about to overcome the flimsy shield and spear of the youth who fought him. His scream as he fell made the others turn and in that turning their death warrants were signed. Farmers’ axes, swords and spears combined with my men’s lances and spears to kill them. By the time my men who had raced on foot reached us, it was all over.

The headman bloodied but unbowed nodded to me, "Timely, My Lord. We would have given a good account of ourselves but we would have perished had you not come."

I nodded. The man I had speared was still alive. My strike had ensured that he would perish but he would linger for a little longer. "Who are you?" I suddenly realised that he was not Scottish. He had the Hammer of Thor around his neck. He was a Viking.

"I am Erik of Ljoðahús."

"You are not Scottish. What are you doing with the Scots?"

He laughed and blood came from his mouth, he did not have long to live. "The Earl of Moray said there was plunder as well as treasure to be had. We thought to take women for the winter." He winced. I saw his hand tighten about the haft of the axe. The headman raised his spear.

I shook my head, "He is a pagan and he is ensuring a safe passage to Valhalla."

The warrior nodded and shouted, as his back arched, "Odin!" He died.

I looked at the bodies and saw that there was a sprinkling of Vikings amongst the dead. "Moray has land close to the isles and the Vikings still rule those lands. He also has connections with Norway and the Vikings there. This is mischief indeed. Now it makes sense. The Scots might have gone home sooner but warriors like this enjoy raiding and see glory in death by combat." I saw that the raiders had with them half a dozen ponies. I said to the headman. "I will leave the bodies for you to dispose of. We will share the booty with you. My men will take three ponies."

"My Lord, but for your arrival we would have nothing. Take what you will."

"No, we shall share. We will spend the night at the abbey." A sudden thought struck me, "Did the bells sound there? Were they attacked?"

"We heard no bells, My Lord."

We headed, as the sun began to set, for Hexham. I hoped we would find a welcome and shelter for the night.

When we were admitted it was not to a quiet, reflective abbey but to a mass of refugees. I was taken to the prior who was tending to a Saxon. The prior told me that the abbot had been summoned to Durham to meet with the newly appointed Bishop of Durham, Walcher, and until then he was in command of the abbey. He looked at the refugees and shook his head. "My Lord, it is timely that you came. Raiders attacked villages and farms to the west of us and these were brought here. This is Ælfgar. He was the thegn of Brougham. He and his daughter, protected by his oathsworn, were making a pilgrimage to Durham. The thegn wished to visit the bones of the saint before he died. They were attacked at Langley. The daughter and her servant were taken. They thought that Ælfgar was dead but he was not. He is a tough man and he was brought here. He does not have long to live. You are a knight, My Lord, speak to him. He has been shriven and can now meet God."

I went over to the man. He looked to be dead already. I was about to turn away when his eyes opened and he frowned and said, "A Norman?" He spoke in English.

I was used to this and I smiled, "Half English and half Norman. I am Sir Richard of Eisicewalt."

His eyes widened, "You are a knight! Then my prayers are answered. You took an oath." I nodded. "My daughter, Ealdgyth, has been taken. The man who took her is Ulf son of Tope. He is a Viking from the isles." He closed his eyes and sighed. He seemed to be trying to summon up strength from somewhere. "They thought I was dead and left me alone. They took my sword, my chain and my rings but left me. I overheard them. I know the name of the man who took her." He grabbed my hand, "He intends to make her his. You are a Norman but you are a knight. Promise me that you will find her and save her."

"I will try."

The last effort proved too much and he expired. The prior came over and folded the Saxon's hands. "That was well done, My Lord. He died with hope in his heart."

He had but he had also given me a burden that I did not need. I would not be returning anytime soon to Eisicewalt. I had a warband to hunt and a maiden to rescue.

Chapter 4

We dined with the monks and I discovered more about the dead thegn. "His manor was a small one close to the old Roman fort. He fought at Stamford Bridge but he felt he was betrayed by the Earl of Northumbria and Tostig. He shut himself away. He had visited me before for he had an illness. We can heal some things but the worm within him was slowly eating him. I believe that he not only wanted to visit the shrine of St Cuthbert but to ask the bishop to make Ealdgyth a ward. His men were all old and he wanted her to be protected."

"What of the man who took her?"

"From others who survived the raids and took refuge here we learned that the warlord was Máel Snechtai mac Óengus. His lands lie close to the isles that are infested by these pagans."

I knew that was not entirely true. Many Vikings and the men of the isles had embraced Christianity but as I had discovered there were still those warriors who adhered to the ancient ways. "So, they will have to head north and west to reach their home. That means they must travel across the high passes." He nodded. "And I must follow."

The prior went to see to the refugees and I sat with my men. I had already worked out who I would take and what I would do but, in explaining it to them, the plans took firmer shape. "We need speed and so I will take only mounted men and…volunteers."

Edward, Bergil, Alfred and Aethelstan all said, almost as one, "Aye, My Lord."

I shook my head, "No, Bergil, someone needs to lead the men back to our home and that will be you."

"Edward could lead the men home."

"He is a squire and he is young. I do not wish to lose my young men on the road back to the manor." He nodded and I stood, "Come let us speak to the others outside." My men were camped in the grounds of the Abbey.

They looked up expectantly as we approached. "This will be our last night together. Tomorrow Bergil will lead most of you to your home and your families. I will take horsemen to hunt for the raiders who have taken a young maiden and other captives. We have eight spare horses and I will take eight of you."

I could see by the looks on their faces that most of them wished to come but I saw debate and doubt on some of them. The first hand that rose in the air was that of the orphan, Elric. I shook my head, "Elric, you do not need to come. This is dangerous work."

"My Lord, these men may not be the same ones that killed my family but they were bred in the same cess pit. Besides, I have a bow and if I can procure some arrows then I can feed us while we travel."

Alfred said, "It is right that he comes, Sir Richard, for if he does not he will have to endure nightmares and horrors in the night. This is the way to expunge those memories, through blood and battle."

He was right and I nodded. We took seven other young men. The married ones I sent home. While I wrote a message for Sir Alain, my four experienced men showed the eight how to saddle their horses and how to learn the rudimentary skills of riding. I decided to take Geoffrey, and Scout would be ridden by Bergil and taken back to my manor. I would not need my war horse. Bergil's horse and the sumpter would carry our treasure and my mail home. I would wear a leather jack. We would be travelling light. Speed was more important than defence. Bergil would take a detour to the new manor of Sir Alain and leave the letter there. He needed to know what I was about to do not least because I was deviating from the orders we had been given. It was also in case we failed.

That done I went to the chapel to pray. I needed God's help. I had twenty men to follow and all of them would be more experienced warriors than at least eight of the ones I would be leading. Even Alfred and Aethelstan might struggle in a combat with seasoned Vikings. I had told a dying man I would save his daughter. Perhaps Edward was right. Spurs could be a curse.

We left the next morning and headed north and west. The year was drawing to a close and it was cold. I wondered how the captives would be coping with the journey. I could not see their captors caring about their condition. They would not take the Roman road and that meant I would be travelling relatively familiar roads for I had hunted Earl Eadwine. They would have to pass through Bellingham. Then they would take the smaller road that led to the border and the unknown lands of Scotland. I had to hope that we could catch them before the border. I prayed that they were driving animals as well as taking captives. If we could take them before the border then life would be easier.

That the raiders had fled along the road became clear long before we reached Bellingham. The farms we passed had either been damaged or the people who lived there came fearfully from their homes to speak to us when they saw it was a knight and his retinue. The numbers were confirmed. There were twenty men and the leader rode a horse. The party had two sumpters and eight women were haltered about the neck and led in a line. They were a day ahead of us. By the time we reached Bellingham we had ridden enough. Four of us were coping well but some of the younger riders were not. We camped at the burnt-out lodge of Eadwine Earl of Mercia. I was not afraid of their ghosts and the eight I led did not know of the battle. Elric had managed to recover eight arrows from the buildings that had been attacked on the road. He was happy and he scurried off to hunt. We had brought food with us but he seemed determined to prove his worth. Already, my pueros viewed him as a younger brother. They offered advice and help.

I was more concerned about his state of mind. He had lost his whole family and I knew how hard that could be. That night, as we ate the stew my men had made, enriched by the squirrels and duck he had killed, I asked him about his family.

"I had a younger brother and sister, My Lord. My mother was a good mother to us all. My father, well, he was a hard task master but we lived better than most families. He was a fine archer and taught me how to use a bow."

I noticed then that while he was still young he was better muscled than many youths. "You trained regularly?"

"Every day, My Lord. It was hard and often I did not want to but my father made me draw the bow. One day I hoped to draw his mighty bow."

"Where is it?"

"The men who killed him broke it when they could not draw it." He looked up at me with a distressed look on his face, "I watched them and I did nothing. Am I a coward, Sir Richard? Did I let down my father?"

"No, you did not. Had you tried to fight them then you would have died and the tale of your family would be lost forever. Your family live on in you. I did not see your father but I am guessing that you resemble him."

He smiled, "I do, Sir Richard but he had a beard."

"Then live in his memory and make him proud of you."

He ate in silence for a while and then asked, "Will he be in heaven, Lord? It is just that he was not shriven in the days before he died."

"He was a good man?"

"He was."

"Then he will be in heaven. I am a soldier and not a priest but at my manor I have a good one, Father Gregory. He can explain it better than I can."

"And is there a place for me in your home, My Lord? Alfred said you were always kind and took in those who were lost."

I smiled, "There is a place for you but it is far from your home. The Wansbeck valley is a wild place compared with Eisicewalt."

"But are there woods?"

"There are."

"Then I can hunt and earn my place in your retinue."

The next day saw us travelling through a midge infested forest over ground that rose and fell. There was no road. It was a track at best and in places even the track seemed to fade. I realised that we had deviated from the main path. Perhaps it was the swarms of insects that distracted me, I do not know, but Geoffrey and the other horses did not like them either. Young Alan had a keen nose and I sent him off to find the path when it became clear we had lost it. The delay cost us an hour and annoyed me.

When he returned his face was ashen, "Lord, I found the path, it is half a mile south of here but…"

"But what?"

He shook his head, "Better you witness it yourself than I try to give words to the horror I found, My Lord."

The body we found was of a young woman. She looked to be no more than sixteen. She had been despoiled and had died as a result of the assault. It affected all of us even though it confirmed for me that we were on the trail of despicable men. They had used and abused the girl and when she had died discarded her. Even though we could not afford the delay we buried her. I spoke words and then we carried on along the road. There would now be just seven captives. How many would survive to be rescued?

The land descended to the Tyne and I hoped that we might be able to see our prey ahead. When we reached the huddle of houses that stood in the cleared land that was Faleston we saw that the houses had been ransacked. I saw no bodies. I wondered if more captives had been added. I called, "Ho, come forth. I am Sir Richard of Eisicewalt and I am here to find the raiders who did this."

The dozen or so people who emerged from the woods were led by three men. The three carried wood axes while two youths behind them carried bows. I dismounted and they approached. Their women and children stayed in the trees.

"When did this happen?"

"This morning, My Lord. We rise early and we heard them as they approached. They spoke in a language we did not understand and, being fearful, I led my people into the woods. They did this." He shook his head, "These are people who just wreck for no reason."

"And I will hunt them."

The man nodded, "Gurth and Leofric, come with me. We will help you, My Lord. I am Arvil of Faleston and the headman. We know the forest."

"Then lead on, Arvil."

The track meant that going on foot was as fast as riding horses. He led us not down the main path but along a hunters' trail. I said nothing but hoped he was making the right decision. The horse dung we had seen on the main path told me the direction the raiders had taken. He was right for his path brought us down to the North Tyne. As soon as I left the cover of the trees then more of the horrible midges appeared. I was going to flick them away when, looking ahead, I saw a movement and I ducked back into the trees. Arvil had already done so and he chuckled, "Aye, My Lord. They have joined this path. They will find the insects there will plague them as they do us. If we stay in the trees then they cannot see us and we can still make good time."

We dismounted and led our horses. Arvil went first and I followed. His two sons flitted ahead of us in and out of the trees. He was right and the main trail would have been little quicker. We had lost sight of the raiders but knowing that they would be moving more slowly than us gave me hope that we might catch them. I guessed they were pushing hard because in a few miles they would pass the invisible line that separated England from Scotland. I am not sure that, apart from the Tweed and the Eden, anyone knew where the border really lay. The ones who lived on the border had disputed it for centuries.

Arvil held up his hand and signed for me to tether my horse. There were plenty of branches and I did so. I did not need to tell the others to do the same. I slowly drew my sword. I did not take my shield. I would draw my other sword if it was needed. I signalled to Elric to go with Arvil's sons up the slope to get on the other side of the raiders. I wanted the three young ones safe and I needed their arrows to force them down the slope. Elric nodded and the three of them scurried up through the trees. They would have a better view down to the river. I turned and pointed to Edward, Alfred and Aethelstan. I made the sign for 'Follow me.' I made the sign for the other seven to follow my pueros. I nodded to Arvil and he moved forward. I stepped next to him.

Ahead I heard a scream and envisioned another of the captives suffering the same fate as the poor girl whose body we had found. As much as I wanted to run I knew that we had to be patient. Arvil was moving silently and cautiously. It meant that if I copied him we would be unlikely to be seen until the last moment for he knew the river. I think we could have moved faster and with less caution for the raiders and their captives were making a great deal of noise. The women and girls had been untethered and it looked to me like three of them were trying to stop the men getting at a young girl. The raiders were going to do what they had done on the trail of the unfortunate girl we had buried. We were close enough now for me to hear their words. The women were begging God to help them and the Danes were cursing in their own language. The result was that as Arvil and I burst out of the trees we were less than ten paces from them.

Three arrows flew from the trees. Two of them hit mail and helmets but the third hit an arm. I drew my second sword as I ran and hacked into a warrior who was drawing his own sword. He managed to block my right arm but my left hacked across his right arm, grating against the bone. Arvil's axe split the skull of a second man. Edward and my pueros were so close to me that we were almost a wedge and we ploughed into the men who, until a few heartbeats earlier, were trying to control women who were fighting off their advances. The raiders grabbed weapons as my young men came from the trees. Thanks to our initial attack we had evened out the numbers a little but they still outnumbered us. The next arrows that came from the trees enjoyed more success as all three found flesh. None were mortal wounds but they distracted the men so that even my young warriors managed to overcome their opponents. I knew who the leader was from his mail, helmet and weapons. Ulf son of Tope hacked and slashed at Aed, one of my young warriors and his sword sliced into Aed's head. The youth had heart but not the skill to face a Dane. The Viking then turned to run for his horse. I was angry. A young man had died and it was my fault for I had not sought out the leader quickly enough. I hurtled after the warrior. I had to run the gauntlet of the surviving warband. While they were fighting my men those who could took the chance to strike at me as I rushed past them. I flailed and slashed with my swords. I blocked most but one blade was heading towards my arm when an arrow slammed into his back and the man fell at my feet, lifeless.

Ulf son of Tope had reached his horse and was trying to mount it. Vikings can and do ride but they are never comfortable doing so and Ulf son of Tope, still holding his sword, could not control his animal. As I brought my sword to slash at him, he blocked the blow. My left hand might have ended his life had his horse not turned in panic. He took out his seax and faced me. He wore an old-fashioned helmet with a face mask. His sword was also an old one but it would be well made and it would be sharp. I knew the seax. It was a nasty slashing weapon that could gut the unwary. I was not wearing mail and I could not take the man for granted. He would be a tough enemy to defeat even with the skills that Taillefer had given me. His horse, freed from control and fearing the fighting, moved away and I was able to face the man on the grassy bank of the river.

He launched himself at me. He could see that which I could not. He was able to watch the fighting behind me. Perhaps he saw that his men were losing.

Whatever the reason he sought to beat me quickly and his hands moved almost as fast as mine in a two-handed attack. I blocked each one but such was the ferocity of the attack that I was forced back. Therein lay the danger for we were both close to the water. He kept up the attack and that meant I had to defend. He was forcing me back as he sought a weakness. My training came to the fore. I was fit and I had practised, when at home, every day. I had fought against Alfred and Aethelstan as well as Bergil and Edward using two swords. I would not tire. He did and in that tiring came a slip. He had to use his left hand for balance as his swing made him almost overbalance. I slashed at his side. His byrnie took the blow but he began to fall and had to fight to keep his balance. If he fell into the river, mailed, then he would drown. I hacked at his right side with my left-hand sword. His mail stopped the blow from cutting him but the force cracked a rib and even behind the face mask I heard the grunt of pain. More importantly, his two slips meant that I was able to go on the offensive. The memory of poor Aed and the sight of the dead, despoiled maiden, drove all mercy from my mind. I rained a flurry of blows at his head as I drove him back the way we had just come. Like me he defended but he had two blows to his side and they now took effect. His hands became slower and in that slowing my swords grew closer to his head. It was my right-hand sword which struck the blow that ended the fight. His seax was too slow to block it and all the power in my right hand helped me to strike at the old helmet. Perhaps it had never been struck as hard before or it might have become brittle with age. Whatever the reason it did not arrest the sword's blade. It struck and split the helmet and sliced through the head protector to sever the skull in two. He dropped like a stone at my feet.

The cheer from behind made me turn. I saw that the raiders were all dead and, Aed apart, my young men had their swords raised and were cheering. Elric held his bow aloft and whooped. We had won.

I took off my helmet and sheathed my swords, "Are any hurt?"

Edward looked around and said, "Aye, lord but nothing that cannot be healed." He looked down. "Except for poor Aed."

I nodded, "Heal the wounded and then we will bury him. This seems as good a place as any."

Arvil nodded, "Aye, it is normally a peaceful place and few pass here. He will lie and be undisturbed."

"You and your sons take what you will from the dead."

He looked at the four tethered sheep, a ram and three ewes, "With your permission, My Lord, we will take the animals. The rest we have no need for."

"Alfred, fetch the horse. Aethelstan, take the weapons and helmets from the dead."

Edward said, "What do we do with them?"

"We have no time to bury them." I looked around. The river had no overhanging trees and there was a large flat rock that jutted out into the river. "We will build a pyre on that rock and burn them. When the next flood comes their ashes will make the way to the sea. Perhaps they will carry them home."

They nodded and I turned to look at the women. Now that I had the opportunity to look more closely at them I saw that all were young women or girls, save for one who looked to be in her twenties, perhaps even her thirties. She had her arms around some of the younger girls. She looked for all the world like a mother duck protecting her young.

"Which of you is Lady Ealdgyth?"

A young woman next to the matronly one stood, "I am Ealdgyth. None call me lady. I thank you, Sir Knight, for our rescue. Did you find the other girl, Nanna? She ran off some days ago and may be lost."

I shook my head, "I am sorry, Ealdgyth, but she is dead." I would not go into the details. Better that they think she had just died rather than have the horror of the manner of her death planted in their memory. "And I have other dire news. Better, I think to deliver it all at once. Your father died. He is buried at Hexham Abbey."

Surprisingly that made her and the older woman smile, sadly, "We thought he died when we were attacked."

"No, My Lady, he lived and was shriven at the Abbey. He died in God's grace and he was able to tell me how to find you. He asked for an oath and I gave it to him. I have almost fulfilled it now." Alfred had brought the horse and I said, "We will leave as soon as we can. Are any of you ladies in need of anything…?" My words tailed off lamely. I was not in a comfortable area speaking of women and their needs.

The matronly one said, "You have saved us, My Lord, and until we return to what passes for civilisation I will continue to watch over these women whom God has placed in my hands."

"And you are?"

"I am Dervilla. I am Ealdgyth's servant and now, it seems, foster mother to these orphaned chicks."

"Then Dervilla, if you need anything just ask. Arvil, can we stay with your people this night?"

"Of course. Leofric, go back to our home and warn our people that we have guests."

It did not take long for the minor wounds to be tended to and my men dug the grave deep. We put Aed's sword in his hand, placed his helmet at his feet and wrapped his body in his cloak. When he was in the grave we put his shield over his face and then piled soil and stones upon it. There would be no marker but every one of those who had left Hexham on the hunt would know exactly where he was buried. We would remember the manner of his death and we would tell the tale. All my men had been shriven before we left Hexham. The prior had blessed our mission. Aed had died in a state of Grace,

"Lord, take Aed to your bosom. His life was ended too soon and I swear that I will do all that I can to ensure that it was not in vain. Amen."

Silence filled the valley and even the birds stopped their chirping. The sun would soon set and peace would come. Every head was bowed.

It was my voice that broke the silence. "Arvil, if you would escort the ladies to your home. Elric and Alfred, go with them and drive the animals for Arvil. We will do what we must for these dead raiders."

Arvil smiled, "You are a thoughtful knight, My Lord. Gurth, lead the way."

The kindling had been laid on the rock and as the former captives disappeared into the trees we laid the bodies on the top. The wind would take the stink of burning flesh away from Arvil's house. I was not sure if the captives had smelled burning flesh before. Its stink was a memory I could do without and I had spared the women from the horror. We knew how to light fires and soon the flames licked the wood we had found. My men had used old wood, much of it was driftwood from when the river flooded. The smoke was swept away from our faces and we saw the flames fanned to ignite the bodies. We waited until the bodies were becoming ash before we turned. Elric stood there watching. He said, "Arvil thought you might need some help to find your way back. Alfred and I have already fetched the horses, My Lord."

"Thank you, Elric, and thank you for the arrow that saved me from the Viking sword."

He looked surprised, "How did you know it was me, My Lord?"

"It was you, was it not?" He nodded. "I just knew, Elric. You were meant to serve me and now it is confirmed."

As we headed up the path to Faleston I wondered if I was meant to save the women too. I knew, better than any, how lucky we had been. If we had not found Arvil then another might have died or we might have failed to surprise them. Our skill, God's hand and our righteous cause had helped but I was not ruling out the hand of Fate.

Chapter 5

Arvil's wife had organised the feeding of the captives and my men. The Vikings had taken much food on their raid, as well as treasure. Most of the food we would leave for Arvil. The treasure we would divide up but that night did not seem the time. The homes were small ones and, the women apart, we would sleep in the open. We all ate outside the house. Hewn logs were used for seats and the women shared wooden platters. My men each had their own spoon, eating knife, coistrel and wood platter. We ate in silence. The silence showed the mixed nature of the feelings of those gathered outside eating. In the case of my men, it was a reflection on the death of Aed and the luck of wounds that would not cause problems in the future. For the women, I guess, it was the relief that they were no longer captives. I suspected that Arvil and his people were wondering at this incursion into their isolated world. Faleston was too far from anywhere to be concerned with who ruled. They lived simple untroubled lives and our visit had merely shown them the true value of their isolation. That the women had been deprived of food and drink on the journey north was clear as they devoured everything that was placed before them. Dervilla had truly taken charge of them. She ensured that they were all fed before she ate herself and even when she ate, one eye was on the women she led. I learned as they ate, their names and ages. Mary was almost fifteen and the closest in age to Ealdgyth.

Next came Elfrida who was fourteen, Beth, close to thirteen, Edith who was twelve and the youngest, Susan, who was ten. Their families had all been slaughtered. They were now orphans. Some had been better off than others but now they were all in the same position; penniless and wearing clothes that had endured a long walk from Langley.

My thoughts, I am sorry to say, were selfish ones. I was now responsible, until I could deliver them back to their hall, and I was forced to look after them. This had nothing to do with the king or the Archbishop of York. I had given myself the burden when I had sworn an oath. What would I do with them when we reached Brougham? I could not simply abandon them. Their men were all dead. I wondered if there was a lord in the west who could take them in. Perhaps the Lord of Craven might offer me aid. He had seemed like a good knight. My mind was like a maelstrom that night and, despite my exhaustion, I did not sleep well. It was nothing to do with the ground but the enormity of my task.

We used the horse we had captured and Aed's horse to carry four of the women. Ealdgyth rode with Dervilla. Beth and Mary shared Aed's horse. The three smaller girls rode behind Edward, Alfred and Aethelstan. Arvil's sons led us, the next day, to the road south to Bellingham. I saw, when we passed it where I had gone wrong. A branch had fallen across the path. We parted just eight miles from Bellingham. I think the youths had enjoyed their adventure. They had fought and killed Danish raiders and gained treasure. They both sported fine swords and daggers now. They also had silver in their purses. Until they went to a town and a market the silver would remain unused but I knew that just having the silver would make them feel more like warriors and men.

As we rode I spoke, first to the three smaller girls and then the other, older two. Two were cousins but all three were orphans. The two older girls, one had been the one about to be abused, were fourteen summers old and were sisters. They were Beth and Mary. The one who had been attacked barely spoke and when I leaned closer to her she recoiled. She would need the comfort of a priest, or perhaps Dervilla could do something.

I spent the longest, on the road from Bellingham, speaking to Dervilla and Ealdgyth. I intended to spend the night at Hexham Abbey and I did not want to camp on the road for obvious reasons. I was not sure if there were any raiders about. The men who were not riding double were in two lines twenty paces off the road. We would have an early warning of an ambush.

"Did my father suffer?" Ealdgyth then shook her head, "I thought that he was dead when we were taken. Had I known…"

I spoke softly, "He was a warrior and he was tough. His end was better than one left on the side of the road. If it is any consolation the healers at the abbey thought that the worm inside him would have killed him soon enough."

"Worm?"

Dervilla spoke, "He visited a physician who told him some months ago, before the first attack, that he had a worm inside him. Your father knew he was going to die and that was why he was on a pilgrimage. He also thought to ask the Bishop of Durham to be your guardian."

I said nothing but I could not see the newly appointed Bishop Walcher taking on that responsibility. Instead I asked, "First attack?"

It was Dervilla who spoke, "Two weeks before we left for the pilgrimage Scots and rebels attacked our home. The thegn fought alongside our men but more than half of our men were killed and the hall was burned down." She lowered her voice and pointed to the other young women and girls, "Their families were all killed and the thegn took them to be his wards. After we buried the dead we left to ride to Hexham. We stayed at Brough and Appleby."

Ealdgyth said, "I think he hoped for help from the lords there." She shook her head and said, bitterly, "They were Normans and wanted nothing to do with us."

Her words were accusatory but I knew that the Normans who had been appointed were not well thought of by the king. I knew not their names but the two remote and poor manors would hardly be considered a reward. Men like Sir Alain Rufus had been given the Honour of Richmond. That was the reward for a warrior. Brough and Appleby, from what I had learned, were two windswept specks on the backbone of England. Brougham was a much richer prize and whoever the king gave that to would be a happy man.

"Not all Normans are like that."

Ealdgyth said, "You speak English well, for a Norman."

I smiled, "And that is because only half of me is Norman, the bastard half. My mother was English."

"Yet you serve the Normans."

"I was brought up, My Lady, in Normandy. My father was a Norman Seigneur. I was always going to fight for the Normans."

The land began to descend towards the Tyne Valley and I knew that soon we would be at Hexham. "We will stay at Hexham until we have wagons to take you and the orphans back to Brougham."

It was Dervilla who answered. She snapped, somewhat ungraciously I thought, "My Lord, were you not listening? There is no hall at Brougham. There are no men at Brougham. If you take us there then dig our graves before you leave to save others the trouble."

I felt scolded. I flushed and said nothing. Ealdgyth reached over and touched my arm, "My Lord, we are grateful to you but all that you have done is deliver us from the clutches of one predator. If you abandon us then it will only be a matter of time before another such man preys upon us."

"It is sad that you feel this way."

She gave me a sad smile, "My mother died when I was born seventeen years ago and Dervilla raised me for my father was busy with the manor. I have seen little in men that fills me with any hope that I might have a happy life. Perhaps I bring bad luck. My mother died, our manor was lost and my father slain."

"Do not say such things, my child. It is blasphemous." Dervilla made the sign of the cross as she spoke and I then reassessed the servant. If she had raised Ealdgyth for seventeen years then she was older than I had thought. I wondered at her story.

What had she given up looking after the daughter of another?

"When we reach the abbey I will ask the prior for advice. He is a wise man."

"Perhaps there is a convent. There I could be safe from the evil that men bring,"

Dervilla shook her head and her voice was firm, "You are too much like your mother to do that."

"I never knew my mother."

Dervilla's voice softened, "I did, for I was her body servant and a kinder woman you never met. You were her only child and she was young when she bore you. She had seen just sixteen summers. We were of an age and, until she carried you, we were like sisters rather than mistress and servant. It was she who taught me to read, as I taught you. Your father could not read. You are right, Sir Richard, he was a warrior. He was wounded at the battle of Gate Fulford and that changed him. He was not at Stamford Bridge nor at Senlac Hill. He withdrew into himself. No, a nunnery is not for you. We will find a way out of this. I owe it to your mother." Dervilla was a woman who knew her own mind.

By the time Hexham Abbey hove into view, I had a much clearer picture of their lives. I still had no answer to my dilemma but I hoped for guidance from the prior.

A great fuss was made of the captives when we reached the abbey. I am not sure that anyone expected us to succeed. They had seen a handful of, mainly, callow youths chasing twice the number of dangerous Vikings. We were lauded too. Once again my men and I camped outside the abbey. I was offered a chamber, along with the captives but I declined as I wanted to be with my men. The captives had their hurts tended to and were found habits to wear while their clothes were washed by the lay brothers. None of them had had the chance to wash. There was blood on their clothes and faces. None of it was theirs but the journey had been a hard one. Water was heated for them and soap provided. The next time we saw them again was when we ate in the refectory. The abbey, in those days, was small and we filled it. The benches were rammed. The captives were now cleaned and looked totally different in their borrowed habits. Ealdgyth looked radiant. I am not sure if it was that the dirt and blood had been washed from her or that the cowl framed her features but she looked angelic.

The prior blessed the food but then went on, at great length, to pray that the curse of, as he called them, 'barbarians from the north', would end. I was hungry when he began and starving by the time he finished. The food was plain but good and there was fresh bread. It was raveled but well made. The soup was also wholesome. I had, however, no chance to talk about the women for Ealdgyth and Dervilla were seated opposite me. Ealdgyth wanted to know where her father was buried and the prior told her. "When we have eaten, Prior, I would go and say goodbye to him. I think it is unlikely that we will pass this way again."

The prior glanced at me and frowned. I said nothing. The abbey had services during the night and as soon as we had finished the tables were cleared. The young women and girls, Ealdgyth and Dervilla apart, retired as did my men. The prior took the two of them outside. I went to see to the horses. That done I waited to speak to the prior but when the bell sounded for compline I knew I would have to be patient. I knew that sleep would be impossible and so I waited outside the chapel. When the service was over the prior emerged and seeing me there smiled, "I thought to retire to my cell, Sir Richard, but I am not surprised that you await me. Ealdgyth spoke to me and I can see your dilemma. Come, let us return to the chapel. It is empty now and God can help us to form my words and our thoughts."

We both bowed and made the sign of the cross when we entered. There were candles burning and they gave an aethereal feel to the meeting as the flickering flames sent shadows and reflected light from the metal objects on the altar.

"I have spoken to Ealdgyth," he smiled, "and the formidable Dervilla. If ever a man was born in a woman's body it is that one. The lady could be a warrior. Neither of them wish to return to Brougham."

"But she could rebuild. It is a better manor than Brough or Appleby."

He fingered the silver cross around his neck, "It is but there are some things about Ealdgyth and her father that you should know. One of his ancestors was Eochaid. Eochaid died almost two hundred years ago in Wales but Ælfgar and therefore Ealdgyth are descended from him." I frowned for what difference did an ancestor make? He smiled patiently as he explained, "Eochaid was the last king of Strathclyde and the last king of Cumbria." It was the Scots who had named Cumberland. I forgot who had told me on the campaign in the north but someone had.

"Then surely that is more reason for her to wish to live there."

He shook his head, "There are many who know of this. Giric was the king of Scotland, although the land was not called that then, who took over Strathclyde after Eochaid was driven into exile. The family of Kenneth mac Alpin were ruthless and all those with a claim to the throne were killed. Eochaid was beyond his reach. The lineage of the kings of Scotland is a mottled map. Macbeth was from the lords of Moray and he ruled Scotland briefly and there have been others with dubious claims. Ealdgyth could be chosen by one who wishes the Scottish crown. It would add legitimacy to a claim. Ealdgyth is a wise woman and she knows this. She wishes to be anonymous. The last thing she needs is to be used as a means to a crown."

I shook my head, "This makes no sense to me but…"

He smiled, "Harold Godwinson had little claim to the throne of Wessex and England until his sister married Edward the Confessor, yet he was crowned King of England when Edward the Confessor died. To men who seek power the smallest thing can prove vital."

"So, what happens to her?"

"The safest thing is for the Bishop of Durham to make her a royal ward. When the abbot returns I will ask him to write to the bishop."

"The bishop cares not for such matters."

"I know but the Palatinate belongs to the king and if she is a royal ward then she is safe."

"Then she would live at Durham?"

"No. I would suggest that she lives with you, at least until matters are settled. Eisicewalt is far enough from the border and close enough to York for her to be safe. You are known as a loyal knight of William and more, you are known for your honour and chivalry. The lady would be safe in your hall."

"Me? My hall?" I was not sure I liked the changes that would be wrought.

"The lady and," he gave a wry smile, "Dervilla think it is a good idea. They both seem impressed by you."

"I am just a warrior, and I will be guided by you and," I waved a hand around the chapel, "God, but I am sure there would be worthier men who could be chosen for this task."

"You are right, My Lord, you have been chosen and perhaps it is God himself who has chosen you."

I made my way back to my camp. My men were asleep and I rolled into my blanket and cloak as I tried to join them. Once more the thoughts racing through my mind fought the need for sleep. On a practical level we would need to build either a hall or an extension to the existing one for the seven new occupants. In the short term we could use the warrior hall that we had built for my warriors. Edward and his wife could return to my hall and my pueros to their mother. The seven would also need to be fed. The manor produced enough food for those who already lived there but another seven mouths could make all the difference. Then I remembered Elric; eight more mouths. Eventually I drifted off to sleep.

Even as I woke to make water I realised we had the problem of horses. The thirty-mile journey to

Hexham had been manageable but we had a longer one to reach Eisicewalt.

"Edward, take these coins," I tossed him a purse, "see if you can buy ponies, sumpters, anything with four legs that could carry our guests."

He nodded, "I will see. How far is it to Brougham, My Lord?"

"We are not going west. We will take them to Eisicewalt. They will be our guests." His jaw dropped and I gave him a wan smile, "I will explain when time allows but we need to get home as soon as we can. We have been away for longer than I wished."

"Yes, My Lord."

I had not been woken by the bells for the services but clearly others had for the women and some of my men were already in the refectory. The prior was absent and I faced Ealdgyth and Dervilla as I ate my porridge.

Ealdgyth smiled, "You slept well, My Lord?"

"I had much to think about." The porridge was hot and I blew on the spoon before tasting it. It was good. The cook had laced it with honey. "The prior tells me that you wish me to continue to be your protector."

The smile left her face as she added, nervously, "Does that meet with your agreement, My Lord?"

"I am both honoured and flattered but you should know that I am unused to the ways of women."

Dervilla laughed, "There are no women in your hall? I understand that the mother of your pueros runs your home."

"She does but…"

"And we are no different from her." Dervilla had spoken and decided that was not an issue.

I ate my porridge and did not fall into the trap of saying that she was different from any woman I had ever met.

Ealdgyth reached over and touched the back of my hand, "My Lord, we will not be a burden to you. I am sure that we can help on the manor. The girls and young women all lived on farms and they know how to tend animals, cook and sew." I nodded and smiled. Before I could say anything she hurried on, "And I can be of help too."

Once more I avoided giving voice to the question that leapt into my mind. How? Instead, I said, "You must forgive me, My Lady, I am a warrior and can think and plan in battle, I had planned on taking you back to Brougham and it is the change in plans that has given me problems, not the provision of a home. When Edward returns we can leave and within a few days we shall be in my manor and by then I will have an idea how we can proceed."

Dervilla laughed, "We are not a military operation, Sir Richard. I can see that I will have to help guide your hand and mind."

I had no doubt that she would.

We had almost eighty miles to go and I asked the prior if there was any food to be had for the journey. Had it been just my men then we could have ridden hard and made the journey in two days. We would only have need of accommodation for one night. He said he would find some. Edward managed to buy three more horses. It meant that only the smallest of the girls, Susan, had to ride double, with Elric who was also light.

The delay meant we left later than I would have liked but we were blessed not only by the prior but by clement weather. We reached the village of Alclud where we camped at the confluence of the Wear and the Clyde. The villagers had little to spare in the way of food but they found kindling for our fires. We cooked a hunter's stew. Once more Elric proved his value and our pot had some meat in it. Surprisingly, the mood was a happy one. The girls seemed to laugh more and the young men had overcome their natural shyness. There was banter and laughter.

Ealdgyth saw me as I observed them. "It is good to see is it not, My Lord?"

"I am pleased but also surprised. After the horror of the journey, you all endured…"

She nodded, "I see the faces of those…, those beasts, in my dreams. I wake up shivering at the thought of their filthy paws touching me but I also know, as the others do, that we were lucky. Poor Nanna was not so lucky and had you not come when you did then Beth might have been abused too. I do not doubt that by the time we reached wherever those animals were taking us, we would all have suffered the same ordeal but you did come. You saved us all. That is why we asked the prior to see if we could stay with you. You and your men make us all feel safer."

I looked over to the others who were washing the platters in the river. Their chatter drifted over, "Even Dervilla?"

"Even Dervilla." She moved a little closer to me, "Let me tell you the story of Dervilla and you will understand her a little more. Her father was slain in battle by the men of Strathclyde. She looked after her mother until she died and then my mother asked my father if she could live with us for they had been friends since childhood. Her father had also been a thegn but the men of Strathclyde had taken everything. She came to us as a pauper. She is pretty and a young man wished to marry her. He was not twice her age as my father was to my mother. He was a young man. When my mother died and she took over my upbringing, she ended the young man's hopes. He died at Gate Fulford."

"How do you know all this, did Dervilla tell you?"

She shook her head, "Dervilla keeps her feelings to herself. It was my father who told me when I was old enough to understand. You can see that I owe all to Dervilla. She has been as a mother to me but more than that, she is a woman who sacrificed everything for me. She gave up a hope of a husband or a family."

"Then the further you are from your home the happier you shall all be."

She nodded, "I know that my heart has become lighter with every step we take south."

We set sentries that night and I took a duty with Elric. We tended the fire that kept away the midges from the river. They were not as bad as the ones in the forest at Faleston but they still liked to bite. "Well, Elric, do you still wish to live with my men and me?"

He grinned, "Even more so, My Lord. I have lost one family but it seems to me I have fallen in with a larger one. My mother, father and sister will always be in my heart but I now have five who could be sisters to me. Dervilla already shows that she is a natural mother and you, My Lord, well, you are like a father to me."

"But I have done nothing for you."

"You have, My Lord. You have given me a place and you have tried to keep me safe. When we fought the Vikings you sent me to a place where I had more chance to survive. Aed died and others were wounded but none came even close to me. Gurth and Leofric noticed that too. It is the little things you do. Alfred and Aethelstan also tell me that you are like their father."

"But I am not old enough yet to…"

Edward had risen to relieve me and overheard the conversation. He said, "Elric is right, lord. I know this better than any. When you took my brother and me under your wing you behaved as a good father would and you continue to do so. My brother ran and that was his loss. When you take a wife, My Lord, and father your own children then they will be truly blessed."

Having spoken to Ealdgyth I was able to see the change in the former captives. When we crossed the Tees at Persebrig and saw the fertile lands of the vale of York before us the mood became even more gay. Here there were forests but they were in the distance. The land to the north had been raided and had suffered when King William had punished the north but the land south of the Tees had escaped his wrath and it showed. We passed farmers and their families harvesting crops under the late summer sun. We saw, in the fields, young lambs that promised prosperity and that all translated to the mood of what I now saw as my people.

As we neared Alvertune where I planned on making our last stop before my manor, I had resigned myself to taking on the responsibility of caring for another eight souls. They all seemed to think that I could do it as did my men. The one who needed to be persuaded was me.

Chapter 6

I sent Alfred and Aethelstan to warn their mother and Bergil of our imminent arrival. They could inform Benthe, their mother, that the warrior hall would need to be prepared. When my pueros rode off Ealdgyth nudged her horse next to mine, "I assume, My Lord, that we are close to your home."

I nodded, "You have a sharp mind, Ealdgyth. I hope that Eisicewalt is not too dull for it."

"I confess that while I am pleased to have a home that will be safe for my people I am also a little worried about how I will fit into your household."

"You can make any changes you wish, Ealdgyth. I want you and the others to be happy. I am new to the running of a manor. Indeed, when you are all settled I must take myself north to see my other manor before the onset of winter."

"You have another?"

"The king gave me Norton. Had the Scots not invaded then I might have been there already. I know little about it except that it lies on the Tees and was Danish."

"The king must think well of you, My Lord."

"I have served him since he fought the Bretons, Ealdgyth. I am his warrior and that is the reason I fight for the Normans, as you call them, and not the Saxons. It is the way of the warrior. I took an oath with my shield brothers. We have kept that oath. I am King William's man."

She nodded, "Did the prior tell you of my ancestors?"

"He did."

"Then you should know that my ancestors were not Saxon. They were closer to the Welsh. My father had an English name and over the years there were those who were Saxons who married into our family. My mother was one but Dervilla, she is also from the land of Strathclyde and her blood is also a mix. What I am saying, My Lord, is that the past is just that, the past. We now live in a land where we have a king who comes from another country, but if the men who fight for him are all like you then there is hope that it will be a safer place. The people do not really care who rules them so long as they are safe and can live in peace. That is my hope too."

When we passed through my gate and into my yard there was already a flurry of activity. Benthe had everyone, Mathilde, Agnetha, Maud and Seara, working like bees gathering honey. At the clattering of the horses Benthe's head appeared from the door to the warrior hall, "My Lord, you made good time."

I knew she meant that I was early. I dismounted and handed my reins to Aedgar, my horse master, "Do not over tax yourself, Benthe. The ladies have spent two nights camped on the ground and…"

"And we can help you. Come, ladies, this is our new home, let us help to make it a happy one. I am Dervilla and you must be Benthe. Your sons have told me much about you." Her winning smile and forthright manner took Benthe by surprise.

"My Lady, we have yet to fill sacks with the straw for the paillasses."

"And I have no title. We have many hands and they will make light of it." She turned, "Mistress

Ealdgyth, while his lordship shows you the hall we will make our nests. Come, my chicks."

I put my arms up to help Ealdgyth from her horse. I smiled, "We have, it seems, been given our orders. I shall show you the hall."

I did not mean to but as I helped her down she fell against me and our faces were close. Neither of us moved but stared at the other.

Aedgar coughed, "I will take the lady's horse, My Lord."

The moment was over and I turned, keenly aware that I was flushed, "Thank you Aedgar. This is Lady Ealdgyth."

She shook her head, "I told you I need no title." She held out a hand to Aedgar, "You must be the horse master. I can see that you lavish good care on his lordship's horses."

He beamed, "I do my… mistress and we now breed our own. My sons and I will try to do something about those poor bidets you have bought, My Lord."

"We had little choice, Aedgar." I held out my arm and she placed her hand upon it, "As you can see the hall is ancient. It was, in former times, a hunting lodge. We have tried to improve it. We now have a fishpond and a hogbog as well as an oven that the villagers use."

She looked through the gate, "The village looked prosperous when we passed through."

"It was not always so but Father Gregory and Ethelred are helping me to make it so."

We toured the outbuildings. When we passed the women they curtsied. Ealdgyth might not give herself the title but my people recognised a lady when they saw one.

Before we entered the hall she said, "Might I walk through the village with you, My Lord? Brougham was not so much a village as a cluster of farms. I am interested to see these people whose community I have joined."

As we walked she made a point of speaking to everyone. When we reached the church she knelt at the altar to say a prayer and Father Gregory, having seen us enter joined us. Ealdgyth enchanted him as she had the villagers. She complimented him on his church and asked the priest to say a mass for her dead father. It was the first time since we had camped by the river that she had mentioned him. The mass would be a way of paying her respects.

It was late in the afternoon when we had finished our wanderings. She had met and charmed old Ethelred who was tongue tied. She had that kind of beauty and her smile simply captivated.

Dervilla stood in the door of the hall, her arms folded across her chest and a stern expression on her face, "Sir Richard, why have you kept my mistress from her rest? We have ridden hard this day and now you have her gallivanting here there and everywhere."

I opened my mouth to speak but Ealdgyth snapped, "Dervilla, it was I who chose to walk the village and I will not have you speak that way to Sir Richard."

I saw the hint of a smile pass over Dervilla's face before she bowed her head and said, "You are right, Mistress. I apologise, Sir Richard. I have cared for this bairn her whole life and it is hard to let go although I know that now she is a woman, I need to become a different sort of servant."

Ealdgyth ran to her foster mother, "You were never a servant, Dervilla. Come, let us go within and I can see the hall. It is the one place I have yet to explore."

I led them both around the hall, keenly aware of Birgitte and others preparing the table for the evening meal while enticing smells rose from the kitchen. Benthe would want to impress our guests.

When we descended Dervilla said, "Thank you for the tour, My Lord and now we must prepare ourselves. Benthe has kindly invited Ealdgyth and me to dine with you. I believe that Bergil and Seara will entertain the other five ladies." Ealdgyth gave me a warm smile as they left the hall.

Benthe came from the kitchen when she heard the door close, "I hope you do not mind my presumption, My Lord."

"What?" I was still bemused by Ealdgyth's smile.

"I invited the two ladies to dine with Edward, Mathilde and myself. The boys said that they would dine in the warrior hall. I cannot think why!" Her tone told me that she knew very well that it was the attraction of the older girls that had been the nectar that drew them from my hall.

"I am content, Benthe, and I am sorry I could not give you more warning."

Her face opened in a smile as bright as a sunrise, "Lord, you are the most Christian of men. It is wonderful that you take so many who are homeless into your home. I mind not although your purse will grow lighter."

"Money is not everything, Benthe. Perhaps my good deeds will help make up for the men whose lives I have ended prematurely."

Her face darkened, "You have never killed anyone who did not deserve it. Bergil, Edward and my boys have told me that. Your place in heaven is assured, My Lord." She made the sign of the cross as she departed.

I had some fine clothes. They had been the ones I had worn when the king was crowned. I rarely wore them but this seemed the right time to do so. I also asked Edward to trim my hair. I was the first one in the hall where we would dine. Birgitte had placed wildflowers in pots around the room and mixed with rosemary, thyme and marjoram, they gave off a pleasant smell. There were good candles on the table and I saw that eating knives were there as well as spoons. When the captives had been taken they had lost everything.

Birgitte came in with a jug of wine she had tapped from the barrel. She placed it on the table next to the beakers. She said, hesitantly, "My Lord, these beakers are good enough for us but you have ladies as guests, perhaps you should think about buying better." I did not answer immediately for I was thinking that she was right. "I am sorry, Sir Richard. I did not mean to be impertinent."

"And you are not. You are quite right. I need to make many changes around here. And Birgitte."

"Yes, My Lord?"

"There is no difference between you, your mother and Lady Ealdgyth. You deserve to drink from a well-made vessel. When time allows we shall all go to York and the market there. It is time I spent some of the money I have been hoarding."

She hurried off smiling the same smile as her mother. They were like two peas in a pod. I poured myself some wine and drank some. It was not the best wine. Sometimes wine did not travel well. That was something else I needed, better wine. I sat in the soft chair that lay before the fire. We had a fire burning all year, even in summer. The old hall had a tendency to dampness. The flickering flames helped me to daydream. I had chests of coins. I had been rewarded many times and I had been frugal. Taillefer had left not only his horse, Parsifal, to me, but also his fortune. Being victorious on the battlefield meant that I had good weapons and mail for my men. I also had the coins that the dead warriors had hoarded. Vikings, in particular, liked silver and kept it about their person. When I had sought Hereward it was the dead Danes who had yielded silver. I would spend as much of my fortune as was needed.

The two ladies had used the hot water and soap provided by my people, I was used to the stink of horses but they were not and both smelled of rosemary when they entered. Ealdgyth said, "Sir Richard, you put us to shame with your fine clothes."

I was appalled by my own lack of thought, "I am sorry, I should have…"

Dervilla said, "It shows respect, Ealdgyth, and Benthe has told me that there is some cloth. We can sew and make our own clothes."

"I had planned on visiting the market in York, and we can buy better cloth."

"You are kind, Sir Richard, but we would not wish to become a burden."

It was my turn to smile, "It is no burden, My Lady, it is a joy."

Edward and Mathilde entered. His wife was beautiful and Edward had married well but she looked particularly radiant. Edward looked like the cat who has just discovered an upturned pail of milk.

I took her hand and kissed it, "You look well, my dear. Is it good to have your husband home again?"

She giggled and said, "It is always good when I do not have to sleep alone."

Like a dam bursting Edward blurted out, "My Lord, I am to be a father. Mathilde is with child."

I could not help but stand and hug him, "And I am pleased beyond words. We have many reasons to celebrate this night."

As if they had been waiting for the news to be given, Birgitte and Benthe entered with the fish. "My Lord, these are fish from our own pond."

"Good."

They sat and looked at me. I nodded and said Grace.

The fish was most succulent and well cooked. Even Dervilla looked impressed. We mopped up the juices with manchet. They had used some of our precious wheat to impress our guests. Ethelred had hunted the previous week and the young hind had been hung for a few days. It too was delicious. We finished with a posset made from cream and the brambles married with the first of the apples from our orchard. The wine had not tasted as bad when supped with the food and we all had the rosy glow of those who have dined well.

Dervilla said, "If we eat as well as that each night, Sir Richard, then we will need much more cloth for our clothes."

"We do eat well but this is a celebration." I was thinking that, for the past many days, the best that they had eaten was the hunters' stew by the river.

I know that I wished the night to go on forever and felt that Ealdgyth did too but the other women determined that rest was needed and Dervilla and Ealdgyth left for the warrior hall. I sat alone before the dying fire reflecting on the changes in my life. That night I had strange dreams that I could not remember when I woke but knew that I had been troubled and I did not know why.

As much as I wished to spend time with Ealdgyth I had much to do on the manor. I took Edward and the pueros with me as we rode first around my farm and then to visit others like Forlan, whose farm marked the end of my manor. I spoke to them all and Edward had a wax tablet with him so that he could write down what I needed to do. Ealdgyth's presence was distracting me already.

As we left Forlan's farm I said, "Aethelstan and Alfred, I no longer need you as pueros."

Alfred was appalled, "My Lord, what have we done to offend you?"

I smiled. Edward was smiling too for we had spoken of this on the way back from Faleston. "I do not need pueros for the two of you shall be men at arms. Aedgar shall breed you two horses from Parsifal and Marie. I will have Uhtred use the mail we took from the dead Danes to make you both better hauberks."

"My Lord..." both were almost speechless.

"You both deserve it. The young men we took to the north will need to be trained and you can help Bergil to do that."

We rode back to the village. Edward said, "The land is at peace now, My Lord. We have time to prepare."

"Hereward is still at large. Hugh d'Avranches is busy with the Welsh border and I cannot believe that the Ætheling has given up his dreams of the crown. We did not destroy King Malcolm's army and the king's rapid departure means that, I fear, the Scottish king will return. We have time but that will be just until the next year. You and I, Edward, will need to travel to Norton before the time of the bone fire. We need to see what problems are waiting for me there."

"Yes, My Lord."

I found that I missed the company of the ladies for I dined with just my two newly appointed men at arms. Their company was pleasant enough but neither was Ealdgyth. I retired early and that meant I rose early. The hall was quiet. Just Birgitte and her mother were in the kitchen and they were making the dough to put in the ovens. Lars had lit the bread oven and it would soon be ready to receive the dough. The villagers would bring their dough later in the day. The fire would be fed all day.

"Do you want an early breakfast, My Lord? I can slice and fry some ham."

"No, Benthe. I will watch the sunrise and smell the new day."

I walked out into the chill air. It was September and now that August had passed it seemed that Autumn was almost upon us. The leaves from the willows had begun to fall and there was a freshness in the air. I regretted not donning my cloak. I walked through the yard at the rear of my hall. Most of the buildings I passed had been built by my men. One of the reasons I wanted to walk was to decide where to put the new dwelling. The former captives needed a home to be built for them and I had to make a decision about its location. I waved to my three labourers who were already busy gathering eggs, milking animals and collecting vegetables. They would breakfast once those important tasks were completed. I strode through the gate at the rear. We rarely bolted it. I passed the pond and saw fish coming to the surface to feed on the insects that hovered upon it. I walked towards the east.

It was as I neared the woods that I saw movement. The warrior in me became alert. I just had my dagger with me but my hand went to it. It was with some relief that I saw Ethelred coming from the woods. Slung over his shoulder was a large dog fox.

He walked over to me, "This one has been taking fowl from the village. He was a bold one, My Lord. I mean we know that he must live but he was brazenly walking into the farms. I managed to get him last night." He seemed to realise that my appearance was more remarkable than his own. "What brings you out so early, My Lord?"

"I have much to do on the manor, Ethelred. Our new guests need housing."

He put the dead fox on the ground, "Aye, Lord, you have made many changes in a short time. I often have to stop and look at the old lodge and try to picture it as it was."

"Are the changes for the better?"

He laughed, “Why, of course they are, My Lord. The people are prosperous. We did not suffer as others did when the king became angry. We have a priest and there will be food on the table this winter. What more could you have done?”

“I don’t know, Ethelred, that is the problem. There is no one to guide me and offer advice.”

He picked up the fox and we began to walk back around the fishpond, “Keep doing what you are doing, My Lord. Your instincts serve you well.”

Just then the sun burst over the eastern horizon and illuminated the fishpond with its golden rays. The still waters made a perfect surface to show the beauty of the day.

Ethelred said, “Aye, this shows God’s grandeur, My Lord. Have you ever seen anything more beautiful?”

“You are right, Ethelred.” I looked beyond the fishpond to my walls and the manor. It was as though God was pointing a celestial finger at my buildings. I clapped Ethelred about the shoulders, “And I now know where to build the new hall for the women. I will add another wing to the hall on the opposite side to the one with the kitchen. It does not need to be large. A room for Ealdgyth, another for Dervilla and one for the other five.”

Ethelred nodded, “Aye, for I think that at least two of those young women will not need to stay there long!” I turned and looked at him. He chuckled, “I have spoken to Aethelstan and Alfred. They still regard me as someone that can be asked for advice. Both have set their caps on two of the captives.”

I had known of their interest, of course, I had seen their eyes when they had travelled back and heard their words when we dined but if they were thinking about marriage then it was a sudden development.

We parted at the gate and Ethelred went to his cottage. It, too, was much changed from the hovel in which I had found him. The yard was bathed in light and I was able to see where we could build the extension. It would be a single storey. We could build it first and then break through. The rooms that were on the other side were for storage. Benthe had already asked me for them to be moved closer to the kitchen. We would add to the kitchen. There was room next to the hogbog.

I strolled into the kitchen and rubbed my hands, "And now, Benthe, I am ready for food. I will eat it in here."

"In here, My Lord? Would not the dining hall be more comfortable?"

"I need to speak to you and to Lars, Drogo and Gandálfr when they eat."

"Very well, My Lord. Birgitte, lay a place for Sir Richard." I knew she was not happy. Benthe liked to do things her way but she would not argue with me.

My three men came in and looked surprised. They hesitated, "Sit, I need to speak to you and we can do so while we enjoy a Benthe breakfast. There is none finer." My flattery assuaged her upset. "I need new buildings and we will require them to be finished before the onset of winter." Benthe laid the bread, butter and fried ham before us. My three workers hesitated. I laughed, "Come, just act as though I am not here. Eat as you would normally."

I sliced a hunk of bread and smeared it with the butter. I took a thick piece of ham and placed it on the bread. The smell of fried ham makes everyone hungry and they soon emulated me.

"We need first to build some storerooms for Benthe here, close to the kitchen and running alongside the hogbog." I drank some ale to wash down the bread and ham and to give them time to take it in. "Does that suit, Benthe?"

"Aye, My Lord. It will save time."

"When that is done and the barrels and pots brought from the other storeroom we will build a wing on the other side of the house to match this one. It will have four chambers within. One large bedchamber, two smaller ones and a room that the ladies can use to sit."

Lars was the senior and we had built a dwelling for him and his wife Agnetha, "Just one floor, My Lord?"

"Just one. We have no time to build stairs. This has to be done quickly. Aethelstan and Alfred cannot live with their mother forever and Bergil and Seara need Elric to be out from under their feet. They need the warrior hall; besides, it is not suitable for seven ladies."

"This is a busy time of year, My Lord. We have much to prepare and store for winter will soon be upon us. The ditches need to be cleaned before the winter rains."

"It will be done, Lars, for I command it but you are right. It needs more than the three of you. Bergil, Edward and I will all help. Aethelstan, Alfred and Elric can also toil."

"Do not forget Ethelred, Sir Richard. He can labour too."

"Aye, Benthe, he can. Get the storage rooms built first. I must visit York in the next day or so. When I return we will make changes. Birgitte, I would like you to come with me. I need to buy cloth and I know nothing about such things."

Birgitte was excited and she beamed, "Thank you, My Lord."

Benthe asked, "Cloth, My Lord?"

"Our guests need clothes to be made. If there is anything that you need, Benthe, then let me know. I will see the smith and make sure he has enough tools made for us to use. All else we have, do we not?"

"Yes, lord. We have enough seasoned timber in the barn." We had cleared a piece of ground of the trees. It had been roughly ploughed and in the spring we would plant beans there.

"Good and you should all know that once the work is done I must take Edward and spend a month at Norton. I have neglected that property."

Benthe wiped her hands on her apron, "You work too hard, My Lord. When do you get time to enjoy being a lord?"

"I am not sure there will ever be such a time, Benthe. It seems to me that being a lord means having more work to do than being a simple soldier."

Over the last couple of years, I had begun to realise why Taillefer had eschewed the opportunity to be a lord of the manor. He enjoyed his life too much.

Chapter 7

I took Edward and my two men at arms along with Birgitte when I went to York. We had a list of the goods that we needed. Egbert and Benthe had compiled it. I think that Ealdgyth would have liked to come but she did not pluck up the courage to ask me. We left before dawn for I intended to sleep that night under my own roof.

As we headed down the road in the lightening sky I gave my squire my instructions, "Edward, I will leave these three with you. I shall give you my purse and let you and Birgitte buy all that is needed." Money was not important and they had the list. I needed little and my search was for information.

"And you, My Lord?"

"I need to speak to Belisarius and the new archbishop, Thomas of Bayeux. They know what transpires in the rest of the country. I need to know, in advance, of any dangers. If we are to spend a month in the north then I have to know if it will be safe to do so."

When we entered the city, through the old Roman gate at Bootham, we passed the minster which had been destroyed by the Danes. I saw it was being rebuilt by the new archbishop. There was scaffolding and the work made the entry to the city from the north difficult. I knew it would be just as hard to leave. We parted at the market. "I will meet you here at nones. Until then the time is yours."

The three younger ones were delighted at the prospect of spending time in the city. Aethelstan and

Alfred had coins they had taken in battle and were keen to spend them. Edward said, with the smile of a young man who was about to become a father, "I will watch over them, My Lord."

There were two castles in the city and I went to the one on the eastern side of the city for I knew that was where I would find Belisarius. When I reached the gate to the wooden castle I was asked my business. As soon as I said my name I was admitted. My half-brother had been in command of the city when the Danes had taken it and Malet was almost a watchword. I dismounted and handed Geoffrey's reins to a guard who told me he would take care of my horse for me. I suspect that it was not just my association with my half-brother that afforded me such consideration. I had a reputation and my twin swords identified me without any mark on my tunic. We had held out at Eisicewalt and defied the Danes. That was not forgotten. I did not have to wait for long to be admitted. Belisarius was seated at a table with a man I took to be the new archbishop, Thomas of Bayeux, and a knight I did not recognise.

Belisarius stood and smiled at me. He liked me. "Sir Richard, it is good to see you. It has been too long. This is the Archbishop of York, Thomas of Bayeux."

The archbishop nodded, "Bishop Odo speaks well of you."

I was always uncomfortable when I was complimented, "I do my duty, Your Grace."

"And this is Sir Ralph de Paganel. He has lands around York."

"And I have heard of you too, Sir Richard. You were Taillefer's man."

"I had the honour to serve him."

Belisarius said, "Sit." He waved to a servant, "Wine. What brings you here?"

I told them of the recent events. They were all clearly unaware of what had happened after the king had left the borders. "I now have seven ladies who need to be housed and that necessitates investment."

Belisarius frowned, "I know the king had urgent business in the south but it seems to me that he might have secured the northern frontier first." He used his stylus to make some marks on his wax tablet. "This means that Brougham needs a lord."

"Yet the land belongs to Lady Ealdgyth."

Belisarius sighed, "It is not as simple as that. King William was already less than happy that the unfortunate lady's father failed to defend the land. He spoke to me about the western marches when he passed through York on his way south. He did not know that Lord Ælfgar had died but I know that he intended to take the manor from him."

"So, the lady gets nothing?"

Sir Ralph said, "From what you have told us, Sir Richard, there was nothing for her to inherit. You said the Scots destroyed the manor?" I nodded. "Then whoever is given the manor will have to begin from nothing." He was practical and matter of fact. It was almost as though the seven women did not exist.

The archbishop studied me as he said, "And are you happy to be her guardian?"

I shifted for guardian was not how I saw myself, "The prior said he would ask the Bishop of Durham to make her a royal ward."

The archbishop waved an irritated hand in the air as though conjuring the words away, "Semantics, Sir Richard. What I am asking is are you happy to protect these ladies?"

"Of course."

"Then there is nothing more to be said on the matter." It was clear to me, following the words of the knight and the archbishop that Ealdgyth's only hope came from me. The Bishop of Durham would probably have a similar view.

I saw a sympathetic look come over Belisarius' face but he had no power. He was one of the king's officials but one who took orders. He said, "And how are Bergil and Seara?"

"They have a son and they are content."

The servant had brought and poured the wine. I wanted to leave but I needed the knowledge that lay in this room. "What news, My Lord, of the outside world?"

Belisarius said, "Better news, Hugh d'Avranches has captured much of Gwynedd. The heartland of England is safe from the privations of the Welsh. Osmund is now Lord Chancellor and Herfast has moved to become Bishop of Elmham."

The political appointments did not interest me. "And the rebellion in Ely?"

"It is over. The Earl of Surrey defeated Hereward. The Danes left after you took the earl prisoner." The archbishop was well informed.

"And Hereward?"

"He is hiding in the Fens but he has no army and he is an irrelevancy."

"It is safe then, My Lord, for me to visit my manor at Norton."

Belisarius frowned, “You have not been there yet?”

I sighed and my voice showed my exasperation, “It is hard to see when I could have done so, for the king had me fight, first Hereward and then the Scots.”

I saw the archbishop’s expression. He did not like my tone. Belisarius saw it too and he said, “Your Grace, while you and Sir Ralph discuss the abbey he wishes to invest, I will speak to Sir Richard about some trivial matters.”

He led me to his office. Piled high with parchments it was clearly a place of work, “Sit Sir Richard.” He smiled, “If you can find somewhere.” I moved some papers and sat on a chair. “What you must understand, Sir Richard, is that this is a time of change for England. Some of the old nobles from the time of Godwinson and the Confessor, have retained their lands and titles but others have lost. Hereward is one such. The laws of Normandy and England are also different. Part of my work here,” he waved a hand around the parchments, “is to try to plot a course through them and present my findings to the king. The two systems need to be melded together and that is tricky. Rome has also begun to take an interest in England. At the moment, Thomas of Bayeux is the highest prelate in the land but Rome wishes Canterbury to have the primacy. York has too many associations with the Danes. You see that you need to watch your words when speaking to men like the archbishop. You are an honest knight but you might think about donning a mask.”

He paused and I shook my head, “I cannot be what I am not.”

"Think of Taillefer. What would he have done?"

I smiled, "He would have acted a part but I am not Taillefer. He was unique. I am just an ordinary knight. I can juggle swords, ride well and fight as a knight should but I am no Taillefer."

"You are anything but ordinary. Now, I will do all that I can to help you. What do you need? Gold?"

"No. Men. I took untrained boys to war and one died. It was just one but that was one too many. If you know of any others then send them to me. I do not think that the Scots are yet done plotting to cause mischief in England."

"Aye, you are right. But for the pressing matter of the rebellion in the east, King William might have taken the war to the Scots. He has not forgotten. King Malcolm will rue his support for the rebels. I will send as many men as I can. I think you are looking for men like Bergil. You seek those who need a home. I will do what I can. You must, however, make Norton secure. It is a crossing of the Tees that we need. There is no bridge but there is a ferry. I know that you will not live there but you need to have men in place who can defend it."

"I will. What can you tell me of the manor?"

"It was the manor of a Dane, Bersi Steanasson. His grandfather had been one of King Cnut's oathsworn. He was a mighty warrior by all accounts. There is talk of a magical sword." He smiled, "There are always such stories. The family was well respected in the valley for he treated those who lived there, the Northumbrians, well. He fought at Stamford Bridge and lost. He also joined in the rebellion of the north. He and his son died. The family," he shrugged, "of them I know nothing but the manor and the farm were destroyed by the warriors the king sent to quash the rebellion."

I knew what would have happened. The king's orders had been clear. The land was to be devastated. If any of the family survived the slaughter they would have to endure starvation. "So, there will be neither hall nor people there."

"It is unlikely."

"Then what is the point of the manor? A manor is not just the name of a piece of land. It is the people who farm there. If there is no one to work the land…"

"You know the answer to that, young Richard, the king will expect you to populate it with your people."

I was almost speechless, "I have just spent years making Eisicewalt strong and you want me to take good people and transplant them?"

"I want nothing." His voice was calm and measured, in contrast to mine. "It is what the king wishes but if you just go there and see the size of the problem then that will suffice until next year or even the year after."

"You just want me to look?"

"That is all."

"Then I will visit. Have you a map?"

He stood and reached up to some parchments. He examined and then discarded some before finding one. He handed it to me. "It is crude, I know, and the distances may not be accurate but it might help you. As you can see there are other places close by. Stockadeton is the largest place and there is a ferry there. I believe people still live in that settlement but the king has yet to appoint a lord of the manor." He looked at me, "He had a man in mind but the man sided with Morcar. He was executed. Until another can be appointed you will be the law." I nodded. I did not like it but I knew the king well enough to realise that argument would be futile. I would have to make the best of it. "And now, before you go about your business, dine with me. The food here is good. The ships that ply the river bring goods from places other than England. You will enjoy it, I think."

He was right but some of the pleasure of eating such fine food and the company of a man I liked was made sour by the way that Ealdgyth had been treated. I knew that she would not mind but to me it was not right. She had lost her inheritance.

It was an hour before nones when I left the castle and led my horse to the market. There I found my squire. He was watching the horses. I saw that the sumpter we had taken was already laden. "Where are the others?"

He smiled, "There were mummers in the square and they asked if they could watch. I saw no harm."

"I do not mind but when they return we must hurry to our home. We will have to leave Eisicewalt for a while." The we told him he was one of those who would have to leave Eisicewalt and his wife. I told him what he needed to know about Belisarius' promise to send men and the urgent need to visit Norton. "I have been told that it will not be a long visit. I will try to make the journey sooner for I am well aware that you will be a father."

"My Lord, I am your man and my place is at your side."

When the three siblings returned they were excited beyond words. A mummer show was exciting and they had enjoyed it immensely.

"And now we return home. You bought all that was asked for?"

It was Birgitte who answered, "My mother made it clear what we needed and we have bought it all."

Edward nodded, "The purse is almost empty, My Lord."

"We can always find more."

We arrived back before dark. Benthe scrutinised the cloth that had been bought as well as the metal goblets. Edward had tried to get the best quality he could but he was told by the sellers that such items had to be specially made. Dervilla and Ealdgyth were more than happy with the cloth that had been bought. They were keen to make a start.

The next morning, I gathered my men and we joined Lars and the others as we began to build the new storeroom. By the end of the day, we had some of the posts in the ground and the wattle and daub plastered across the willow. The new sleeping chambers would require more work but by the second day we had a roof and Benthe was satisfied that we could start to use it the next day. So long as the rains held off then all would be well.

Ealdgyth came to speak to me at the end of the second day, "Sir Richard, why do you labour with your men? You are a lord."

I laughed, "It is my land and I want to be part of the manor."

"But the chambers are to benefit us."

"And the prior made you my responsibility. I do not mind toiling, Ealdgyth. When I grew up I was brought up as a servant."

She touched my hand with hers, "You are kind beyond words, My Lord. I cannot think of many others who would do this without having an ulterior motive."

"It is the way I was brought up."

The next day saw harder work. We had many stones that the ploughing of the new field had dragged to the surface and we had collected them. While Lars and Drogo made the mortar we used a wheelbarrow to carry them to the site. The last posts were embedded and stones rammed in. The first of the mortar was then poured into the holes. We made sure that they were level and upright before we gathered willow to make a frame for the next wall we would build.

I bathed that night. The mortar we had used seemed to cling everywhere and the hot bath I enjoyed made me feel more like a civilised person.

The posts had set well and we fastened the willow to the two sides. We began to fill the trench we had made with the stones. After each layer we would pour more mortar and then add more stones. By the end of the day, we had a low wall that reached to my waist on three sides. The harder work would be reserved for the next day. Until we broke through to the main hall we would have to climb over our work. I was loath to break through until we had walls the height of a man. By the end of the day, we had our walls complete. They would take some days to fully dry out. I consulted Ethelred who was the master of such matters and he told me that there would be no rain. We did not bother with a temporary roof. By the end of the week, we had broken through and we had a roof in place. There were two wind holes and shutters fitted but until the plaster had dried it would not be used. We had built a fireplace and chimney on the outside wall. A fire would be lit each day to help the plaster to dry. It meant that Edward and I were free to visit Norton. It was something that I dreaded but it had to be done.

Chapter 8

We left the others continuing to work on the new house as well as completing the many tasks the time of year demanded. It was a two-day ride north to the Tees. There was a village at Stockadeton but I did not know if it had suffered in the destruction of the north or if people had moved back. I thought when we reached the river that we might have to swim, but there was a ferry of sorts and when the man on the north bank saw my spurs he came across. It cost me more that I would have liked for the passage but it saved a dousing. I pointed to the village, "You survived?"

"When others rebelled we simply hid and waited out the storm. We watched until there were no warriors prowling around and we came back. We found that our homes were still intact. They had been used but were neither destroyed nor damaged too much. We are a resilient people." He waved an arm around and said, "Thornaby was destroyed by the Danes many years ago and that was a lesson to us here. We use the clay that is found around here to make pots. We make goods and sell them. Ships travel up the river and take them hence. That way we have profits and we can begin again. We are survivors."

It seemed to me a practical and pragmatic solution. Fields could be destroyed and would take time to replant. Animals that were slaughtered could not be easily replaced but digging clay from the earth and turning it into goods seemed less trouble.

Once on the other side I asked him about Norton.

"It is a place of ghosts, My Lord. No one survived the anger of the king. Their headman went to war and lost." He shrugged, "We were lucky I think but Norton… the men died and then a plague struck them and the rest all died."

"The plague?"

He shook his head, "Some disease or perhaps they starved to death. You should ask our priest; he buried them."

"Where does your priest live?"

"He has a dwelling by St. John's Well." He pointed and I saw the house.

The ferry had been overpriced but the information was valuable. We walked our horses over to the small house and as we neared it the priest came out. He frowned when he saw my spurs and mail. "Here, north of the Tees, there is nothing left for you Normans to take. What more do you want? Our lives?"

I spoke in English, "I am only half Norman and the rest is English and I want nothing from you, Priest, except information."

He kept the scowl on his face as he said, "What sort of information?"

"I am the new lord of the manor of Norton and the ferryman said that you buried the dead."

He shook his head, "You have a manor of corpses, then. Aye, I buried them. Had I known of their predicament then I might have visited earlier. It might have been that I could have saved some. They were proud and did not ask us for help. Pride is a sin and it cost them their lives."

"Was it the plague?"

"I do not think so. They had no food and I think that they starved to death. Billingham is also deserted. I buried the dead of Norton but I had no corpses in Billingham. I said prayers and that was almost a year ago. I am not dead and have no illnesses."

"Thank you." I mounted Geoffrey. I looked down at him, "I hoped for a Christian welcome. It seems I came to the wrong place."

"Your King William has much to answer for."

"My friend, like it or not, he is now your king or would you have the weak willed one who invites the Scots over to ravage our country?" I did not wait for an answer but spurred Geoffrey on the signposted road to Norton.

It was not far to go but it was a depressing ride. The land rose and fell as we passed the many streams that covered the land. Woods had been cleared and there were signs that the fields had been tilled but now they were weed covered and wild shrubs were reclaiming land. I saw burnt out farms and not a single animal. The land rose as we neared what had been a prosperous manor. Belisarius had told me that in the time of Cnut it had been a rich one. There had been a mill, a church and even a quay for the Danes to tie up their ships. As we rode through the blackened remains of a palisade I saw a weed covered fishpond. There were buildings that had not been burned but they were tumbled down. As we rode through we saw the vermin which now inhabited the remains of Norton. We dismounted and approached the graves which, a year on, still stood starkly bare against the green of the weeds. The wooden church had been burned too but somehow the tower with the cross still stood defiantly against the sky. We walked through the village. We found one dwelling that looked habitable. It lay some twenty paces from the last tumbled down house and fifty paces from the last one that had been burned. Tying our horses to a post we entered. There was dust and dirt which had blown in. Cobwebs abounded but it had been lived in.

"This must have been the place where the survivors lived." I looked at the chairs and the table. "If disease came then it is no wonder that it took them all." Then I recalled that the priest had said starvation had been the cause. We passed through the house and saw that, at the back there was a path that led down to, I presumed, the river. We headed along the overgrown path and found what had been a wooden quay. It was no longer usable. Floods, tides and winter storms had wrecked it. I saw, beneath the waters, the remains of a fishing boat or knarr that had sunk.

We headed back to our horses. Edward said, quietly, as we untied them, "There is nothing. We do not even have a place to rest our heads this night."

"We can camp by the fishpond and as for there being nothing, you are wrong. When we were a mile or so from the ferry I could still smell woodsmoke and I smelled it again just now by the river. Animals do not light fires. Men do. There are still people living somewhere but they do not blazon their presence. They are still fearful and we might well terrify them. Tomorrow we leave our horses here and explore on foot. We shall be as though we were scouting in enemy land except we seek the weak and not warriors."

We rode back to the pond and made a fire. Edward had fishing lines in his bag and we used them. The fish, untouched since the devastation, had prospered and we caught four large ones. We could have speared them they were so bold. We ate well. The next morning, we took our horses back to the one dwelling we had found and put them in the rear where they could graze. They would be hidden from sight. I took out the map. "There is a causeway to Billingham on the north side of the boggy land that used to be the course of the river. We would be spied on that path. Let us look at the two that are close to here, Rus' Worthy and Rag's Worthy. The third, Pers' Track is further away."

Edward shook his head, "What is a worthy?"

"I know not but I am guessing it is a Danish word. They look to be within walking distance and seem to me to be close to where I smelled woodsmoke." We headed back down the road to Stockadeton. We had left our helmets and mail with the horses. It was easier walking without them. Our shields and spears were back in my hall. We had not come for war and our swords would have to suffice if there was danger.

I saw a signpost with runes upon it. I could not read it but I followed one of its arms. The track we found was overgrown but as I knelt I saw signs that feet had trodden it and recently. There must have been rain and I could see the imprint of a boot. We headed along the track. The map showed that the first worthy lay close to the road and I saw the tendril of smoke ahead. There was a dwelling and someone lived there. The land was not devoid of people. I wondered why the priest had not mentioned the fact.

"Let us leave this path and try to approach the house unseen. I do not want to scare away whoever lives there."

The fields that were close to the track were untended and elder bushes and trees had taken hold. There were wild brambles too. They afforded cover. The smell of woodsmoke grew stronger and although I could not see the dwelling I knew we were getting close. The bleating of a goat confirmed it. I stopped when I saw, through the branches of the elder and hawthorn trees, the house. It was a long low building with a turf roof. Smoke trickled from the chimney. I saw movement and spied a woman and children. The woman was milking the goat and the children were picking brambles from the bushes that lay between us. I saw no man. I waved a hand for Edward to squat. We would wait. I heard laughter from the three young children. The woman shouted something but I could not make it out. The milking finished, the woman entered the dwelling and she called for the children to join her. I took the opportunity of moving closer to the house. I found a place where we could see and yet we were hidden by a single mighty oak that had been left standing. I studied the farm, for that was what it was and saw that there was a stream that ran close to it. The building looked longer from this angle. The Danes and Vikings lived in long houses. This had been the home of a larger group than the three children and the woman.

Our patience was rewarded when I heard voices from our right. There were two of them and they were taking the path that Edward and I had used. I saw a man and two youths coming along. They had, between them, a small deer that they had hunted.

"Elfrida, we are back!"

The woman and the three children came from the house and the children whooped when they saw the deer. I waited until the six had gathered before I stood and left the shelter of the tree. "A fine kill!" I spoke in English and I kept my hand from my sword.

The man whirled as did the youths. Their hands went to their daggers. I held up my hands to show the open palms. "I mean you no harm. My squire and I just wish to talk to you."

The man, when he spoke, had an accent. It was not Danish but Northumbrian. "Who are you and why do you hide?"

I took a few more steps closer to them. I stopped when I was five paces from the man. I saw his eyes flicker to the two swords across my back. Edward stood to the side, his hand kept away from his body. "I am Sir Richard fitz Malet of Eisicewalt and," I paused, "Norton. This is my squire Edward. King William has asked me to ensure that this land, the land close to the manor of Norton, is safe. Who are you?" He hesitated as though by telling me his name he was giving away some secret information. "Come, I have given you my name and I know that your wife is called Elfrida."

"How?"

I smiled, "We watched your wife milk the goat and the children pick brambles. We heard you call out. Had we intended harm we would have done so already. Please, tell me your name."

"I am Ragnar of Rag's Worthy. These are my sons, Ragnar and Walter. You have seen my wife and daughters already. We do not need Normans in this land."

"Yet we are here and the land is now ruled by King William but I am half English and I can swear to you that you will be safe, safer perhaps, than when the land was ruled by Harold Godwinson."

He snorted and waved a hand, "Safer? Tell that to the people who lived in Norton or Rus' Worthy or Pers' Track. They were butchered and slaughtered."

"But you were not."

He nodded, "God saved us. We were visiting my wife's father in Durham for he was ill and were away when the warriors came. We left Durham before it too was scoured and we hid. God favoured us and our home was left intact. We just wish to be left alone."

"And I am happy that this is so but you should know, Ragnar of Rag's Worthy, that I have spent some weeks fighting the Scots who came to the Teesdale and they took captives and killed the men. What would you do if they came here?"

He looked around as though the Scots were upon them. "We would hide."

"When I am able, I will have warriors in Norton and they will guard this land."

"Now?"

I shook my head, "I do not lie nor do I make promises that I cannot keep. I am here to see the scale of the problem. I will not return with men until the new grass comes. I need to know who else lives in this land."

He turned to his wife, "Take the children inside. Walter and Ragnar, gut the deer. I will speak to this Norman and then we can be left in peace."

I could see that the children were fascinated by Edward and me but they obeyed their mother. The elder youth took out a seax and slit open the belly of the deer. The guts began to tumble out. The second youth pulled them to the ground.

When we were far enough away not be overheard, he spoke, "The men of Stockadeton never liked us for we were of Danish blood. When the rebellion began we were shunned. They did not rebel. Neither did I. I saw no point. The other Danish settlements were all destroyed and their menfolk killed. Even the mighty sword of Bersi Steanasson availed them naught." He shrugged, "When Tostig fought King Harold it turned many of the Northumbrians against us. We might have survived but for the rebellion further north. We had no part in it. We just wanted to live our lives in peace but when the Normans came, they destroyed."

"There are none left in the valley except for Stockadeton?"

"There are some who live closer to the sea, to the east of Billingham. They eke out a living in the salt marshes close to Greatham and Bewley. We call them the marshmen. I think they must have escaped from Billingham and avoided the wrath of King William's knights."

I nodded, "Then I have a task that would tax Hercules but I know my duty. I will return, Ragnar, and I hope that I find you and your family well."

"You speak well for a Norman and your words, if they are true, give me hope but in this land hope is a dream and the edge of the sword and the burning of flesh is the reality."

There was little point in investigating the other places and so we trekked back to Norton. As we neared the depressingly empty settlement I said, "Tomorrow we try to find these people of the marshes. We will ride for it strikes me it is too far to walk."

The horses had enjoyed a day of rest and better grazing than we might have hoped. We ate fish again and slept, once more, in the open. The next day we mounted our horses and headed for the sea. We headed towards the causeway and saw, closer to the river, the burnt-out houses that had been Billingham. Not all were destroyed but there was no smell of woodsmoke and no movement. It was a ghost town. The land ahead was undulating. From Ragnar's words I had deduced that there were swamps, marshes and streams as well as dunes. I soon discovered the truth of the matter. We ended up leading our horses for with our weight, we were mailed and helmed, upon their backs, they sank into the swampy ground.

I almost gave up for I thought that no one could eke out a living here but then I smelled woodsmoke and knew that ahead, for the breeze was bringing the smell from the sea, were people. We were just a mile from the causeway and we had passed dwellings that were empty but had not been destroyed.

I stopped to work out the best route to the origins of the smoke. It was then I spied a mast. It was to our right and the river lay in that direction. The warrior in me took over. "Edward, I do not like the sight of that mast. In these waters a mast means an enemy. Let us investigate but follow my lead."

"Yes, My Lord."

My fears were confirmed when I heard the screams and shouts. I finally saw the smoke rising and knew that just ahead lay a settlement. "Mount." The ground was a little firmer this close to the dunes.

As soon as I clambered on the back of Geoffrey I saw the four houses, little more than hovels, and the river beyond. I could now make out the Viking longship. It was not one of their dragon ships but a smaller variety. I had heard them called a snekke or snake boat. It held just ten men or so but as they would all be armed it was a serious threat. As I urged Geoffrey across the small rise before us I saw another ship in the river. It was a knarr. They were the wide ships that carried cargo. This was a slave raid. I drew a sword. The people were fleeing. They knew better than to stand their ground. Even the three men were running. They had no swords, just fire hardened spears and the Vikings had helmets spears and swords. The warriors knew their business. They were in a long line and were channelling the people into a human net. The only thing that would stop them would be us.

The attention of the raiders was on the people. The men on the outside of the line must have been younger for they were faster and they were catching the slower ones, the old.

"Edward, take the left."

I urged Geoffrey to the right. We passed across the front of the women, children and old women who looked up at us in terror as we trotted past them.

The three men from the settlement were in the middle. I wanted Edward and I to have the best chance of success and that meant taking on individual men rather than trying to fight a couple. They saw us and I heard a shout, I assumed in Norse. The man who was closest to me looked young. He had a pot helmet, a spear and the inevitable round shield. Seeing a horseman, he stopped to face me. I had given those on my side a chance, I did not hesitate but rode Geoffrey directly at him. He thrust at me with his spear. If he had been an experienced warrior he might have gone for my unprotected side but he went for my sword arm. I hacked at the shaft and used Geoffrey's weight to send the warrior tumbling into a bog. I wheeled my horse around and the next raider found that he could not bring his shield around quickly enough and so he tried to turn his body. I brought my sword down and struck his helmet.

Their leader shouted something and the men began to try to form a shield wall. There were only two of us who were mounted but we both had well trained horses. Our animals responded to our commands and we charged. We were aided by the three men who had turned to fight the ones in the middle. I leaned from the saddle to avoid the spear thrust at me and I brought my sword over the top of the raider's shield to hack across his face. The blood and bone splattered the men on either side of him and with Edward's horse snapping and biting behind, not to mention the threat of the three men who were fighting for their families, he stepped away from the animal. The wall broken the men tried to fight as individuals. We were mounted and the slavers had not expected to fight trained men. We hacked and slashed at men who wore no mail. The raiders decided that they had endured enough and they ran. Edward brought his sword across the back of another warrior and just four men and one wounded man made it to the snekke. We could have pursued them but there was little point and I reined in.

After sheathing my sword, I lifted my helmet. One of the three men who had been attacked by the slavers had a wound and a woman was binding it. The elder of the three men looked at me. I could see the confusion. I looked Norman and he would not know how to address me. I made it easier for him, "I am Sir Richard fitz Malet of Norton and this is my squire, Edward." I dismounted. A man on a horse, especially a mailed one, always looked threatening.

"I am Algar of Belasis. Thank you for coming to our aid." He hesitated, "Had we seen you first we would have fled from you."

I nodded, "I know. King William wishes this land to be productive once more and I am sent to see how the manor of Norton stands."

"Had he not destroyed so much, My Lord, he might have found it a prosperous place."

I was coming to realise more and more that some of the Normans who had come with the king had exceeded his commands. He had wanted the rebels punished but I saw that they had tried to make it easy for themselves by killing everybody. "That is the past, Algar, and we cannot change it." I waved a hand at the two ships as they used the tide to head out to sea, "Just as we cannot undo their attack all we can do is to make sure that we defend against them the next time they come."

He nodded his agreement and they began to walk back to their homes. I saw that they were crudely built dwellings, little better than the hovels soldiers used on campaign.

"Tell me, Algar, why do you live here? Surely there are better places to raise families. This swampy ground must become pestilential in summer."

"It does, but the bogs also make it harder for an enemy to get to us. We collect samphire from the sand and hunt the seals. We catch the salmon in our nets and we eke out a living. This is a good place."

"Unless they come by sea."

"Aye, we thought the threat from the east was gone."

"No, my friend, King Sweyn of Denmark still seeks his English crown." I handed my reins to Edward who led our horses to a pool that I hoped was not brackish. "Norton has a dwelling still where men might live. There is a pond there that can be fished."

He frowned, "I know but it is your land. The punishment for poaching is harsh is it not, My Lord?"

"It is but this would not be poaching. I am the lord of the manor and if I give you permission then it is called gamekeeping."

He smiled, "It would be better than this. We lived across the causeway in Billingham and I always envied the life they led in Norton. They were Danish and favoured by their kings."

"I will be returning to my home further south for the winter. You and your people are more than welcome to winter in Norton. Ragnar of Rag's Worthy and his family survived and I will be bringing some of my people to settle here in the valley when the new grass comes. Do not decide now for you will need to talk to your people about this."

"You do not sound Norman."

"That is because I am only half Norman and that half is the bastard line. I am Saxon and English through my mother and my grandfather who was a housecarl."

His face changed and he smiled, "Then, perhaps, we will take you up on your offer."

I held out my hand and he grasped it, "This day began ill but now we are well met, are we not?"

"We are, My Lord."

I waved over Edward and the horses, "Take what you will from the dead. If nothing else this day has shown us that there are enemies everywhere and men must defend themselves."

Algar went to his hut and came back with a bundle, "It is little enough, My Lord, for we are a poor people but take this seal skin. We have them in abundance. They make fine capes, boots and hats for they keep away the water." It was a beginning.

"Thank you, Algar, I will return." As we rode back to the causeway path I said, "Did you suffer any wounds, Edward? I had little time to see."

He shook his head, "No, Sir Richard, but I confess that riding over the swampy ground made me fearful."

"It was not the best ground over which to ride but you did well. The raiders should have made a shield wall sooner. They might have won."

That night we ate the last of our supplies. "Tomorrow we return home to Eisicewalt."

"Will you return here, My Lord?"

"I have no choice in the matter but I do not think that I will make this my home. I will find another to be my steward here and to defend this place. It could be a good home. It is on higher ground and is easier to defend than Eisicewalt. Would you and Mathilde like to live here?"

He shook his head, "No, My Lord. My place is by your side. When you decide to take on another squire I will join Bergil and be a man at arms. I do not have the wit to run a manor."

I smiled, "I think you do but this is not the task for a commanded man. It is a task for one who chooses to pick up the burden. If I cannot find such a man I will return here and see if Ragnar or Algar are the men for the task."

"You think Algar will come?"

"I think that within a few days he will be living here. Where he lives he cannot farm. He and his family fish, forage for samphire, hunt seals and make salt. Such a diet cannot be good. Here he can farm. There are fields and whilst he has no draught animals the men can pull a plough. I saw such tools in the wreckage of the buildings. I do not doubt that if we were to look we might find some old seed somewhere or perhaps a sack of dried beans that might be planted. When I come again I have much to bring. This manor might yield a good return but before that happens I will need to invest. I shall visit with Belisarius and tell him of my discoveries. Norton's ghost can be exorcised."

Chapter 9

It took two days to reach my home. We both had empty bellies for there was little to be had on the road between the Tees and Eisicewalt. My home looked welcoming after the devastation that had been Norton. I was also welcomed not only by Benthe, Bergil and my people but also by Ealdgyth and Dervilla. We had only been away for a short time but, it seemed, they had missed me. Ealdgyth and the girls were keen to show me the first of the clothes made with the cloth I had bought for them. Birgitte had chosen well and all the women of the manor had helped with the sewing. While food was prepared I went with Ealdgyth, Dervilla and Bergil to inspect the new chambers.

"The plaster is still drying, My Lord, but within a week it will be ready for the ladies."

Dervilla frowned, "Not wishing to sound ungrateful, My Lord, but these are little better than monk's cells at the moment."

"Dervilla!"

"No, Ealdgyth, Dervilla is right. We need furniture. My men can make some, the beds and tables but we will visit York and see what the craftsmen there can create."

"That sounds expensive, My Lord."

"It might be, Ealdgyth, but it is necessary. I had planned on visiting York in any case. Perhaps if you two ladies came with me we could buy what they have. We will take a wagon this time."

I did not plan on making many more visits to York before Christmas but this one was vital. I had to speak to Belisarius. He would report to the king and I hoped that the king would heed the advice of Belisarius. My brief visit to the north had shown me that it was in great danger. An enemy could easily take the land. The king had emptied it of those who might defend it.

Bergil came with me and I left Edward at home. There was no need for him to be away from his wife again. Alfred and Aethelstan, now men at arms, came too as escorts and as muscle in case anything we bought was heavy. I rode a new horse bred by Aedgar. It was sired by Parsifal and the mare that had been bought a year ago. It was meant for Alfred but I was a better rider and Aedgar thought I might school the animal on the way to York. Goldy had his father's colour but the gentler nature of his dam. I enjoyed riding him. Alfred drove the wagon and Bergil and Aethelstan flanked me.

"You have not said much about Norton, My Lord."

"No, Bergil, for there is much to do there, perhaps too much. I will visit there again in spring but this time I will take men with me. Hopefully the land hereabouts will be safer by then." I told him what we had found and his face fell as I described the devastation.

This time we visited, not just the market, but also the craftsmen. There were places to buy pots, furniture and even jewellery. They had samples of their wares but any items would need to be ordered and made specifically for us. I let Dervilla and

Ealdgyth choose the design and I paid for the work. "And you will deliver to Eisicewalt?"

"Yes, My Lord." The quick answer told me that I should have haggled more and that I had paid too much.

As we left I said, "I need to speak to Belisarius. I will go alone and leave you, Bergil, to watch the ladies." I handed a purse to Ealdgyth, "Use this for whatever purpose you see fit."

"My Lord, you are too generous."

"My lady, you have nothing. It is a Christian thing to do." I turned to Bergil, "When you are done return to the manor. I will come home when I am done."

"Alone, My Lord?"

"Alone."

This time Belisarius was not in conference. He was working in his office. I was admitted. He sat back and put his inky fingers together, "Well? You visited Norton?"

"I did." I gave him an account of all that I had seen.

He made notes on his wax tablet and then said, "The king, when he last visited, expressed some disquiet about the dangers to his northern border. The Scottish threat remains as does the Danish one. Norton will need a strong hand."

"And that hand will not be mine. Do not worry, Belisarius, it will be a firm one but I will choose the man. And that brings me to my next question. Did you find me any men?"

"I did. There are four Bretons who came from Brittany to serve, as they thought, with Alain Rufus.

For some reason he did not wish them to be his men. They are seeking another master."

I frowned, "Sir Alain is a good warrior. If he does not wish them to follow his banner then I do not want them."

He shrugged, "Perhaps you should ask him. He is here in York consulting with the archbishop. He wishes a good priest appointed to Richmond. You will find him by the minster. The archbishop spends most days there supervising the work. If Sir Alain is not with him then the archbishop will know where he is to be found. I will, in any case, continue to seek out men for you. From what you have told me Norton needs men with strong backs and stout courage."

I left my horse with Belisarius' men and headed for the minster. I did not reach it for I met with Sir Alain and his knights as they headed for an inn. He was pleased to see me, "Sir Richard, this is well met. Let us hie to a tavern for you had interesting adventures. I was told of your hunt after we parted and I would hear the details." He smiled, "I heard the gossip and I would like to hear the truth."

"I would be honoured." I liked the Breton and happily followed him and his knights. Sir Ulric was amongst them. He had clearly been forgiven for the error that had almost cost us.

Sir Alain insisted upon ordering and paying for the drink and the food. While we waited for it to arrive I began to tell him the tale of the hunt for the captives. When I had finished he said, "And you have taken on the burden, I hear, of caring for the seven women you rescued."

"What else could I have done?"

"An interesting point and had that been my choice would I have done the same?"

I could not tell, from his face, what he might have done. I knew that I did not regret making my decision. I was already fond of Ealdgyth and I wanted her in my life. However, until we had the decision from Durham, my life was in abeyance.

"There is another matter I wished to speak to you about, Sir Alain. It is why I sought you out."

"Speak, I am intrigued."

I had to be honest and I told him what Belisarius had said. "You see, Sir Alain, I need men but if these warriors from your home are unsuitable then I would not have them serve me."

In answer he glanced at Sir Ulric who sighed and said, "That is my fault, Sir Richard. It is I who cannot serve with them. The brother of one of the men, a knight, was killed by me in a tourney. It was an accident but I feared that the four men might harbour a grudge."

"Then why did they seek to serve Sir Alain?"

"They did not know I served the count. I only joined his retinue after Senlac Hill."

"And if I took them on would this cause you a problem, Sir Ulric?"

I saw hesitation and Sir Alain snapped, "I will make that decision, Sir Ulric. You are a fine knight and a worthy member of my retinue. I value your sword. I acceded to your request not to hire these four men because I have enough men at arms but I can tell you, Sir Richard, that you may hire these men and Sir Ulric will swear that there will be no trouble." He looked at Sir Ulric.

"I so swear."

"When we return to my home, Sir Ulric, we will make that more formal." He sighed, "I thought the king was the only one who had petty disputes to disrupt his life. It seems I was wrong."

"The king?"

He smiled, "You have been away from court for some time. You do not know about his sons."

"I know that there are three who are warriors: Robert, Richard and William. The fourth is but a toddler yet."

"Robert does not get on with his two younger brothers and they squabble and brawl all the time. It does not help that the favourite of their father is Richard, his second son. It is a problem for the king. You and I have no such problems yet, eh? However, when we sire heirs it may be, perhaps, these trials are sent to help us become better parents." He stood and waved over the innkeeper, "And now we need to ride. You are lucky. Your home is a short distance away. It will be dark before we reach our Richmond."

I returned to Belisarius, "I will take on these men. Where are they to be found?"

"They are in an inn by the river, '***The Saddle***'. As I am paying for their accommodation I chose somewhere not too expensive."

"You were paying for them?"

"An investment. They are good warriors and I knew that someone would need them."

"You mean me."

He smiled, "I feel that I owe you, Sir Richard. I will sleep sounder knowing that you have more men to guard the northern gate to York. Tell the innkeeper to send his bill to me."

I mounted my horse and rode through the crowded streets that led to the busy river. Ships could navigate all the way to York. In winter, when there was often flooding, it was the fastest way to reach the heart of the city. The inns there did a good trade but they were not the sort of places I would have taken Ealdgyth and Dervilla.

I let the ostler watch my horse. I took the opportunity to examine the horses I took to be the Bretons. They were easy to spot. They were not war horses but the lighter horses bred by the Bretons for the light horsemen. The mounts told me much about the men. When I entered the inn it was crowded and the cheaper tallow candles gave it a smoky look. It was like peering through yellow fog. It stank of spilt ale. I spotted the four men immediately. They wore their hair short at the front and shaved at the rear. As I made my way towards them I saw that they were older than I had expected. One of them looked to be older than I was, older, even, than Bergil. For some reason I had expected younger men. Older warriors often preferred to stay close to their homeland and yet these had left Brittany and come to England.

My movements attracted their attention. I saw the older of them glance down and recognise my spurs. He said, as I stopped at their table, "My Lord, can we help you?"

"Perhaps I can help you. Belisarius sent me to you." Hope sprang in their faces. I had known enough professional warriors to know that idleness does not sit well with them. They liked to be employed. "I am Sir Richard fitz Malet." Their faces told me that they knew my name. "I seek warriors to serve in my two manors, Norton and Eisicewalt.

Belisarius sent me to you. Are you willing to be my warriors?"

The older one said, "Just like that? You need know no more of us?"

"I have spoken to Alain Rufus. I know all that I need to know. I have been told of the problem and the count made it quite clear to me that he would have taken you on. The question is…?

The older warrior said, "Conan, My Lord, of Vannes."

I nodded, "The question is are you willing to serve me?"

He smiled, "Belisarius told us about you, My Lord. You are the knight trained by Taillefer. We hoped that you would ask us to be your oathsworn."

"One more thing. At times we may serve with others. The reason the Count of Richmond did not hire you was because of a feud."

A man at arms with a maimed hand, shook his head, "When my elder brother was killed it was an accident. I bear the knight no grudge. We all know that using blades and spears, even in training or in tourneys, can result in wounds and, as in my brother's case, death. If I was angry with anyone it is the Duke of Brittany who chose not to give me my brother's land."

The answer satisfied me, "Then you are hired. Do you need anything from York?"

"No, My Lord. We have spent enough time here. There is just the matter of the bill."

"And that is taken care of. Get your gear and I will meet you in the stables."

I spoke to the innkeeper who seemed happy with the arrangement. I reached the stables at the same time as the four men. Conan nodded approvingly, "A fine horse, Sir Richard and, I dare say, expensive."

"We bred him ourselves so there was no expense." I mounted and flipped a coin at the ostler. "The ride is not a long one and will allow me to get to know you all a little better."

Their names were Alan, Robert and Bertholt. They had all served together for some time. I discovered that they had fought against William when he was the Duke of Normandy. When the pay disappeared, they contemplated taking service in Italy and Sicily but it was cheaper to find a passage to England.

"There is a warrior hall but you will not be able to use it for a week or so. The ladies who live there are waiting for their chambers to be habitable. Until then you will have to use the stable. Is that a problem?"

"So long as we are fed, My Lord, we are content. We are warriors all."

I told them their pay and they were also happy with that. I knew how much men at arms and sergeants were paid and I used the top rate. I understood the value of good soldiers.

We passed Forlan's farm and I said, "This is the southern extent of this manor. My land runs through the village to the woods to the east, the crossroads to the north and to the beck to the west."

"Beck, My Lord?"

I nodded, "A local word for a stream. I do not know how good your English is," we had been conversing in Norman, "but it will need to improve. Bergil is the captain of my men at arms and he can teach you. His wife is English as are all the women in the manor. I will give commands in English."

Bertholt said, "We live in England, My Lord, we should speak the language. We will learn."

The wagon was already back and had been unhitched. We had gates but no one guarded them during the day. There was no need. We dismounted, "I will lead you to the stables."

As we neared it Aedgar came out. He said, "And how did Goldy behave?"

"He is a good horse and we can give him to Alfred. These four are joining us and until the warrior hall is vacated they will sleep here."

He nodded, "I will have Harold and Absalom make a space for them. My sons need as much work as I can give them and these four horses will do just that."

"When you have sorted out your belongings then come to the hall. You shall dine with me tonight. Aedgar, have one of your sons show them the way."

"Yes, My Lord."

I went in through the kitchen. "Benthe, we have six more guests this night. I have hired new warriors and I would like Edward and Bergil to meet them. Tell your sons that I do not need them this night but soon they will have to return to the warrior hall. I need all my men to be as one." The slight frown was the only sign that I had caused her any inconvenience. "Ask Walter of Bootham to inform them."

"Yes, My Lord."

I walked through the house and went to the new chambers. I found Dervilla, Ealdgyth and the young women there. They had bought a small table and must have made a pair of small tapestries to hang over the wind holes.

Ealdgyth said, "When we have time we will sew something better. The beds will be delivered by the end of the week."

"End of the week?"

Dervilla busied herself with the fitting of the tapestry as Ealdgyth smiled and said, "Dervilla returned to the man who was making the beds and encouraged him to have them finished by the end of the week."

Dervilla sniffed and said, "It is not as though we asked for anything fancy, My Lord."

"And will the walls be dry enough by then?"

Dervilla nodded, "They are dry enough now, My Lord."

"Good, for I hired four more men today. They are Breton warriors and will need my warrior hall."

The ladies all began chattering away and I realised that I should have invited them too. It was too late now and I would not give more work to Benthe. Perhaps when they moved into the new chambers might be a better time. Once they were living in the main building then they would eat with me.

Bergil and Edward arrived first and I explained to them the circumstances surrounding the men. Bergil nodded, "I can see why the count was reluctant to hire them. As I discovered to my cost anything that disturbs the unity of warriors is to be avoided."

"But they might cause dissension here, My Lord."

"I think not, Edward, however, I will rely on you, Bergil, to keep an ear to the ground." I hesitated and then spoke, "I think it would be better if you dined, for a while, in the warrior hall. I know you have a family…"

"If it is just the evening meal that would not be a problem, My Lord. Seara is expecting another child and she likes to eat early."

The four men entered and I saw Bergil assessing them as they did him. I introduced them and said, "You can move into the warrior hall by the end of the week." I called, "You can serve the food now."

It was Maud and Birgitte who brought in the food. Benthe would have enough to do in the kitchen preparing for hungry men.

I said little during the meal, instead, I studied them. They all had scars. Bertholt's was on his face. Robert had lost one of his fingers. Conan had a long scar running up his arm and Alan had a white one on the back of his right hand. All had hair in the Norman style, that is to say shaved at the back. I saw, on Conan's head, a couple of white hairs. These four men had been warriors for a long time. Bergil, and occasionally Edward, questioned them about the wars and battles in which they had fought. It was what warriors did. I liked that they did not boast but spoke in a matter-of-fact manner.

What I saw was that Robert, who looked to be the youngest, had eyes for Maud whenever she brought in food. For her part she smiled at him. I was pleased about that. Maud had come with Seara and Seara had saved her from the rapacious attack of a Dane. She was fey around men, even the gentle men who served me. She smiled at Robert and that made me glad that I had hired him. If she rejoined the normal world then I would be pleased.

As the food was finished I ended the evening, "Tomorrow we begin to train as one. I will join you. Come Sunday I want the men in the village to join us after Father Gregory's service. We have the autumn and winter to make the men of Eisicewalt into a fighting force. By then Aedgar and his sons will have bred us more horses and we can eventually become a mounted band."

I saw the excitement on their faces.

"One more thing. When the spring comes my warriors, the men around this table and my two men at arms, will ride to Norton. There we will labour and make that manor strong once more." I paused, "One of you will be the one who runs that manor for me. I will not command the appointment but I hope that one of you will choose to take on the task." Their faces told me that none of them relished that thought. It gave me a sour end to the evening. I had thought that one might show some spark of interest but I saw that Edward and Bergil had wives and families to think of. The four Bretons had come as one and endured as one. I could not see them changing. That night, as I retired, I would have to pray that Belisarius would find me another warrior who might take on the task.

We assembled in the yard after a good breakfast. While my labourers could fight if the manor was threatened, they had too many other tasks to spend time simply wielding weapons. They would have to be trained with the villagers on the green. Similarly, Aedgar would not come to war. He was the horse master but his sons Harold and Absalom would join Elric. Ethelred would also be there but as a trainer.

We were all dressed in leather jacks. Thanks to our successes in war, we had many weapons stored in what passed for an armoury. Most were only fit for training and so I had Alfred and Aethelstan fetch them. The three youths each had a leather jack. They carried their bows. Elric had already demonstrated that he was a good archer. Harold and Absalom also had bows but I knew nothing of their prowess. I looked at my men. It was a small band and I did not know, yet, their worth as a warband but I knew from my time with Bruno and the others that we could be better if we all worked as one.

"We have all come from different places but we are gathered here as the men of Sir Richard fitz Malet. For the next three days we will train on foot." I smiled at the Bretons. "I know that our Breton brothers are more comfortable seated on the back of a horse and when we practise mounted we shall see their skills, but we have had to defend the manor from our walls and I would like us to be such a force that none dream of taking Eisicewalt from us." I saw the three youths looking around, "Ethelred."

He stepped forward, "Aye, Lord."

"These three will be both our scouts and archers. You have skills in the woods that are unsurpassed. For the next days I would have you teach them your skills and to make them better bowmen."

I could see that it pleased not only him but also the three youths, "Aye, My Lord. My eyes maybe getting rheumy and my hearing dull but I shall make these three the eyes and ears of the manor with teeth as sharp as any. Come my fine young game cocks, let us see what an old man can do with you."

When they had gone I was left with eight men. I smiled. I had seen Bergil and the Bretons weighing each other up. Each would be keen to show the others that they had superior skills. It was the way of the warrior.

I was about to begin when Dervilla and the ladies came from the warrior hall to go to my dining hall for food. Seeing the men there they paused. My men would have an audience. I nodded to the pile of weapons and shields, "Each of you choose a shield and a sword. You need not blunt your own weapons." They did so. I sat on the tree stump that was used to chop kindling upon. "I have seen my men at arms and squire fight but you Bretons are unknown to me. I wish you eight to spar with each other and I will watch. When I call your name and tell you to hold then that contest is over. The swords are blunt ones but I do not wish us to bring out the vinegar and honey. Understand?"

They all chorused, "Yes, My Lord," and went to the weapons. The weapons and shields might be of little use in a real battle but these men all knew what they needed and every weapon and shield was chosen carefully.

When they all had a shield on their left arm and a sword in their right hand, I said, "Bretons, defend yourselves." I had deliberately not given them any warning.

Bergil was quick thinking and he took on Conan. It was his way, he saw himself as, me apart, the best warrior in the manor and he would fight the one he thought was the leader. Edward went for Robert as he stood next to Conan and that left my two youngest men at arms fighting Alan and Bertholt. If

Alan and Bertholt thought that they would have an easy time with two young men who looked like they had barely begun shaving they were in for a surprise. The presence of the young women ensured that Alfred and Aethelstan would want to show off their skills.

The sounds of sword on sword and metal on shield made the young women cover their ears but I could see joy on their faces. I realised that this was a good thing. It would exorcise the ghosts of the Danish raid and the slaughter they had witnessed. Alfred and Aethelstan fought well and even made the two Bretons fall back but the old soldiers had memories of battles past to call upon and it was Aethelstan who was the first to lose. "Bertholt, hold."

Aethelstan's head drooped. Bertholt put an arm around his shoulder, "You did well my young friend. Perhaps I can teach you a few tricks, eh?"

Alfred lasted a few more strokes. I suspect that seeing his brother lose disheartened him.

Edward, however, was more than holding his own. I am still unsure who would have won if Robert had not slipped on the horse dung. Edward had his sword at the Breton's throat in a heartbeat. Edward shrugged apologetically, "I am sorry, Robert, but in war a man takes his chances when he can."

He held his hand out for Robert to take and the Breton pulled himself to his feet, "Do not apologise, squire, you have skill and a warrior who has skill and luck is to be admired."

Conan and Bergil's battle was a closer one than any of the others. I think, in the end, the reason why

Bergil won was because Conan was like a sword that had been left too long in its scabbard. He was slow to react to a sudden shift of Bergil's feet and the sword was poised above the unprotected head of the Breton. "Hold!"

They stopped and smiled at each other. There was respect there. The seven captives clapped. They had enjoyed the spectacle.

Conan said, "You have good warriors, My Lord. They are well trained."

Alfred said, "That is because it was my lord who trained us. He can defeat any two men."

Conan shook his head. "In my experience two men will always defeat one."

Bergil smiled, "My lord, would you care to show them?"

I did not want to for I did not like to show off but I caught the look on the face of Ealdgyth. Her eyes were wide and wished, I could tell, to see me fight. I nodded, "Very well. Alfred, Aethelstan, your swords."

They handed me their swords. I had noticed that both swords were similar. They were not my swords but the balance would be the same. I tossed them in the air and caught them. It was not showing off. Taillefer had taught me that it was a good way to warm up. I smiled, "Well Conan, which of your men would you care to help you?"

"Come, Robert, and let us hope there is no dung this time." They were the two who had lost and he wanted the chance to show his and Robert's skills.

The two were taking it seriously. My four men joined the women to watch. I saw eager anticipation on the faces of my men. The other two Bretons stood apart. They did not yet feel part of my familia. The two Bretons did what I expected and came at me from two sides. Conan had made a boast and he had to ensure he won. I did not move and I waited. It was Robert who came at me a heartbeat before Conan. He held his shield before him and had his sword raised. Conan, on the other side, held his sword before him. I stepped to the side and using my left sword smacked away Robert's blade. I had quick feet and he bundled past me. His movement blocked Conan's attack and I smacked my right sword across Robert's back. In battle he would be hurt. My men and the women all cheered.

I turned to face them, "Let us call that luck, eh. Once more."

I had the measure of them now. Robert was the reckless one and Conan was more measured. Robert would also be angry that he had been defeated so easily. They came again but this time were side by side. Conan would not risk being blocked by his brother in arms a second time. I used that to my advantage. I ran at them and took them by surprise. I blocked both their swords and then whirled behind them. I brought both swords down and they were forced to raise their shields. I used my shoulder to barge into Conan and as Robert lunged at me trailed a leg so that he fell sprawling at my feet. My sword tapped the back of his head and my right hand darted out to stop a handspan from Conan's nose.

The Breton laughed and bowed, "My lord, such an exhibition I have never seen." He turned to face my men, "I apologise for my foolish boast. Two swords and you wielded them so fast that they were a blur."

I tossed the swords to my two men at arms who caught them easily. I put my hand out and helped Robert to his feet. He shook his head, "I have seen enough of this yard already, My Lord. I can see that we have much to learn."

I turned as Dervilla said, "Come ladies, we have watched enough sport this morning. We have much work to do once we are fed. These warriors need their hall."

My men all bowed as they passed. I saw that not only Alfred and Aethelstan were looking with doe eyes at the women, but the Bretons were too.

Ealdgyth paused as she passed, "My Lord, you must be the mightiest knight in Christendom."

I found myself blushing, "I was well trained but I think there are many who could best me. I thank you for your kind words."

The rest of the morning was productive. I showed them the methods I used and they saw the benefits of juggling. "Your left hand can use a shield but you need to be creative about its use. What happens if you lose your shield? We have all had to fight with sword and dagger. That is all that I do but I have trained myself so that my left hand is almost the equal of my right." I pointed to Robert's missing digit, "If a man is wounded in the hand then, unless he can use his other as well, he is a dead man. I like having luck but I want skill more."

By the end of the day there were bruises and even a cut or two but we had achieved much. I had Maud and Birgitte fill baths. I saw the smile exchanged between Maud and Robert. As they left us I said, "Birgitte, ask your mother to ensure that there is enough food for all of us."

She hesitated and then said, a little fearfully, “My Lord, my mother took it upon herself to cook enough for the men and for the ladies from the warrior hall. She thought to lay the table for all of you. She hopes you are not offended by her presumption.”

I smiled, “Tell her that she has read my mind and I am pleased.”

I was the first to bathe and after I had dried and dressed I went to the yard to wait for Ethelred and his scouts. They dragged their weary feet towards me but their faces were animated. I saw Ethelred speaking to them as they approached. When they neared me they stopped and bowed, “How was the day?”

Ethelred nodded, “They are raw clay, My Lord, but young enough for me to form it. Young Elric here has skills with a bow the like of which I have not seen before this day. Had we had such archers at Gate Fulford then our foes would have lost. I have told the other two to emulate him. They can all now see sign but, as you know, My Lord, such skills take time.”

Elric was excited, “And Ethelred said he will tell us more tales of Gate Fulford and the times when the Danes came here, My Lord.”

I gave Ethelred a stern look. He shrugged, “My Lord, you saved this manor when you fought the Danish champion, I thought that they should know.” He turned, “Well, my little band, tomorrow we will see if you can find me. I will be in Ethelred’s wood and your task, when you rise, is to find me!” He was making a game of it and I saw the response on the faces of the three youths.

I said, “Thank you, Ethelred.”

"Thank you, My Lord." He gave me a sad smile, "They could be like grandsons. Perhaps my task, when you rescued me from my pit of despair, was to make three in my image. I now have even more reason to rise each day."

The meal that evening was more like a feast. It was not the food that made it so. It was good food but no different from that which we normally ate. It was the company, the banter, the smiles and the fact that we had everyone around my table. The hall was filled. Birgitte and Maud spent as long as they could in the hall and it was not just duty that demanded their presence. Elric also dined with us and I think he might have been overawed had not Ealdgyth, who was seated next to him, taken pains to help him with matters that had not arisen in his humble home. Her kindness touched me. Elric responded with smiles and '*thank you*'.

The four Bretons were struggling with the English that was spoken around the table. Dervilla surprised me when she was able to translate some of the Breton words. She brushed off my thanks saying, "Some of the words are similar to Welsh and I had a Welsh servant when I was a child. I had thought I had forgotten the words she taught me."

No one, least of all me, wanted the evening to end but I knew that it must for we had much to do and a short time in which to do it.

I stood, "Thank you all for coming this evening." Benthe had come to help clear the dishes away. I said, "Benthe, I am in your debt. I should have thought of this but I fear I am just a soldier who does not think of such things. We shall make this a weekly event." I smiled, "I would not like to impose on either you, Benthe, or the limited resources of Egbert and Walter."

"It is a delight, My Lord. This hall needs laughter and young smiles. I am content."

I stood at the door as they all left. Dervilla squeezed my hand as she left and said, "This was well done, My Lord. My chicks can now preen their plumage for they have good cause." I saw her glance at a beaming Conan, "as do I."

Ealdgyth had a flushed face. I do not know what prompted it, perhaps too much wine, but whatever the reason I took her hand and kissed the back of it, "My Lady, thank you for what you did for Elric. It was kind."

She squeezed my hand and her blush became redder as she said, "My Lord, these are our people, are they not? For my people, I thank God that it was you who came to rescue us, I do not think our lives would have been as good had it been another. Thank you."

I was reluctant to let go. Dervilla coughed and said, "Come, Ealdgyth, otherwise we shall be here all night."

When they had all gone I waited while Benthe and the two young women cleared the table. She paused at the door to the kitchen, "That was well done, My Lord. It is good that you now look to yourself. It is time." She said nothing more and she left. I went to my bedchamber. Despite my tiredness I was loath to sleep for I was running the evening through my mind. I had not wanted it to end and my last conversations had given me more questions than answers. Eventually I did sleep.

Chapter 10

Over the next days we practised on foot and then on horses. It was when we were all mounted that the Bretons showed their true worth. Bergil and Edward could not match their skills. They were able to lance the hoops suspended from the beam of the barn. They were able to stop their horses in an instant and they had the skill to weave their animals down a narrow obstacle course. It helped that they had slightly smaller horses but even Aedgar was impressed by the way they could control their animals.

When Saturday came I left Conan to continue training the men in riding for it was time to make the move for the ladies. The wagon had arrived late on Friday evening with the furniture and I used everyone in my manor, apart from my warriors, to help. Ethelred and his scouts were involved as were Lars and the labourers.

It was Dervilla who took charge. She commanded and instructed. She realised I was getting in the way and said, curtly, "Sir Richard, if you would just supervise then the work will proceed much more quickly."

The only break we had was at noon when we stopped for ale, bread and cheese. By late afternoon all was done. The fire made the chambers warm and it looked cosy.

I thought our work was done but Dervilla said, "And now we make the warrior chamber as welcoming as this, our new home. Come ladies, we have work before we dine."

I said, "Benthe, you and those who are needed in the kitchen should attend to your duties." I turned to Dervilla, "While I am still the lord of the manor."

Dervilla gave me a coy look but there was mischief in her eyes, "My Lord, I just thought to do as Benthe had done and think of those things that do not enter a warrior's mind."

The manor changed that night. We now had another seven young women in the hall and that meant there were more females than males. I do not know why but it seemed to make a difference. Elric, Alfred and Aethelstan joined the Bretons in the warrior hall and with Bergil and Edward in their own homes the only men I saw on a regular basis were Egbert and Walter.

Sunday was the first one where my Bretons attended the church. The seven women had all been before but my four new men made us a larger contingent and I saw the villagers looking apprehensively at them. Father Gregory always gave a sermon in English and he welcomed the new men. I had spoken to him before the service and he told all the men that there would be weapon practice on the green after it had concluded.

While the men went to fetch their weapons the women of my hall and the manor chattered like magpies. Uhtred and his sons were the closest to the church and they returned quickly to talk to the Bretons about weapons. Ethelred had his bow, and he, along with Elric, Harold and Absalom were setting up the marks that would be used.

By the time the men returned we were ready. I spoke first to all my warriors. I was keenly aware that Aed's parents were there as well as his younger brother and sisters. My words were intended for them too.

"The men of Eisicewalt have already shown their courage when they obeyed the command of the king and rescued the seven maidens here. That it cost the life of a warrior was upsetting. Our Sunday afternoons will be spent in weapon training so that no more young men die in the service of the king. Ethelred will work with the archers and slingers and Bergil will lead the training of the men. I will watch so that I may better judge the quality of the men I will lead into battle."

I had brought Scout and I mounted him. Every eye swung to me as I rode towards the church. It was a good vantage point.

Bergil shouted, "We will form a shield wall. Conan and Sir Richard's squire will be the centre. Form up on them." Bergil and I had discussed this. By having our mailed men in the centre, we were ensuring that we had a good rallying point. Alfred and Aethelstan stood next to Edward. In a real battle I would be where Edward was and Bergil next to me. As I had expected it took longer for the men to do as they were asked and Bergil had to chivvy and chase them. Eventually, we had three ranks and while Ethelred took the young men through their paces, Bergil marched the men of Eisicewalt up and down the green. I wondered if my Bretons thought that this was beneath them. After all they were horsemen, but their faces told me that they saw it as necessary.

When Bergil was happy with their marching he sent the four Bretons and Edward away.

"Let us assume that the five who are heading for the hall are incapacitated. What do you do?"

Alfred and Aethelstan knew the answer but they kept silent. Eventually Uhtred said, "We fill the gap." He pointed to Athelgar and Hob. "You two bring those next to you and fill the gap. Close up the centre."

Bergil caught my eye and I nodded. We had found the natural leader of the men. I had wondered if it would be Aedgar who did so but he just nodded too.

They were still forming when hooves were heard and our five horsemen with spears whose heads had been removed, charged from the far end of the village. Bergil said nothing and Uhtred roared, "Lock shields and brace yourselves."

Edward led the Bretons and they were in a small wedge. Edward had improved dramatically as a rider since the Bretons had arrived. They galloped at the shields and spears. I knew that they would not strike home but my heart was in my mouth as they waited until the last minute to, after tapping the shields with their spears, wheel and ride around the side. The grins on the faces of the men in the shield wall were a sign of their relief.

I rode Scout and placed myself before them, "If you want to know why we have marched you back and forth then this is the reason. We wanted you to get used to being as one. That was just five riders. There may come a day when we have to face ten times that number. They will not stop but all of you showed great courage this day. None of you faltered. No one fled." I shouted, "Egbert, Walter, the ale!"

Benthe had brewed some dark ale and the two men wheeled the cart to the green.

"Enjoy the ale. This day's training is done."

They cheered and took their coistrels from their belts. I dismounted and joined my oathsworn. "You did well, Bergil."

He shook his head, "Everyone did well, My Lord. We have made a start. Let us see what they are like when December comes and we are doing this in the rain and sleet."

I turned to Conan, "This was not beneath you?"

"No, My Lord. We are warriors and we eight cannot fight a large number. We need to have the men of the manor with us. This is good."

I noticed that he had said eight. I was pleased that he had said we but he had not included me, "There are nine of us, Conan."

He smiled, "Aye, My Lord, but I did not like to presume."

Over the next weeks the men grew closer and we were able to use different tactics. We tried using our horses while the men of the village acted as a block of infantry to hold off an enemy. By the time November was almost done Ethelred and the archers were able to support us. Despite his youth, it was clear that Elric would lead the archers and slingers. He was not as old as some of those who used bows but he was better than them all. Since he had come to us he had filled out, Benthe fed him well and he had taken to accompanying my gamekeeper, Ethelred. He hunted every day and Ethelred imparted unique knowledge to him. He was not ready to lead yet but when we were next called to the muster then he would.

It was also at the end of November when the messenger came from the Bishop of Durham. There were regular riders sent between Durham and York but the one on the last day of November had a letter for me. It had the seal of the bishop upon it. I went to my hall and slit open the wax.

Dunelm,

My Lord fitz Malet,

The Prior of Hexham has presented the case of Lady Ealdgyth of Brougham to me and I have consulted with the king on the matter. She is to be a ward of Durham but placed in your care. Her lands are to be given to another but, until she marries, there is a stipend of five gold crowns a year, payable from the Palatinate. When next you visit your manor at Norton I pray you visit with me so that we may discuss the matter further.

You are further charged to ensure that all those who were captives of the Danes remain safe. Lady Ealdgyth apart, you may choose the suitors for any of them. Lady Ealdgyth's hand can only be given with the permission of myself as the king's representative in the north.

Walcher

I folded the letter. I do not know why but I was disappointed. I had thought that Ealdgyth might be given land. The stipend was almost an insult. It would not change their circumstances. I was more concerned that it would be Walcher who would determine her husband. He was a churchman and he would make a political decision rather than one that might suit the lady.

I stood, "Walter."

The old man shuffled in. His arthritis had become worse of late. I wondered when it would be time to ask him to retire. I knew he would not want to, he enjoyed being useful but I did not think it was fair on him to have to work. I would have asked Egbert but he was in York buying what we needed for the Christmas celebration. We had heard a ship with spices was due in. He had taken Maud and Birgitte with him.

"Yes, My Lord?"

"Ask Lady Ealdgyth and Dervilla to join me, would you?"

"Yes, My Lord." I saw pain in his face and the claw like hands.

"You need to take life easier, Walter."

He smiled and held up his hands, "You mean the arthritis? It is just God's way of saying I am lucky to have lived as long as I have. The Danes would have taken my life but I found sanctuary. Each day I wake and feel the ache in my bones I know I am alive. I do not mind the work, My Lord. What else would I do?"

The man had a good philosophy.

"Benthe, bring in some wine and some goblets."

She called from the kitchen, "Yes, My Lord."

She arrived back before the two ladies. When they came with hair groomed I knew the reason for the delay. Benthe poured the wine and Lady Ealdgyth said, "My lord? This seems ominous."

I smiled and shook my head, "I have received a missive from the Bishop of Durham." I pushed it over. I nodded to Benthe who left us. She closed the door for privacy.

I poured some wine for us all. The two ladies read the letter and then sat. Ealdgyth looked unhappy when she had read and digested the letter. "I do not like this, My Lord. I did not want Brougham as I did not wish to be a cow at the market. It seems to me that I have merely changed my owner and the bishop is the one who will be selling me."

I spread my hands, "I can do nothing. I do not like it either. I do not think that this was what the prior intended."

"If I was to be the ward of anyone I would have you as my guardian."

I said nothing.

"You do not wish to be my guardian? My Lord, I would rather it was you for I know that you have my best interests at heart."

I looked at Dervilla for help. I was in an unknown land.

Dervilla put her arm around Ealdgyth, "Ealdgyth, you are putting Sir Richard in a difficult position."

"How so?"

Dervilla drank some of the wine and then looked me in the eye, "Because I do not think that Sir Richard wishes you to marry anyone…"

"What?"

"Who is not the Lord of Eisicewalt."

I could not meet her gaze and my eyes dropped. Ealdgyth's hand came across the table and her fingers touched mine. It was like the shock of icy water in the morning. My eyes widened and met Ealdgyth's, "Is this true?"

"I want you to be happy, Ealdgyth, and marry a man that you choose. I would not have you marry one who is chosen for you or one for whom you feel gratitude."

"You goose! Yes I am grateful to you but I am no fool and I know that you do not marry a man because you are grateful. You marry a man because you wish to spend your life with him and bear his children."

I turned my hands over and grasped hers.

Dervilla sighed, "Sir Richard, I know you are the bravest of knights and I know that your men view you as the cleverest of men but this…" She shook her head, "Ealdgyth would be your wife. Would you be her husband?"

I turned and spluttered, "Of course but…"

"Then you need to write to the bishop and tell him what you both wish."

"Is that what my lady wishes?"

She squeezed my fingers, "Of course it is. I have loved you more each day until now I can barely sleep without your face drifting into my dreams."

"Of course," interjected Dervilla, "the bishop might well have his own suitor in mind."

She was right and I stood, "Then I must do all in my power to ensure that Lady Ealdgyth has the right husband. Me. The messenger will stay this night in York. I will ride to him. If anyone can see a way to ensure that this will happen it is Belisarius." I shouted, “Walter, have Edward bring our horses around.”

“Yes, My Lord.”

“You would leave me?”

“I would never leave your side if that were possible but Dervilla is right. I must do this and do so with all haste.” I kissed her hand. She threw her arms around me and kissed me hard on the lips.

Dervilla said, “Ealdgyth!”

Ealdgyth laughed, “I care not if you think me a wanton, Dervilla. I have wanted to do that for so long. Tonight my dreams will be sweeter.”

Edward was in the stables when I arrived, “What is amiss, My Lord?”

“We have to get to York and I must speak with Belisarius. I will tell you all as we ride.”

Telling Edward helped me to focus on the words I would use and to find a solution to the problem. Perhaps Bishop Walcher viewed Ealdgyth as a bargaining tool. Whilst she had no land she had a heritage and a family tree. There were lords who valued such things. King Harold had benefitted from his sister marrying King Edward. When we reached York I left the horses with Edward and sought Belisarius. I was told that he was with the archbishop and I would have to wait. It was an hour before the meeting ended and Belisarius emerged. He saw me and nodded. He put his fingers to his lips and waved for me to follow him. We went to his room and entered. The corridor was empty.

“I know why you have come, Sir Richard.”

I shook my head, “You may think you know but while the cause of the problem may be known to you events have transpired which I must tell you about.”

He frowned and then sat back. “Go on.”

“The lady is unhappy with the letter from Bishop Walcher.”

“She is now a ward of Durham and he can do as he wishes with her.”

I took a breath, “She wishes to marry me and I her.”

His eyes widened and he leaned forward, “I am an old man who lives in the world of men. I did not see this coming but it changes nothing. You should know, Sir Richard, that the bishop has a suitor for her already. Oengus mac Máel Snechtai is the Mormaer of Moray. Mormaer is a term that ranks with a lesser king. He has a son, Lulaich. The boy is but ten years old, however, if the mormaer can arrange a marriage to Lady Ealdgyth, it strengthens his claim to the crown of Scotland.”

“I do not understand.”

“The bishop is playing politics. He hopes to destabilise King Malcolm by causing dissent in Scotland.”

“You do not know this king of Scotland. I met him on the Aln and he is a clever man. This mormaer will not show his hand until his son is married. This plan will not stop the Scots from supporting the rebels and invading England. They gain Cumberland and Northumbria by doing so.”

He smiled, “Interesting. Archbishop Thomas said much the same thing.”

“Then there is hope.”

“Do not get ahead of yourself. There are politics of religion here. At the moment the archbishop is head of the church in England but there are moves, from Rome, to give Canterbury the primacy.”

"That is a matter for the future. The now, Belisarius, is that we can take action and marry Ealdgyth to me."

"That would make you an enemy of Walcher and the mormaer."

I laughed, "I have enough enemies and I fear neither man. I will marry Ealdgyth and if that means defying Bishop Walcher I will do so. I can leave this land and return to Normandy."

I did not want to do that for I was attached to Eisicewalt but for Ealdgyth I would do so.

"That is hasty and may not be necessary. I happen to agree with your thoughts. King William spoke to me when he passed through about the danger from the Scots. He had already planned on chastising the Scottish king next year. Wait here and I will speak with the archbishop."

It was only an hour I had to wait but that was the longest hour I had ever endured. I watched each drip of wax from the candle as it made its way to the pewter base.

When Belisarius came back his face was as stone, "Well?"

"It took some persuasion for the archbishop does not wish to make an enemy of Bishop Walcher. He is drafting a letter to the bishop. He says that he wishes to take over the guardianship of Lady Ealdgyth and he warns the bishop of the threat from Scotland. I am to send a report to King William. In that report I will put forward the case that you should marry Lady Ealdgyth."

"Then I can marry her."

"No!" It was almost a shout. "You will do nothing until the king has decided. All must be done properly. Letters need to be exchanged and the king must have his say. If King William chooses to support Bishop Walcher, and he might well do, then I am afraid she would have to marry the son of the mormaer. I know it is not the answer you wished for but it is, at least a hope."

I stared at the latest drip of wax as it slipped down the candle. I could just pre-empt a bad decision and flee back to Normandy. It would mean leaving my people to suffer at whoever King William replaced me with but Ealdgyth would be happy. Even as the thought came into my head I knew that Ealdgyth would not agree and I could almost hear my grandfather's spirit telling me to do the right thing. There was an oppressive and embarrassing silence in the room.

Belisarius broke it, "On a more positive note, Sir Richard, I have found you another three men. Englishmen this time. They left England after Senlac and went to Byzantium. They did not enjoy life there and have returned home. They are housecarls although they have returned almost as paupers with neither mail nor helmets but they are good warriors."

I looked at him. The soldier in me came to the fore, "They were at Senlac?"

"No, they fought at Stamford and were slightly wounded. They left from York after the defeat at Senlac and have returned to their home. They are good men."

"And I need all that I can get. Send them and," I stood, "I pray you send me word of the king's decision as soon as you know it."

"I will."

As we headed back in the twilight I told Edward what had been said, "You cannot go against the king, My Lord."

"I know." I was already thinking about my stepbrother. He might be able to offer me sanctuary. He was not a minor lord but a companion of the king. Perhaps flight back to Normandy might take the lady away from the machinations of the bishop. My stepbrother owned me much and surely he would offer her sanctuary.

It was only when I returned to my hall that I realised how close the women in the hall had become. Benthe was with Dervilla and Ealdgyth, along with Maud, Birgitte, Seara and Mathilde. Of my men there was no sign. I had sent Edward to the stables with Scout. As I opened the door to the dining hall every eye swivelled to me. I saw that Ealdgyth had been weeping. She said, "Well?"

I hesitated and Dervilla said, firmly, "Sir Richard, you are master here and we all bow to your wishes but this concerns Lady Ealdgyth. Everyone in this room has an interest in this. Speak for we would all hear."

I looked at Ealdgyth, who nodded. Benthe sighed, "My Lord, a trouble shared is a troubled halved. We may not be warriors and we cannot fight with swords but we all stand by Ealdgyth and you. Whatever is to be done know that you have the support of everyone in this manor. We all know what we owe to you. We would see you happy."

I went to Ealdgyth and took her hands, "You are sure that you wish all to hear this?"

"They are my friends, Richard, aye. I wish them to know all."

I nodded and faced them. “I will not honey my words but tell you everything even if that is upsetting. You wish to know the truth and I will give it to you. Bishop Walcher wishes to marry Ealdgyth to the ten-year-old son of the Mormaer of Moray.” Dervilla took Ealdgyth’s hand. Maud’s eyes welled up with tears. “I have asked the archbishop to intervene. He has written a letter to Bishop Walcher. It cannot be there for some time. Belisarius and the archbishop will also write to the king on the matter. I have been told to do nothing in the meantime.” I smiled at Ealdgyth, “If we were to marry here then it might undo any hope we have of happiness. Our future lies in the hands of others.”

“I will not marry a boy who merely wishes my lineage. I would…” I could see that she had not thought it through. What would she do?

I took her hand again, “We have to hope that the king makes a wise decision but, if he does not, then I will ensure that you do not have to marry against your will.” I paused, “We could leave Eisicewalt and find a home somewhere else.”

If Benthe had been stoic until then my words opened a floodgate, “My Lord, you cannot leave us. You have made this a happy place. It prospers. If you left it would wither and die.”

Dervilla said, calmly, “And where would we go?”

I smiled, “I do not recall inviting you, Dervilla, for this would be a dangerous road Ealdgyth and I took.”

She snorted, “Where my lady goes so go I.” She faced me defiantly.

I nodded, "Normandy and if I was not welcome there then take my sword to Italy. The Hautevilles value knights. I would begin again."

Ealdgyth stood, "Then there is hope and I am content. I trust you, Richard."

"But all must be done well. There can be no impropriety. I will not jeopardise our future."

Dervilla smiled, "And that shows that you are both chivalrous and noble. I can see a happy ending in all this."

Benthe said, "And now, ladies, Sir Richard needs to be fed." She shooed them away like a farmer's wife with geese. Ealdgyth's fingers lingered a little longer on mine and she smiled as she left.

I looked at the flickering flames in the fireplace. Was I burning all that I had built up? I was loath to leave this place. Men had died here to keep it safe and would I discard it for a hope of happiness with Ealdgyth?

Edward must have been waiting outside. He came in when they left. "I have spoken to Mathilde, know, My Lord, that I will follow you to Italy."

"I thank you but let us hope it will not come to that. Before I forget, we have three warriors who will be arriving tomorrow. Tell Conan. They are housecarls."

"Housecarls? Will that cause a problem with the others?"

I shook my head, "There were not at Senlac. They fought Northumbrians and Vikings. If they appear to be a hazard then I will not hire them. Now go to your wife. Leave me with my thoughts."

Birgitte brought in my food and placed it before me. Maud brought the wine. Birgitte said, "My Lord, do not leave us. If you do and you take your men with you then hearts will be broken." From the glance she gave Maud I guessed that Maud would be one of those affected.

"The matter will take time, Birgitte. We have winter. Nothing can be done until the new grass comes. Know this, I will not allow Lady Ealdgyth to be married against her will."

They both smiled and curtsied. I had said the right thing.

Chapter 11

The manor was too small for secrets and after I had breakfasted and gone outside the whole manor knew what had gone on. I was surprised at the smiles and happy faces. It was Bergil who explained why, "They think that what you do is right. They believe in the goodness of God. They pray that He will change the mind of the bishop."

"It is good that they pray but I have met senior churchmen and more are like Bishop Odo and not St Cuthbert." I changed the subject, "We have three housecarls arriving today. Speak to them and find out all you can. They come with nothing but if they served in the Varangian guard and fought at Stamford then they will be a worthy addition to the familia."

"That they will. We need a stiffening of the men who fight on foot."

Knowing that events were now out of my hands I threw myself into work. I had been distracted and there were things that needed my attention. However, the first task, the visit to Father Gregory, was already planned, and I also needed to tell him what had happened. He would have heard the tale but like all such tales it might have become distorted. Better to hear it in my words.

I passed Ethelred and his now almost constant companion, Elric. Ethelred waved, "We are off hunting, My Lord. I think there is an injured stag. We will try to take him."

"Be careful, Ethelred, I would not like to lose either of you."

He laughed, "I am too wise and this one is too quick for that, My Lord. It is why we work so well together."

Father Gregory was making some repairs to the roof of the church. It was still a wooden one. We both had plans to build a stone one but that took masons and coins. He came down the ladder, "Sir Richard," he paused, "I heard about your problem, My Lord. Would you like to talk?"

"I think that is necessary."

We went into the church. The tallow candles gave it a smoky feel. I told him everything, including my plans. He nodded, "I am a simple priest, My Lord. I confess I do not like this politicking. I ask myself in these situations, what would Jesus have done and I know in my heart that he would wish Lady Ealdgyth to be happy. The Lord would wish her to be married to you."

"The plans are made and now we wait on the whims of others. The reason I have come to speak to you is that the recent arrival of the captives has caused a stir amongst the young men of the manor. I think that some may come to you to ask you to marry them. I want you to know that I am in favour of all such marriages. The captives have no father and I am still responsible for them. I suspect the suitors will come to you first. If so then know I give my blessing. Those young women endured enough on the journey north. I would want them to be happy and not wait upon the whim of a lord."

"And you, My Lord, deserve to be happy too."

"The lord of the manor has less freedom than you might think, Father Gregory."

It was noon when the housecarls arrived. They looked thin, their clothes were torn and I doubted that they had soles on their boots but they carried themselves proudly. Each still had his sword on his baldric and a long axe over his shoulder as well as his round shield slung over his back. They had their long hair tied behind them and I saw the tattoos that told me they had Danish forebears. They looked younger than I had expected them to be.

They entered the yard and looked around them.

I strode up to them, "I am Sir Richard fitz Malet. Did Belisarius send you?"

The tallest of them spoke, "He did, My Lord. I am Galmr of the Varangians. This is my brother Folki and my cousin Haldir."

I had served with a man called Galmr before Senlac and I took it as a good omen. "You have Danish names and yet you speak English."

"We were born to the east of here and our fathers were Danish. They came over with King Cnut."

"And I hear you tried the Varangian Guard and served the emperor. They are a most prestigious body of men and feared throughout the eastern world."

"They are and we were proud to serve with them. We fought alongside them for a year but…"

"But?"

He sighed and explained, "Sir Richard, it is so hot there and fighting in mail…we endured it as long as we could and then returned."

I liked his honesty from the off. "Somewhat poorer, I see." I nodded to their clothes and their footwear.

"My Lord, the journey back is a long one and filled with robbers, bandits and men with no honour. There were six of us who left Byzantium. We buried three on the way back. We had to sell our mail and helmets to pay for a passage home and we have eaten little but what we could forage from the road. Belisarius was kind and we fared better at York." I nodded as I studied them. "My Lord, we are warriors. We have sought work in York but found none who were willing to take us on. It is as though they did not trust us. You need to know, Sir Richard, that we are loyal Englishmen. Belisarius has told us how you fought against all those invaders who would have taken lives here close to York. We would be honoured to serve you."

I nodded. I had already decided to give them the opportunity but I wanted them clear about my hierarchy. "Then, if you can take orders from a Norman lord then I can use three more experienced warriors." I waved over Bergil who, along with my Bretons, was watching the interchange. "This is Bergil, the captain of my guard. Can you take his orders?"

Galmr nodded, "We can and we can fight."

I looked at Bergil who nodded, and he said "Aye, they will do, Sir Richard, but we cannot have men fighting for the greatest knight in England dressed like that. Come, we have, in the warrior hall, boots, mail and helmets. That done we shall see if Mistress Benthe can provide food."

"Hold, before you do that there is something I should like to do. Conan, bring your men over, too." They came and stood in a half circle before me, the new warriors towering over the Bretons. "Take a knee." They dropped to one knee. I drew my favourite sword, the first one given to me by Taillefer. I reversed it and held the blade. "I am an old-fashioned man. I believe in the old ways. I would have you all swear an oath on my sword."

Galmr grinned and said, "And we would too, but, My Lord, would you do us the honour of holding the hilt? We would swear a blood oath."

I looked at Conan who also smiled and nodded, "I like these men already, My Lord. We will do the same."

I reversed the sword and held the hilt. They all grasped the blade. It was razor sharp. Their blood ran down to drip on the ground. It was almost as though they had rehearsed it for they all said, almost as one, "We swear to be the oathsworn of Sir Richard fitz Malet."

I nodded and grasped the blade myself. It cut me across my right palm, "And so it is done and we are sealed in blood."

They rose and clapped each other on the back. Bergil said, "Come, let us bathe those wounds of honour in vinegar. Edward, see to his lordship."

It was only then that I saw the looks of disappointment on Alfred and Aethelstan's faces. They had not been given the opportunity to do as these seven new warriors had done.

Ealdgyth and Dervilla had come from the hall when they heard the commotion. They saw my hand as Edward bathed it in vinegar. He would apply honey and a bandage to seal the wound. Ealdgyth looked shocked, "Why did they do that, Dervilla?"

"It is the act of a warrior. It is a good thing, Ealdgyth. We shall all be safer for these eight are now bound in blood."

By the end of the week the wounds were itching, my new men were dressed as warriors and the letter from the bishop seemed to be forgotten. The missive had made a difference, however. Despite that fact that it was winter, it was though it was spring for the young women of the manor put flowers in their hair and bathed in rosemary water. The young men, Aethelstan and Alfred in particular, had taken to shaving the backs of their heads to emulate the Bretons and they took more care with their appearance. The biggest surprise, however, was the blossoming relationship between Conan and Dervilla. I would not have believed it before the arrival of the Bretons but Dervilla began to behave like a young girl. She smiled more. She, too, took greater care with her appearance. The new cloth helped and the clothes they wore were more flattering than the rags they had first dressed in. Conan, for his part, was at first tongue tied when Dervilla spoke to him. It was the second of our feasts when I spotted that she was seated next to him. I was not aware of their interaction but Birgitte, who noticed such things, took delight in telling me that she thought they were enamoured of one another. I was too wrapped up in my own problems and the fate of Ealdgyth but once it was drawn to my attention it became clear. I sought counsel from Father Gregory. I could have asked Benthe but the gathering of the women following my return from

York had made me wary of them. I knew that Benthe would tell Dervilla and I did not want that.

Father Gregory was somewhat surprised by my question but he answered it, "My Lord, I know little of women and I cannot abuse the confessional but from what I have seen in the church on Sundays, there is a closeness between the two. It should not surprise you. Dervilla has devoted her life to Ealdgyth and you have promised to take on that burden. She will soon, God willing, be free to determine her own destiny. Conan, too, has served others. He is now in the latter part of his life. Perhaps, he now seeks that which others have, a family."

It made sense. I had seen Conan looking enviously at Bergil whenever Seara brought young Richard out to see his father. If Bergil, a warrior, could have a family, then, why not him? I suspected that Father Gregory knew more than he was saying but I respected his reticence. I began to notice more things as November passed. At our weekly feast, now attended by three Varangians, I tended to speak to Ealdgyth who had taken to sitting on my right. We both wanted intimacy but I had promised Belisarius restraint and as my dream was to have Ealdgyth as my wife, I would not put that in jeopardy for a furtive kiss. I saw that Aethelstan would sit close to Mary and that naturally put Alfred next to Elfrida. Until I spoke to Father Gregory I put it down to a happy accident. I now saw that the two couples kept their heads close. There was always laughter and the passing of platters always resulted in an accidental touch. By the same measure Robert and Maud also showed a growing fondness for each other. The difference was that as Maud served at table they could only speak when she entered.

Ealdgyth and I talked also. We could not say the things we wished to say for it was around a table but we said enough with our eyes and occasional touches. When Seara was noticeably pregnant Ealdgyth asked me, “Do you think Bergil yearns for a daughter or another son? He is a warrior.”

I shook my head, “I do not think it matters. So long as the child is healthy and survives the parlous early years they will both be content.” She nodded. We both knew of many infants who died within weeks of their birth. Two had been buried in the village since the captives had come.

“And you, My Lord, do you want an heir?”

I found myself blushing again. I thought I had rid myself of the weakness but her question prompted other thoughts. “A good question for I would not wish my people to be dispossessed because I had no sons, but I would like a daughter. I would like her to look as beautiful as you.”

It was her turn to blush, “Richard!” I had weaned her from using, ‘My Lord’ or ‘Sir Richard.’ “I should like a son who takes after his father, but a daughter would be welcome. Just so long as she gets to choose her own husband.”

“Sadly, we know that is not the reality, Ealdgyth. Great lords make such decisions and if they are your liege lord then you have to obey.”

“Would that be true in Italy too, Richard?”

“As they are Normans and use the same system then, aye. From what Galmr has told me it is different in Byzantium. There, women can own property. They can even be the empress.”

"Could we go there?"

I put my hand on hers, "We can go wherever you wish, my love."

She squeezed my fingers, "Let us wait until we have the letter from the king before we discard this little piece of paradise."

That winter had started early. At the end of November, we had endured our first frosts. They were followed by rain of Biblical proportions and there was flooding. The fishpond was our salvation. Thanks to its position the floodwater drained to it and the pond became a lake but it did not threaten the fields nor the houses. Our ditches took away the surplus. York was, as usual, inundated. The two rivers there combined to make a huge lake and only those buildings on the highest ground were untouched. The waters only began to recede a week into December. Egbert had already bought our spices and all that we would need from York and we were well prepared for Christmas.

Ethelred came to me not long after the waters receded, "Sir Richard, now would be a good time to hunt the food we shall eat over the long nights. The waters ensure that the animals will be on higher ground."

He was asking me for a larger hunt with more men than just him and Elric. It was a good idea for it would give all my new men the chance to endure risk and danger but not in war. Men sometimes died or were hurt whilst hunting. "We will hunt on foot. Which day will be best?"

Ethelred knew the land and the weather better than any man I had ever known. He looked at the sky and sniffed the air. "The day after tomorrow will be best. The waters will be lower. Will you organise your men, My Lord?"

"I will."

"Elric, Lars and I along with the other labourers will be one group. We shall use bows."

"And I will ensure that we have boar spears as well as javelins."

"I have not seen as many signs of the wild pigs, My Lord. I think the new boar is more cunning than the old one and he leads his herd well." He chuckled, "A lot like you, My Lord."

I sought out Edward and told him of our plans. "I want both our new men and old to hunt. Tell them that we do so on foot. I know the Bretons will be disappointed but the boggy ground will not suit horses. Absalom and Harold can come with us. It will be good experience for them."

I rose early the day of the hunt. It would be a day for stout leather jacks and boots that would keep our feet dry. I had used the seal skin that Algar had given to me and had boots made for me. There was enough left over for a hat but as we would not be hunting in the rain I would not need that. It would be cold and I would need my oiled cloak too. My swords I could leave at home but I strapped on a pair of daggers. One was a wicked looking seax taken from one of the Danes we had killed. It was longer than a dagger and with just one edge made a good tool for gutting. Others were up early too but I was the first to break my fast. I had almost finished when Dervilla and Ealdgyth entered with the other young women. I noticed then how quickly even the youngest of them, Susan, was growing. In the months they had lived with us good food and the security of my walls had made them blossom.

"It will be quiet today, My Lord, without the clash of steel as your men practise."

"For the next month, Dervilla, there will be less time for swords. We will use axes to copse the wood and store kindling for the winter. But for the rains and the flooding we would have done so a month ago. I do not know what life was like at Brougham, but here we have a pattern. There is a rhythm to the seasons. It is a fool who tries to fight nature. We flow with it. When the nights are long we stay within and prepare for the longer days to come."

Ealdgyth nodded, "I had an idea to keep the ladies and myself occupied, Richard, I thought that we could make a tapestry for this room. It would brighten it up and keep it warm."

"A good idea."

"When we were in York we heard that Bishop Odo has commissioned a tapestry recording the achievements of the Normans."

I looked at the young woman who would become my wife one day and said, "You would make one that illustrates the Norman victory?"

She laughed, "No, Richard. I would honour the people of Eisicewalt. Benthe has spoken often about the time the Danes raided and you fought their champion before the walls. We have spoken of this and thought to make a triptych. Three panels will show the Danes coming, your fight and Edward's rescue of you. That way we could include the faces of the people of the village. It would honour them."

"That would be a fine thing to do but it is a lot of work."

"And as you say what else have we to do until the new grass grows? Those women who are married have families to care for and create more babies. We are spinsters and better occupied than pining over what we cannot have, yet." Her hand brushed the back of mine and I nodded.

"You have all that you need?"

"We do and Dervilla has organised us. We will make a start this day while you hunt. Take care, Richard."

"I will."

We gathered in my yard. Edward and Bergil had arranged the weapons. We had three boar spears and each of us had three throwing spears, javelins. Ethelred and Elric appeared. They held their bows, as yet unstrung. I said, "Today we obey Ethelred as my gamekeeper. He knows the land, the paths and the animals. Know that I am not precious about being the one to make the kill. We hunt for food." Many lords would punish men who threw a spear before the lord of the manor. I was not one. "Tell us what we need to know, Ethelred."

"Elric and I have found the spoor of a large herd of deer. There are too many to survive the winter and they need to be culled. His lordship needs a healthy herd. Go for the old and the slow. Let the young live to prosper. No one is to touch the stag. He has won the right to rule the herd by his strength."

Conan asked, "What do we do if we are charged? We are not mounted and cannot flee."

Ethelred looked at me for the answer. "Conan, this is to prepare us for war. If the stag comes at you then those around must make a barrier of spears. He will just be seeking a safe path for his hinds and does."

Galmr said, "I have hunted on foot before, Conan. It is a greater test of courage than hunting from the back of a horse. Any animal can outrun a man. Do not worry, my shield brothers and I will be close by."

There was no intention, I do not think, to make a challenge but I saw from the faces of my Bretons, that they had seen it as such.

Ethelred said, "We have two miles to walk and the paths are treacherous. Elric leads and I will follow. Keep in our footsteps and I want silence from all. We are not magpies and there will be no chattering. We use hand signals. Watch closely for mine. I shall not make them twice."

The cold wind that came from the east was in our faces. I pulled the cowl of my cloak over my head as I walked behind Ethelred. We walked in silence. The wind was in our favour but until we saw the herd we would have to rely on Ethelred and his hand signals.

Once we neared the wood Elric took us down a path and then left the path. He stopped and Ethelred used his hands to command us into a long line. He pointed to Bergil to take one end and Conan the other. The rest he spread out. The two hunters were in the centre and then me. Edward guarded my right. I handed him all but one throwing spear. Ethelred and Elric strung their bows. The barbed hunting arrows they would use were in an arrow bag but both of them took three arrows and held them next to the bow. The two of them then stepped forward. We followed. Edward and I now had Bretons to the right of us and the Varangians to our left. Harold and

Absalom followed behind with spare spears and their slings.

One advantage of the recent rain was that the leaves that had fallen were soggy. They did not crunch but no matter how careful we were there were still noises. The boots of the others slurped in the mud. For some reason the sealskin boots were silent by comparison. When I went to Norton the next time I would see about getting more skins for my men. Algar's gift had been a good one. The canopy of trees had shed many of its leaves but there was still enough cover to make shadows. The ground undulated and there were hollows and bumps. Saplings sprouted and there were wild bushes with brambles and autumn raspberries. Most of the bushes were bare but they were still a barrier that we had to avoid.

Someone to my right had just slipped when Ethelred held up his hand. I was unsure if it was because of the noise or if he had heard something. I peered ahead and spied a movement. If this was war, my hand would have gone to my sword. I saw the small deer and knew that we had found the herd. Ethelred turned. I dropped the cowl from my head. Every face went to watch him. He pointed to Conan and signalled for him to move further to his right. He did the same with Bergil. He was extending the line. He waved to Harold and Absalom and they filled the gaps. He waved us forward but made the sign for '*go carefully*'. We all looked down to place our feet where we would neither trip nor make a noise. We each held our spear ready to throw. With the wind in our faces the smell of the deer came at us and they would have no indication that we were close. The deer's attention was on the food they ate. The exception, of course, was the stag. I saw his antlers as they rose and fell. He was vigilant and was both eating and watching.

We made it to within thirty paces or so before we were seen. We were lucky to make it so close. As soon as we were spied the stag gave a warning and his females obeyed his command. They turned to flee. Ethelred shouted, "Now!"

I scanned the herd and saw one who looked a little lame. I pulled back my arm and threw a javelin. All along our line men had spears ready to throw but, like me, were obeying Ethelred's command and looking for weakness. It gave the herd of deer the chance to flee. Luckily our long line limited the escape routes. My spear struck the old hind in the rump. It was not a killing blow. I held my hand out and Edward gave me a second. I was lucky. Folki's hurriedly thrown javelin missed the wounded hind but sent her towards me. I did not throw the spear but held it in two hands. The animal came at me and I was able to ram the spear into her chest. The force of her movement pushed me back until Edward placed himself behind me.

Apparent confusion reigned. The herd was panicking. I heard the sound of javelins being thrown and then the stag bolted towards Robert. Ethelred shouted, "Ware Robert!"

The stag was far bigger than the hind I had killed. If it struck Robert he would at best, be badly wounded and, at worst, dead. The mud was almost his undoing. He slipped and fell. All that he would be able to do would be to roll away but as the herd was following him he would be trampled to death.

The arrow sent by Elric was his salvation. My young archer, the youth from Wallington, sent an arrow which hit the antlers of the stag. I know he was not trying to kill the animal but it went so close to the skull that the stag veered to its left. Bertholt and Conan had made a gap to allow the herd to pass and Robert was able to roll to his left. As the herd passed the Bretons and Absalom, they stabbed with their spears at the weaker ones who passed. In a few heartbeats the only sounds to be heard were the deer in the distance and the dying animals as they thrashed to their deaths.

"Robert?"

He stood, "I am well." He walked over to Elric, "And I owe you a life. That was as fine a flighted arrow as I have ever seen. Thank you."

Elric picked up the arrow where it had fallen and shrugged, "I was lucky as were you. I could have missed."

Ethelred unslung his bow, "Elric, I know your skill better than any. I knew you would not miss. You were right though, Robert the Breton, we were lucky. We managed to kill more than I hoped. By my count there are seven dead deer. While we see to the animals Elric, take Harold and Absalom, see what else you can hunt."

It took an hour to gut the animals and to cut saplings to help us carry them back. We had not taken Ethelred's hounds but the offal we took would feed them. When we did not use our men to hunt Ethelred and Elric needed the hounds.

The three youths brought back some birds they had killed. They managed to bag four pheasants who had strayed into the wood for food. With the seven deer on saplings, we marched back to the hall. We could have fried the hearts and liver and enjoyed those in the woods but we were close enough to the hall to be able to return and enjoy fresh bread, cheese, onions and ale. It would be a fine lunch and we would be able to talk about the hunt in my dining hall. As we walked back Edward said, "If we had more archers like Elric, My Lord, then think what we might do on the battlefield."

"Archers like Elric are rare. Ethelred will tell you that. He is still young and will get both better and stronger with age. His skill will train others like Harold and Absalom so that they can become a little better than they might have been otherwise."

We reached the hall a couple of hours after it was noon. The rest of my people had eaten already. We hung the animals in the larder. We would eat first and then skin and butcher them. We washed and took off our muddy boots before entering my hall. None would risk the wrath of Benthe. The blazing fire, food and ale made the hall a most convivial place. We were making a great deal of noise and Dervilla and Ealdgyth entered. The noise ceased.

Dervilla had a mischievous look on her face, "My Lord, there was so much noise I feared for our lives. We thought we were being attacked."

Ethelred snorted, "My lady, what you heard was a celebration of a most successful hunt. When we dine at Christmas we will enjoy the finest of food."

She curtsied, "Then, Master Hunters, we are in your debt. Come, Ealdgyth, back to the tapestry."

I saw that Ealdgyth was reluctant to leave. Her eyes were on me and the blood-spattered jack. I smiled, “The blood is that of a deer. I came to no harm.”

“Then I am content.”

I turned and saw the grins on the faces of my men. Ethelred said, “The sooner the letter comes from the bishop the better, My Lord.”

He was right, I was ready for marriage.

Chapter 12

Eisicewalt, Christmas 1071

Christmas came without a letter. While everyone was disappointed it was not unexpected. In the grand scheme of things, the fate of Ealdgyth was relatively unimportant to the king, the bishop and everyone outside of our manor. The disappointment was put to the backs of our minds as we threw ourselves into making the celebrations the best that they could be. The hall was decorated with greenery from the woods. We had plenty of holly for, in harsh winters, we could use it to feed our animals. We took the ivy to stop it clambering over the trees and the cutting of the mistletoe was a throwback to the pagan times. It was seen as a sign of fertility. The hall was transformed. We gave three of the deer we had hunted to the villagers. I knew that most lords would not have done so but to me it made sense. We did not need more than four deer for our feast and they would eat well for the whole period of the winter solstice. When January came the women of the village would still be using the bone stock to make soups and stews made from old beans and what greens they could forage, palatable. I knew that in my hall we were luckier. We had spices and the meat from the culled animals we had killed in October was now made into puddings and pies that would be eaten over the Christmas festival. The meat was enriched with the fruit that would not last until March and stale bread added to it. I had heard of the tradition from my mother and grandfather. My first

Christmas at Eisicewalt had been a revelation. When I had first arrived we had not enjoyed spices. Now I knew the value of them. We had plenty of them and Benthe guarded them like gold. With fish from our pond and game birds hunted by Elric we ate well. Bergil and Seara hosted the meal that was enjoyed in the warrior hall. The workers and their families ate in the warrior hall while the household and my warriors ate in my hall. Benthe and her family ate with us. We were tightly packed.

I think Ealdgyth was the most excited amongst us. Her father had not celebrated as much as we did and the packed hall, food, decorations not to mention the good humour and banter made her smile. Father Gregory dined with us and it was he who said Grace. He sat at one end of the table next to Benthe and I sat at the other next to Ealdgyth. Everyone was dressed in their finest and Ealdgyth wore, about her head, a garland made of flowers that had been dried in summer and bound with rosemary. That hardy plant grew all year and was also intertwined in the holly, ivy and mistletoe.

I stood, "We shall not stand on ceremony. It is not my way and if others do not like it then I care not. Let us celebrate the good fortune that has come our way." I put my hand to my side and Ealdgyth grasped it. The simple gesture was greeted with cheers and clapping.

Benthe said, "Serve yourselves, Sir Richard has given us the day off and I, for one, intend to enjoy it."

This would not be an organised feast. The pudding apart, the rest of the food was placed upon the table and people chose whatever they wished to eat. Once the food was on the platters then with spoons and eating knives we devoured the feast. For some, like Maud and even Father Gregory, this was richer food than they were used to. The wine and the ale were both good and were in plentiful supply. The smiles became broader.

It was in a pause as we all drank something to help the next dish to go down that Mathilde made an announcement. Her cheeks were flushed for she was unused to the wine she was sipping. She suddenly said, "Ooh."

"What is it?" Edward looked concerned.

She shook her head and put her hand on his, "The baby kicked. It will be a boy, I am sure."

Benthe and Birgitte gave each other a knowing smile. Women like that knew such things. I could see from their expressions that they also thought it would be a boy. From the concerned reaction of Dervilla and Ealdgyth one might have thought the three of them were sisters.

I stood and raised my goblet, "Here is to Edward, Mathilde and the child who will be blessed with the best of parents." Everyone stood and toasted them.

As I sat Ealdgyth said, "And when Seara's child arrives that means there will be at least two new babies in the manor, eh, My Lord?" I nodded, "I pray that the bishop's letter comes soon for I would make it three."

She said the words so quietly that, with the hubbub around the table, only I heard. I shook my head, "You wanton!"

She pointed up. We were sat beneath the mistletoe. It was a sign, in the old religions of fertility, Christmas was as much about the pagan traditions as Christian ones. Ealdgyth said, "And as I like the old ways…" She kissed me on the lips.

It had not gone unnoticed and there was a roar from the room. It seemed to be taken as an invitation and all those who were seated beneath a bough of the white berries, emulated us.

Father Gregory laughed, "I should take out holy water and bless this room. The pagans have taken over." It was his way of giving his consent.

I noticed that Robert and Maud, seated next to each other, did more than just peck as most did. When Ealdgyth nudged me I saw that Dervilla and Conan were also more passionate than most.

When the pudding was brought in and aquae vitae poured on it to ignite the dark dessert, it seemed that it was a sign of better things to come. When the flames died down Benthe carefully portioned the pudding and everyone was given a small piece of the rich dessert. With cream from our cows it was as fine an end to a meal as any.

No one wanted the night to end but it had to. Egbert came from the warrior hall to tell us that the celebration there had ended and that the warriors could return to their home. Benthe rose and said that the table needed to be cleared and so the feast ended. I held Ealdgyth's hand as I walked her to her chamber. I looked above the door, "Next year we shall have more mistletoe collected."

She laughed and kissed the back of my hand, "Now who is the wanton?" She smiled, "Tonight bodes well for the future, Richard. The bishop cannot gainsay us. We just need to be patient."

Dervilla shooed the others in. I had seen Aethelstan and Alfred kissing Mary and Elfrida. The two were giggling as they came in. Dervilla gave me a slightly unsteady hand to kiss, "My Lord, that was well done and I thank you."

I kissed it, "And I thank you, Dervilla, for keeping your chicks safe."

"And soon, My Lord, they will no longer be mine to watch over." With that enigmatic comment she went into the chamber and the door closed.

It was Robert who approached me as the first snows fell at the start of January. We had been sparring for an hour. It was too cold and wet to do more and we had finished for the day. He said, "My Lord, a word, if it pleases you?"

I smiled, "Of course, but can we speak inside my hall where it is warm."

We went into the hall, shaking the wet from our cloaks. As we passed Walter I said, "Some ale, Walter."

"Yes, My Lord."

I stood at the fire the better to warm my hands. After putting in a poker I moved to the side so that Robert could join me. He shook his head and began to ring his hands, "The cold always affects my lost digit, My Lord. It feels as though it is still there."

"You were lucky it was on your left hand."

"Aye, I intend, when I can, to have mail mittens made. I hear that Uhtred is a good smith."

"He is. But for the Danish attack York would still be enjoying his services. We are lucky."

Walter brought in the ale. I took out the poker and plunged it first into Robert's ale and then mine. "Food, My Lord?"

"No, Walter, we will wait for the others at noon." He left us and I said, "Well?"

"I am a blunt man, My Lord. I would wed Maud."

I nodded. I was not surprised but I needed to ask some questions. "You have the maid's permission?"

"Aye, My Lord."

"And you know what happened to her?"

"That a Dane tried to rape her? Yes, My Lord."

"Then I will give my permission. You shall need to speak to Father Gregory."

"I will."

"And you know that you must continue to live in the warrior hall."

"We understand that, My Lord. The others intend to partition part of it to give us privacy."

"And Maud is content?"

"She says this feels like family and the presence of my shield brothers makes her feel safer."

"Then all is well. Go fetch her so that she may know you have my blessing."

Maud's face when I told her I had given my permission touched me. Her eyes filled with tears, "My Lord, my father is dead but you have been a better foster father to me than any could have hoped. I pray that you will find happiness too."

"And that is my earnest wish too."

The wedding was held four weeks later in the village church. As their vows were exchanged and the marriage blessed I realised that soon I would need to build a larger stone church. Thanks to the many refugees who had come to us the numbers of villagers had grown and at the wedding we filled it. Maud was popular with the villagers. They all knew her story and admired her stoic manner.

When next Aethelstan and Alfred came, this time with their mother to seek permission to marry Mary and Elfrida, it seemed that the first marriage had threatened to open the floodgates and yet the one who wish to be married, more than any other, was me and that was still denied Ealdgyth and me. Each time a rider passed through the village on their way to York my heart raced and then I fell into a deep despair when the horse continued without stopping.

It was April when they were all wed. If it was any comfort, and it was scant comfort, it was the knowledge that Dervilla and Conan also wished to be joined but Dervilla would wait until Ealdgyth was married.

It was May when the messengers came and it was not from the north but the south and it was late in the afternoon. A pair of riders arrived from York. They were armed and helmed. Clearly they were both soldiers but the quality of their horses told me that they were pueros. They dismounted and the slightly older one said, "I have come from King William, My Lord. I had a message to deliver to York and I have one for you. There is another for Durham and finally we are to deliver one to the Earl of Northumbria." He hesitated, "Could we stay the night, My Lord, it is a long way to Durham?"

"Of course," I nodded, "Harold, stable these horses. Absalom, warn those in the warrior hall that there will be two extra guests. Come." I led them inside and said, "Walter, tell Mistress Benthe that we have two more guests in the warrior hall this night."

We entered the hall and the letter was handed over. Birgitte came in with wine, bread and cheese. The two men looked hesitantly at me, "Eat, drink and warm yourself by the fire. If you have come from the south you will have found the clime is colder here than there."

"Thank you, My Lord. It is raw out there."

I sat down to read the letter. It was not in the king's hand, I knew that. Some scribe had written it. The letters were formed in the same way as those from the Bishop of Durham. I knew it was not Belisarius' hand for he had a unique way of writing.

Robert fitz Malet,

You are charged with mustering, for the king's pleasure, thirty men of whom eight should be horsemen. You are to muster at Durham on the fifteenth day of July. We are to chastise the rebellious Scots and ensure that they acknowledge us as their liege lord. The muster will be for forty days. There will be payment; ten silver pennies a day for you, two pennies a day for each horseman and one penny a day for those who fight on foot. Food will be provided from Durham once the muster begins and the service will begin the day you reach Durham.

I stopped reading and poured some wine. The two messengers were enjoying the freshly baked bread and the excellent goats' cheese we produced. I knew that when I turned it over there would be the usual caveats and conditions on the other side. This was an order and parchment was not to be wasted. I would read it once I had digested the news. The news meant that I could not go to Norton in the Spring, as I had planned. Algar would have to fend for himself. This was an order from the king and could not be disobeyed. We would be away for half of July, all of August and, depending upon how far into Scotland we campaigned, some of September. They were the harvest months. The men I took would be determined by their occupation. The farmers I would leave. I would take Harold and Absalom as horsemen. That they were not yet horsemen was immaterial. I would take Ethelred. I would have him command my archers. He would be able to continue to teach Elric his skills. Walter, Uhtred's son, could come as well as Athelgar. The others I would need to find by visiting my people.

I turned over the letter. I read the caveats and conditions. They were as expected but my eye was arrested by the last paragraph.

It has been brought to our attention that Lady Ealdgyth, whom you rescued from a fearful fate, has been promised to another. It is not in England's interests to have that marriage take place. It is for Sir Richard fitz Malet to decide whom she marries. It is his decision to make and his decision has royal approval.

William, King of England and Duke of Normandy

I saw the seal and ran my fingers over it. I could marry Ealdgyth. I was so stunned I just sat holding the letter. To make sure I was not hallucinating I re-read the paragraph three times to see if I had misunderstood. I would confirm all by riding to speak to Belisarius before I told Ealdgyth. If I was wrong I did not want to get her hopes raised and then dashed. She deserved better.

I was distracted that evening but I am not sure anyone noticed. Our two guests were plied with questions. Whilst neither were knights they were both clearly from good families and serving as pueros to King William would do them no harm. I was trying to control my feelings and emotions. If I had read the letter right then I could plan a marriage but if I was wrong and King William merely wished me to arrange a marriage for Ealdgyth to another then my hopes and my life lay in ruins. I was also a little concerned not only about the reaction of the Bishop of Durham whose plans I had thwarted but also the more dangerous Mormaer of Moray. I had already crossed his path when I had rescued the captives. Suddenly the Danish raiders became a little more sinister in my mind. Had they been sent to specifically take Ealdgyth? They had been part of the warband sent by the mormaer. Their detour away from the Aln now made more sense. The mormaer had sent men to aid the king but, perhaps, they had their own mission too.

All of this meant that, towards the end of the meal, Ealdgyth put her hand on mine and said, "Richard, you have been quiet. Are you ill?"

I was not familiar yet with the ways of women but I thought that she needed to be told, not the truth but something that would put her mind at rest. "I am distracted and I apologise. I have to choose the men whom I will lead. It will be a hard choice as I need men who can fight but I have to leave behind men who can till the land. The king has chosen a time to fight that is inconvenient."

She frowned.

I explained, "The king leads men whom he pays. They can go to war at any time. Men like me who are lords of the king's manors have warriors who work the land. My farmers might be the best warriors to take but if I do then we may not have enough food next winter. It is a treacherous path I tread."

"And when we are wed then I can shoulder some of the burden, Richard. It is not right that you have to do so much."

"When I was younger, Ealdgyth, I thought, as the bastard son of a Norman who barely acknowledged my existence, I would never be anything other than a disposable warrior. I embrace my role and I know that both my mother and grandfather would be pleased with me. I keep their memory in my head and they are the judges of what I do."

She persisted, "And I will be there to help you make those hard decisions and to take some of the weight from your shoulders."

The house was awake early the next day. The two messengers were keen to get to Durham and Edward and I had to get to York. I explained to those who breakfasted with me that I needed to ask for clarification from Belisarius about the nature of the campaign. It was a lie but a necessary one. I did not tell Edward about the last part of the letter. I kept that to myself. We took our best horses. Edward had a horse sired by Parsifal. Soon we would have horses sired from both Scout and the offspring of Parsifal and Marie. I had high hopes for those animals. It meant that we were able to reach York far more quickly than if we had taken lesser horses.

The city seemed both busier and livelier than I had remembered. I suppose that it was early summer and the news of an impending campaign meant that there were many men who would profit from the campaign. These would not be those who fought but the ones who made weapons, leather goods, saddles, horse tackle, wagons as well as those who would source the food that would be sold to the king. In Durham there would be many more who would anticipate a profit.

We had to push our way through the crowds and we did so on horseback. Normally I might have led my horse but I could not wait to see Belisarius. The two swords across my back marked me as Sir Richard fitz Malet and that knowledge was reinforced by the sight of the magnificent horse I rode. We were not hindered as we headed to Belisarius' quarters but we were slowed as I was greeted. Men wished to speak to me. I was seen, in York at least, as something of a saviour of the city. People like Uhtred, Seara, Egbert and Maud had been saved because of me and those who had survived the Danish incursion remembered me and my actions. I also knew that there would be Danes in the city who harboured more malevolent thoughts. There were many who had hoped that King Sweyn would succeed.

We discovered that Belisarius was at the castle at Bailie Hill. It meant we had to recross the river. I wondered why he was there. The castle had been badly damaged during the attack on the city and like the minster was being repaired. We rode through the gates which had already been mended and after dismounting I handed my reins to Edward. "Wait here while I seek out Belisarius."

I found him by the inner bailey where he was supervising some workmen who were making new inner gates. He turned and beamed, "Sir Richard. What brings you here? I believe you had good news from the king?"

"Did I?" I took out the letter and handed it to him.

He looked confused, "It says you can marry Lady Ealdgyth. Where lies the problem?"

I took the letter and read aloud, "*It is for Sir Richard fitz Malet to decide whom she marries. It is his decision and his decision has royal approval*. It does not say that I can marry her."

He laughed and it was so loud that men working on the gates turned. He waved a hand for them to continue their work and said, "You are looking for problems where there are none. When I wrote to the king," he nodded at my look, "aye, I did not just rely on the archbishop, I made your feelings quite clear and my advice was to let you marry the lady for it would make Eisicewalt a stronger bastion." He smiled and tapped the letter, "Marry her, you have the king's blessing and, I might add, mine. It would be good to see some good come from the bloodshed of the last years. I am an old man and in you I see hope for this land. I do not doubt that there will be more blood spilt and men will die but with the blood of Sir Richard fitz Malet and Lady Ealdgyth of Brougham then England will be a stronger country."

I stuffed the letter in my belt and took his hand in mine. I shook it, "Thank you, Belisarius. You have ever been a good friend and Ealdgyth and I will be forever in your debt."

"Just be happy and that will be enough for me."

I turned and headed back to Edward. "Well, My Lord?"

"Well?"

"Did you find out more about the campaign?"

I cursed myself. My lie was catching in my throat. "Aye, all is well. We will call at the market. I should like to buy some things for Lady Ealdgyth. You can see if there is some good quality cloth for your child. A new baby needs such items."

He beamed and I had taken his mind off his question.

What I really wanted was a ring. I knew the size of Ealdgyth's ring finger as she had once tried on my signet ring. It fitted her well and we had joked as she had waved it about that she was now the mistress of Eisicewalt. I knew there was a goldsmith close to Middlegate and while Edward sought out fine cloth I headed for the goldsmith. Such men had their property protected. He had a shop rather than a stall and I had to ask the man at the door to let me in. My spurs and my two swords brought a smile. He bowed, "My master will be honoured to have Sir

Richard fitz Malet as a customer." He peered up and down the narrow street before opening it. He saw my questioning look and said, by way of explanation, "We have those who hide close by and wait until the door opens. They think to gain entry and steal my master's gold." He patted his short sword. "If they do then they will die."

He opened the door without looking within and when I had entered he closed it behind me. The goldsmith and his apprentice were working. They did not use candles but an oil lamp which light gave a more controllable light. They looked up and ceased their hammering. Unlike the doorman they did not recognise me and the man said, "I am Tobias of York, My Lord, how may I be of service?"

"I am Sir Richard fitz Malet and I require a gold ring."

"A signet ring, My Lord? You have a design in mind?" My signet ring had been given to me by my stepbrother and I did not need another. The two stars that were my mark suited me.

I shook my head, "I need a ring for a marriage." I took off my signet ring and handed it to him. "That is the size of the lady's finger."

He smiled, "Then do you wish a design upon it?"

"I wish it to be plain but made of the best quality gold."

He took the ring and placed it on a measuring device and then used a stylus to make a mark on his wax tablet, "The problem, My Lord, is durability. I can use the finest of gold but it would be more likely to wear. If I use some baser metal to strengthen the gold, the ring will still look as good but last longer." I frowned. I did not want to give something cheap to my future wife. "It is what all lords do, My Lord. Perhaps I could inscribe it? There would be no extra charge for that. A marriage ring is a sacred object and I would be honoured."

Perhaps the engraving might be a good idea, "To Ealdgyth from Richard."

He said, "That would be appropriate. When do you need it for?"

"We marry within the month."

"It shall be ready. Now the sordid matter of the cost." We agreed a price and I gave him half. He promised me the ring in a fortnight.

I rejoined Edward who looked for purchases, "You bought nothing then, My Lord?"

The lie I told came easier this time. Perhaps I was getting used to it. "I saw nothing. Better to return empty handed than with a gift bought because there was nothing else."

By the time we had reached the Bootham Gate it was noon. The minster was still being repaired but the bells sounded the hours. Once free of the crowds, it was pleasant to ride the open and empty road. Those who were visiting York were still there and the hour meant that few others would be travelling. Merchants from the north would not be entering until late in the afternoon. As I had discovered, north of Eisicewalt there were few safe places to rest.

Shipton was still being rebuilt. The Danes had destroyed it and slaughtered the people who had lived there but it was a good place for a village and hardy folk had taken the opportunity to begin to build new dwellings. The new houses would not be exactly where the old ones had been. People were superstitious that way but the land that had been farmed would be farmed again. It would be easier than finding virgin land filled with rocks and stones.

I was in as happy a mood as I had ever been. For once things were going well for me. The campaign against the Scots was the only cloud on the horizon. I was about to tell Ealdgyth that we could be married. That would please not only her but also Conan and Dervilla who would be free to find their own happiness. Perhaps it was that air of joy that distracted me. I should have spotted the ambush but I was just a few miles from home. I could almost see Forlan's farm, and my mind was daydreaming. The crossbow bolt that was sent at me should have killed me. I wore just a tunic and no helmet. Luckily, the bolt struck neither flesh nor skull but the two scabbards across my back, and fate directed the bolt to smack into the place where they crossed. A bolt might penetrate a leather scabbard but not two, and certainly not two swords. What it did do was send a shock of pain down my back.

Edward was slightly behind me and he shouted, for he saw the bolt fall to the floor, "Ambush! Crossbow!"

The three men who rode from the trees ahead must have thought that their crossbowman from the woods had wounded me for they rode at me with swords in their hands to finish the job.

Edward shouted, "It was a crossbow, My Lord, sent from the trees."

I dropped my reins and drew my swords. I shouted, "Edward, deal with the crossbowman." Edward knew the danger of a crossbow. It might take time to reload but without mail we could not rely on luck a second time.

"Aye, My Lord." Drawing his sword, he wheeled his horse to ride back to the place of concealment.

I urged Scout on. I had trained him to move without the use of reins and just the prick of my spurs. That was another skill passed on to me by Taillefer. Scout could ride with just direction from my knees. I was taking on three men but Scout was as much a warrior as any man. The three men who rode at me were riding nags. They were not good horses. I took in that, and, while they all wore helmets, they had no hauberks nor did they carry shields. They had their left hands on their reins and their swords were in their right hands. I steered Scout to go between two of the men. My horse would know what I intended. He was as much a weapon as the two swords I held. The third man I would leave until I had the advantage. I could use both my hands but the one I had the most confidence in was my right hand and as I blocked the two swords that came at me almost simultaneously, I riposted with my right-hand sword and slashed down as I deflected the blade. The edge raked down the helmet and then gouged a line in the man's cheek. It was then I noticed the Danish axe hanging from his saddle. His helmet was also Danish. It was a Danish ambush. He squealed and his hand went to his face where blood spouted. I wheeled Scout. I think he must have anticipated my command for he did so instantly and I saw that I was now between the other two men and slightly behind them. Both had slowed and were trying to turn. They were not skilled horsemen and their animals got in each other's way. Scout snapped at the horse on my left and it baulked. I slashed with my sword and this time the helmet of the warrior did not slow by blade. It hacked across the back and shoulder of the man to my left and as he was wearing neither mail nor mittens the edge sliced into his arm and severed it to the bone. The sword fell from his hands and he used his left hand to pull away.

The only one whom I had not struck tried to escape. He wheeled his horse and was ten paces away from me by the time I turned. I saw that the one whose face I had slashed was forty paces up the road. I doubted that I would catch him but the one without a wound could be taken. He was following his wounded companion. I sheathed my left-hand sword. I would not need two swords for one such killer. Scout responded to my spurs and he began to catch the other horse stride by stride. As I neared him and saw, in the distance, Forlan's farm I stood in my stirrups and brought my blade down. It not only tore through the leather and ripped flesh, but it also broke his back. He fell from his horse and was dead before he hit the ground. I wheeled Scout and rode back. The man whose arm I had severed was still seated on his horse and he was trying to stem the bleeding as his life blood pumped away. Even before I reached him he had fallen from his horse and lay on his back. Edward galloped up the road towards me. I dismounted and as Edward reached me I handed Scout's reins to him.

I knelt by the man. He was dying and I doubted he had more than a few heartbeats left to live. "Who sent you?"

He spat some words out but they were not in English. I guessed they were in Gaelic. He tried to raise himself but the effort was too much and he lay back, dead.

"The crossbowman?"

"There were two but the second one was slow to use his infernal machine. They are both dead."

I nodded, "I wounded one and the other lies dead. The question is who sent them? I have not annoyed anyone of late. And why would a Scot and Dane conspire to kill me?" Then it came to me. The letter from the king. The Mormaer of Moray and the Bishop of Durham must have learned of the king's decision. The letter concerned the muster and the news of the king's decision was almost an afterthought. There were always spies at court and the news of the king's decision could have reached the mormaer. The man had spoken in Gaelic. I tore open his tunic. Beneath it he wore not only a Christian cross but also a hammer of Thor. That suggested someone associated with the Danes. It explained the Danish connection. I searched his purse and found a gold coin amongst the silver. I did not recognise the face on the coin. That was not a surprise. Coins were coins and could be used anywhere so long as they were made of gold, silver or copper. It was his helmet that gave me the information I needed. It was a helmet with a nose piece and above the nose piece was a herkumbl. In the past leaders had given these signs to their men. This one bore the arms of Moray. The Mormaer of Moray had not given up trying to get Ealdgyth. If I was dead then he might still achieve his ends. We inspected the other bodies and it confirmed what I thought. These men had come from Moray.

We tied the bodies to their horses and took the four dead men back to my manor. As we neared the hall we were spotted and my men came into the yard.

Bergil said, his eyes drawn to the corpses, "My lord…"

I dismounted and held up my hand, "First, did a rider pass the hall not long ago?"

Harold said, "Yes, My Lord. He was a warrior and was riding as though the devil was behind him."

I shouted, "Conan, mount your men." Conan nodded. "The warrior who rode through the village was one of these ambushers and he tried to kill me. He escaped and I would know who sent him. It may be a fruitless search but he might stop to tend to the wound I gave him."

Conan asked no unnecessary questions but led his men to the stables. They were galloping up the road even before we had taken the bodies from the backs of the horses. The commotion brought others to the yard and when Ealdgyth saw the blood on my tunic she ran to me, "Richard!"

"It is not my blood and I have much to tell you but not here. Go within and I will join you when we have dealt with these men."

"Of course." She smiled although her face was pale, "You are alive and that is all that matters. I will have wine and food for you and fresh clothes." She was already thinking like a wife and she returned inside the hall.

As the four horses were led away Bergil and my men took the weapons from the dead. They would join the others in our armoury. "The bodies, My Lord?"

The men were not shriven and I did not want ghosts haunting my manor. "Take them and burn them where the stink will be taken by the wind."

"We will, My Lord." He hesitated, and then turning said, "My Lord, I am your captain and I issue you a command. From now on you do not leave this manor without an escort of four men."

"It was only a ride to York, Bergil."

"And yet five men attacked you and we allowed one to ride boldly through the village. We have grown complacent, My Lord, and that ends now."

Some lords might have resented Bergil's manner but I knew he was right. We had grown complacent and that had to stop.

Chapter 13

I entered my manor house and went into the dining hall where I knew that Ealdgyth would be waiting. Dervilla was with her. It was Dervilla who asked, "Where have the Bretons gone, My Lord?"

She was really asking after Conan. I said, "One of the men who attacked us escaped. They seek him. I doubt that they will catch him but it is as well to make sure that he is not still around."

Ealdgyth burst out, "But who were they? What did they want?"

I sat opposite Ealdgyth and held her hands in mine, "The king has given us permission to marry. I do not know for certain but I believe that the killers were sent by the Mormaer of Moray who still wishes you as the bride for his son."

It took some moments for the news to sink in. She was still thinking about the attempt on my life. I glanced up and saw the look of joy on the face of Dervilla. She knew what it meant. As the realisation dawned so Ealdgyth's face changed and she rose, "We can be wed?"

"We can but as the muster is to be in July then time is pressing, unless you wish to wait until the autumn after the campaign is done."

She shook her head, "I would be wed as soon as we are able."

"Then tomorrow we speak to Father Gregory." I looked at Dervilla, "Conan does not know."

She nodded, "Then I shall be the bearer of those glad tidings." She smiled, "And I will leave you two now."

When we were alone Ealdgyth stood as did I. She kissed me and we held each other tightly. She smiled and seated herself on a seat. She patted the one next to it, "Tell me all and do not spare me. I know now what happens when men fight. If I know what you did then I will not be as afraid when you leave me to fight in the north." I would not lie any more. I told her all. I saw her eyes widen as I did so. When I had finished she said, "How did you know it was a bolt from a crossbow?"

"I did not know for certain. I just knew I had been struck. A bolt hits you like someone striking at you with a hammer. I have been hit when I wore mail and a gambeson."

"And the one that escaped, will Conan catch him?"

I shook my head, "He had too much of a head start but I had to send my men to ensure he was not watching us. I will know him again for he had a Danish axe and his face is now marked by my sword."

"When he evades them he will return to whoever sent him."

"The mormaer."

She nodded, "And you go to fight against the Scots do you not?" It was my turn to nod. "He will try again."

"Of course, he will."

"Then I bring you nothing but trouble."

"You cannot think that way. You can do little about your antecedents. My life might be easier as an Englishman if I did not have Norman blood and easier as a Norman but for my English connection. We live our lives with what we have and not what might be. I am content and if this mormaer sends men against me in battle then I will have my men around me and I know that the men in my familia are better than any and in that I include the king's men."

As I had expected, my Bretons did not catch the man. It did not sour the evening for the news I had brought made the whole hall joyful. Dervilla's life had been not her own until her charge was married. She could now begin a new existence. For the leader of the Bretons the news was even more welcome as Conan had not expected to have a wife before he joined me and now he would have one. It was not just him who was happy but, following Robert and Maud's marriage, his other two men saw hope for themselves.

Both marriages were hastily arranged. That was forced on us by the king's muster. Like Robert before him Conan would have to use the warrior hall but he did not seem put out by that. Dervilla looked less than happy and I wondered if we might have to build a house for them. Dervilla was a lady and sharing a warrior hall with so many men was not right. Even though we were preparing for our own marriage Ealdgyth and I talked through the potential problems.

Ealdgyth had a keener insight into the running of the manor than did I. "Your men at arms have married Elfrida and Mary. They do not seem to mind living in the warrior hall. The three youngest might also be happy enough living in the warrior hall and then we could allow Dervilla and Conan to live in the new quarters you built. There is no rush. While you are away the warrior hall will be empty and I shall find out what the wishes of the others are."

"Already, you are lady of the manor taking decisions to ease my task."

"You have enough to worry about, Richard." She paused, "And Beth has said to me that she finds Galmr a most attractive man."

"My Varangian?" I had not seen it.

She nodded, "I know, he looks rough and wild but he is most gentle of speech and they get on. Such things do happen, Richard. We can never know what attracts a man to a woman."

For one so relatively young my bride-to-be was wise, "I know but he has said nothing to me."

She laughed, "And why should he? He is a man and men are, I believe, close mouthed about such things. Say nothing and let things blossom."

I did but I made a point of watching them and my observations confirmed Ealdgyth's words.

As it turned out the date that we chose for the wedding, Midsummer's Day, was a perfect one. Sometimes the weather could be unpredictable in June but that year it seemed to behave itself. The skies were clear and it was as though God himself was smiling upon the weddings. The villagers had decked out the church in summer flowers and the air was heavy with their perfume. The two brides had new dresses made for the occasion and while they both looked beautiful Ealdgyth was stunning. Her beauty radiated like the sun's rays. As we stood in the church even the light from the candles could not help but make her glow. When I slipped the ring on her finger and it fitted perfectly I felt a shock of pleasure race through my body. The goldsmith had done a fine job. The inscription was hard to see in the church and I did not mention it. I would let her discover my hidden gift at her leisure. It might be a pleasure she enjoyed when I was at war.

Ealdgyth had been keen for the village to enjoy the occasion and we had tables on the green so that everyone could enjoy the day. Ethelred and Elric had hunted and we had game aplenty. None went hungry. I had bought some fine wines and Benthe had brewed special ale for the day. It was, quite simply, perfect. We walked back to my hall and my men at arms formed a guard of honour with drawn swords as we entered. We had a smaller celebration in my hall with just those who lived there. When we retired I felt that the day could not have gone better. The night proved to be even more of a success. It was dawn when we finally drifted off to sleep. We had made love and we had talked, it seemed, all night. I would rise late in the day for the first time in my life.

The next day I felt different as my wife and I walked into my hall. The smiles from everyone were silent ones but their eyes told us both of their approval. The only cloud on the horizon was the prospect of leaving for war. The days seemed to fly by and all the things we wanted to do were marred by the knowledge that we had to prepare the whole manor for thirty of us to leave.

I felt guilty at taking Ethelred. He had begun to look older in recent months. The time he spent with Elric gave him a twinkle in his eye but they looked rheumy. His hands had the claw like look of one afflicted with stiff joints. I began to regret my decision to take him and I went to his cottage to speak to him, "Ethelred you need not come with us on this campaign in the north. You have trained the archers well and…"

He snorted, "If you do not wish me to come, My Lord, then just say so. You need not dance around an old man. You need not worry about my feelings but know this, Sir Richard, I want to come. I am not the drink ravaged empty shell of a man you found when you came here. I have purpose and I am your man."

I nodded at his hands, "Yet you are not the man you were, Ethelred. In the last years you have aged."

"As we all do. True, I cannot draw a bow as well as Elric but here," he tapped his head with a crooked finger, "I have knowledge that can only be attained through war and I can still wield a sword. The archers of this manor are young and Elric will be their captain. We need this campaign for me to pass on my knowledge and skills. You need me to command them and they will obey the grizzled old man who fought alongside their grandfathers at Fulford Gate. I have no bairns left to follow me but Elric is like a grandson to me. When we return from Scotland then I shall hang up the sword and watch the new Ethelred be the gamekeeper and captain of archers."

"You are certain?"

He smiled, "You have made great changes here, My Lord, not least with me. I think that had you not come I would have died before even the first attack by the Danes. Let me do something useful in the twilight of my years."

He was sincere and he had convinced me, "Good. Then all is well."

This would be the first time that the old man had come to war with me and I had Aedgar find him a horse. Of course, the old warrior objected but I was firm with him. He was no longer a young man and while we needed his expertise and experience we did not need a man who would be exhausted by marching to the borders. We used all the nags and bidets we had acquired to mount as many men as we could. In the end, thanks to Aedgar's skill, we were able to mount all of us. That, in itself, helped everyone as we could delay our departure. We could ride to and reach the muster in two days as opposed to the four or five days it would take to march. We also ensured that every warrior we took, even the archers and slingers, had a helmet and either a seax or a short sword.

The night before our dawn departure I lay with Ealdgyth in my arms. "We have not had long as husband and wife, Richard."

"No, but the time apart will be short although I doubt that it will seem so. Forty days is not a long time."

She snuggled in, "It is forty days and forty nights. I shall miss you here in my bed."

I laughed, "At least you shall have a bed. My men and I will have the ground, a cloak and a saddle for beds and pillows."

She was silent for a while. "I will be the lady of the manor while you are away. I will make sure that all is done as you would wish it to be. The fields will be tended and the animals will prosper."

"I am leaving enough men to ensure that you are all protected but you must remember to have the gates barred at night." I was still worried about the mischief that the Mormaer of Moray might cause.

I felt her stiffen next to me, "You think that we are in danger?"

"No, but if you are not prepared for danger then that is when it strikes. Barred gates and doors will deter any who seek to bring harm to the manor."

In contrast to our wedding night that last night was very short. As much as I might wish to tarry I had to rise and prepare for the long day's ride north. By dawn we had breakfasted, dressed and were already marshalling outside. There were tears from many. Mathilde and Seara both had babes in arms. Even Dervilla looked tearful. Ealdgyth was showing that she was a lady. She kept herself under control. She comforted a weeping Maud who was also with child. I knew that inside she was just as upset as the others but she masked it well. Some might have thought our parting was perfunctory. It was not for we had said our real goodbyes in the bedroom. Mounting Scout I raised my arm in farewell and led my men through the gates of my manor. We passed through a village that had united to wave us goodbye. There were tears there too as we headed north. Aed was remembered. Would other families be seeing their men depart for the last time? Once we had left the last house silence reigned amongst the men. Every man was alone with his thoughts. I suspect that the younger ones were excited but the mood of the majority prevailed. There would be songs, banter and laughter but not yet. Until the memory of loved ones left behind was sent to the back of the mind, the part we called home, there would be reflection.

We camped at Persebrig. The villagers there had been mustered and, not having horses had left the day before. It meant we had a warm welcome from the families there and we were fed. It was not a feast but it saved us having to cook. We reached Durham a day ahead of the assigned date and the army filled the loop in the river. I suppose I could have asked for a chamber in the newly built castle but I preferred to stay with my men.

What I had prepared myself for on the ride from our camp to Durham, was the cool reception I would receive from the bishop. I had thwarted his plans for Ealdgyth and even though it was supported by the king he would be but a temporary presence in the north. The bishop was the effective ruler north of the Tees. The king had yet to arrive and so the hall was not filled. I had not expected to be at the table with the bishop but neither was I relegated to the lowest seat. I was amongst the lords who had travelled from the Honour of Craven. I was something of a celebrity, thanks to my association with Taillefer and my exploits since. I spent the evening speaking with them about the last campaign and the prospects for this one.

The bishop retired first. He pointedly looked at me and after he had left a tonsured priest came and spoke in my ear. “The bishop would speak to you after the service at prime.”

I nodded. It meant I would have to rise earlier than most of the other barons and knights.

The bells for Lauds woke me and I slipped out of the tent and headed for the river. The gates would be barred but I was well known enough to know I would be admitted. I went to the bridge over the river to watch the swirling waters beneath. Was I fated to have a complicated life? Even my old friend Bruno seemed to have a simpler life, although the wound he had received in our last battle together meant that he would rarely be required by the king. Was he better off than I was? As the light started to brighten the eastern sky I reflected that a man had to deal with whatever life threw at him. It was the mark of a man that those who were successful dealt with the vagaries of fate and endured. I hoped that my candle would not be snuffed out as quickly as Taillefer's. My brief time as a husband made me yearn for more.

I headed for the castle and was admitted. I went to the bishop's quarters as I heard the bells for prime. I waited outside his office. The proximity of the bones of St Cuthbert were a comfort. He had been a good man and he had faced far greater danger and adversity than I had. It calmed me.

"Sir Richard, you are prompt that, at least, is courteous." The bishop's tone was polite but told me that he was unhappy with me. We entered his office and he sat. He did not invite me to do so and I stood. He put his hands together and closed his eyes. Silence hung heavily in the room. I wondered if he was trying to intimidate me. He opened them and patted a letter on his desk. "I have been commanded by the king to sanction your right to approve the marriage of Lady Ealdgyth." He stared at me, "Whilst I understand the reasons I am not happy about the situation. I am a man of God and unlike some clerics the pleasures of a woman are not for me. I am responsible for protecting the north. Had I been allowed to arrange the marriage then I could have removed the threat from Scotland. Heaven knows we have enough domestic foes without adding the Scots. You may be responsible for many more unnecessary deaths in the future." He poked a finger at me, "I hope that when men die you remember that."

I became angry inside but I kept my voice calm as I responded, "My Lord Bishop, with due respect your plan had little chance of success. Whilst dissension in Scotland might have delayed an attack on England it would not have prevented one. Why do you think King William comes north? He wishes to end the threat in the only way possible, by force of arms. This Mormaer of Moray with whom you entered into a covenant is an evil man. He has tried to abduct the lady and made attempts on my life."

The bishop shrugged, "You are one man and Lady Ealdgyth is but one woman. The sacrifice of your life and her happiness would be a small price to pay for peace in the Palatinate." He gave a thin smile and waved a hand as though to dismiss the words I had spoken, "It is done but I wanted you to know that any deaths from Scottish incursions in the future are laid at your door."

I nodded, "My Lord Bishop, you are a deluded fool. Stay in the church for the world of war is beyond your ken."

I knew I had angered him from the glaring of his eyes but he merely waved a hand for me to leave. I did not regret my words for they would not have changed his opinion of me. The problem would be Norton for that lay within the Palatinate. He could not hurt me in Eisicewalt but Norton was a different matter. As I headed back to my camp I knew that I would have to plan carefully when I appointed someone to run the manor for me.

When the king arrived, he brought fewer men than I had expected. There were just two hundred knights along with a hundred men at arms. All were mounted but none were what I would have called his senior leaders. William de Warenne was missing as was Bishop Odo. I knew many of the other knights. Most were the younger knights from Senlac Hill. I knew that they would be hungry for war. They did not have the huge estates such as those won by King William's companions. If they did well here in Scotland then the newly conquered manors in Wales and the north would be theirs for the taking. I knew that as soon as I spoke to them. They asked me about the manors in the north and the problems of the tenants.

I shook my head, "If a knight treats them well then they are not a problem. If you try to treat them as little more than thralls or serfs then they will resent it. If we are to win this land for King William it must be with the consent of the people." I pointed a finger towards the north. "The threat comes from across the border. It is the Scots whom our people fear." I thought of the Dane I had recently slain. "And the Vikings. They are still a threat. When we defeat them then we can expect support and cooperation from the people of this island."

"But they do not grow wheat."

I laughed, "Sir Humphrey, as much as I like manchet, I can live with raveled. If you like manchet so much then buy wheat. This is a good land. The winters are harsh but the land teems with game and there are forests that can be hewn." I knew the knight had come from Normandy as a pueros. "In Normandy you might have enjoyed wheat but the chances of a fine manor?"

He nodded, "Aye, Sir Richard, you have a good head on your shoulders and I can see from your men that you have good warriors that you have attracted. Are they Varangians?"

I nodded, "And I have Bretons. All of them are happy to be living here in the north."

Sir Guillaume asked, "And the Scots that we fight, are they like the housecarls we fought at Senlac Hill?"

I shook my head, "No, but they have a good weapon that you will not have encountered in England."

"And what is that?"

"The land. They will use the land to ambush and to slow us. Our horses will not enjoy the open fields for which they are well suited. I hope you have brought archers for they will be needed."

Sir Humphrey shook his head, "The king is relying on the men of the north for that."

"You mean there are no others coming north? You have no archers nor slingers?"

"No. What you see is the entire force from the south."

My heart sank. We would struggle.

Chapter 14

The king spent that first day in conference with the bishop. We feasted together but he seemed distracted and did not speak to any save those seated close to him. I was summoned to a meeting the next day. The bishop and Lord Robert of Craven were there along with Prince William, the king's third son. Known by all as Rufus because of his red face he was not addressed as such except by his brothers and father. I already knew that King William's sons did not get along. It was telling that the king had yet to have all his sons with him at one time. It seemed that he liked to keep them apart. I wondered why he was here. I also wondered at my inclusion. My rank was far below the others.

King William was always business like. I knew there would be no reference to my marriage to Ealdgyth. I was not his friend, as Taillefer had been. I was a tool. I was a weapon to be used to secure his kingdom. As he nodded to me I reflected that my inclusion meant a special task for me.

He began straightaway and his voice was forceful and confident, "I do not intend to tarry here in the north. Matters in France and Normandy demand my attention there and I have wasted enough time on Edgar and King Malcolm. We will chastise them and bring them to heel like the dogs that they are."

His son said, "Do we conquer the land?"

"For what purpose? There is nothing to be had except for forests and rocks. The Romans showed us that this was a desolate land when they built their wall. We will make them obey our commands and then the bishop will build castles along the Tweed. We will make Carlisle into a bastion in the west and then have castles built along the Tyne." He looked at the bishop, "We will watch this campaign to see who shall be given the responsibility of having lordship of those castles." The bishop nodded. I knew that he would be thinking how to do that. Castles were not cheap to build especially if they were to be made of stone and, as the Romans had showed, stone and not wooden walls were needed here in the north. He would also be thinking of which knights could be given the responsibility. The bishop was a political animal and he would choose the men who would suit him. "Now, let us move on to the campaign." He nodded to me, "You may wonder why you are here, fitz Malet. The reason is that while my son will command half of the army he needs someone with local knowledge and experience." He gave a rare smile, "And someone who has an insight into the minds of the people of this land. That will be you and all will answer to you save my son."

"Your word is my command, King William."

"The Lord of Craven will bring his men with me. I will command that half of the army. My son will command the men of the Palatinate. We will all march north from here until we reach the Tweed. William will lead his half of the army to the east of the river and I will take the rest to the west. King Malcolm will have to divide his forces. I have a fleet of ships filled with Earl Waltheof and foot soldiers sailing up the coast even as we speak and more men will be landed at the Forth. We keep moving north until King Malcolm yields." He sat in the chair that was close to him and poured himself some wine. He was allowing us time for questions. I now understood the reason for the arrival of so few men from the south. The men on foot and the archers would be in the ships. Horses would have been discomfited by the voyage but foot soldiers would be transported quickly and with less fuss. King William was a clever commander.

The bishop said, "You have not mentioned which men I am to command, My Lord."

"I have, Walcher. You are to build castles and the first one will be here. This is as fine a defensive position as I have seen in this land. The loop of the river gives you a natural moat. Count Alain is, even now, doing the same at Richmond. This campaign is a diversion. We shall not need many men to shake these Scots into submission." He poured a little more wine and said, "We leave on the morrow. The ships will arrive on the Forth one month from now." We all bowed and the bishop, the Lord of Craven and I bowed and turned to leave. The king said, "Sir Richard, wait a while." I turned back. The king said to his son, when the three of us were alone, "Sir Richard here held out in his manor when York was lost. He has yet to fail to obey my every command. You shall heed his advice for it will be well judged."

Prince William looked at me, seemingly for the first time. His father had clearly not shared his plans with him. The prince was ten years my junior but I know that I was not an old greybeard like his uncle, Bishop Odo. His father's words were to be heeded but I knew he would not be happy with my relative youth. "I shall take all the advice that you offer, Sir Richard."

The king said, "Good. Now there is a personal matter I need to discuss with Lord Eisicewalt. Go and see that all is ready for our departure." The king's son did not look happy to be dismissed, especially to perform a squire's duty but no one disobeyed the king's orders.

When alone I expected him to speak about my marriage but he did not. "My son is young and he has never commanded. You are to ensure that he does not make mistakes. You are a fine rider. Regard my son as a colt that needs to be schooled. A firm but fair hand is what is needed. William has much to learn. You shall not be apart from the army from long. It is not far from the Tweed to the Forth and I hope that the news of the arrival of the fleet will cause King Malcolm some problems." The king was clever. He knew that there had to be spies in Durham and word would soon spread about the fleet, not to mention his plan to divide his army. He had not asked us to keep his orders secret. By dividing his forces, the king was forcing King Malcolm to either defeat one of the two armies heading north or to fall back north of the Forth. The king could defeat King Malcolm and I was flattered that he thought I could too. "I want my son to keep his sword pricked against any opposition that we find. If you can defeat any enemies so much the better for that will weaken the Scots and give my son confidence. I need all my sons to be battle hardened. One day one of them shall rule this land and I do not want it to be lost in the future because of an error. You shall do with William what Taillefer did for you."

It was not the same situation and the king knew it. I had been a pueros when Taillefer had taken me under his wing and William Rufus was the son of a king. I had noted that he had not once referred to his son as prince. Thinking back, I realised that none of his sons had ever been accorded that title by the king. He wanted them to earn it. "And how many men will be in our half of the army, My Lord?"

"The bishop has provided fifty knights and squires. There are," he picked up a piece of parchment and read, "fifty men at arms, forty archers and slingers and three hundred spearmen." He tossed the paper to the table and shrugged, "The quality of those spearmen is debatable. I doubt that even half will have a spear and a shield. My son has fifteen men in his familia. All are, like him, young."

In my head I calculated. We had less than five hundred men. If King Malcolm had any sense then he would try to take us first. We were an easier morsel to digest. I knew then that we were bait. The king had enough sons to risk one, especially the third one.

"You may wonder why Gospatric is not here and the reason is simple. I do not trust him. I have decided that his cousin, Waltheof would be a better earl. I gave Gospatric one task when I was last here in the north and he failed to do all that I asked. You and Count Alain did more and your lands are further south. I gave him the chance to redeem himself and he failed. When we have scoured the north then I will have Gospatric replaced. He squats in Bamburgh and wonders what I plan for him. Let him wonder. The men of Northumbria are untrustworthy and I would rather have a smaller army but led by men I trust than have vipers close to my bosom." He saw my face and smiled, "I am relying on your natural ability to survive, fitz Malet. You have shown a great propensity in that area. You are also lucky and that is something a general should never ignore. There will be rewards for you. Eisicewalt and Norton are but the start. Now, you have much to do. You need to ensure that the knights you lead know who wields the whip."

I was dismissed and I left. As I did so a couple of clerks entered. They had been waiting without and, no doubt, had heard our words. The king's son would know of them too. As I headed back to my camp I knew that I could not share the king's commands and opinions with anyone. What I could do, however, was to share with them my fears for the future. If we were bait then I would use my men to ensure that we survived.

I did not reach my camp for the king's son was waiting for me. He was alone. "A word, Sir Richard."

"Of course, My Lord."

I saw that four of his familia were hovering nearby. They were beyond earshot but I knew that they would be there to keep others from overhearing our words. They were slightly older than William but each had spurs.

"I am young but I have my own ideas." He paused but I said nothing. "I will heed your advice but I will not brook being commanded. Your advice shall be private."

I nodded and then spoke, "My Lord, have you fought in a battle yet?"

He flushed and his red colouring became scarlet, "I have read of battles and been told of them."

"Telling and participating, My Lord, are as different as practice and combat to the death. One is easier than the other." I paused and chose my next words carefully and measured my tone, "When we split from the main army we will be a target." I saw his eyes widen. He had clearly not thought of that. "You are the son of the king and we lead the smallest element of the army. We will be the one they try to attack." I did not say that his father was using us as bait. Hopefully, he would work that out for himself. "We will be on Scottish soil and they will defend it. They know the country and we do not. In theory the land to the east of the Tweed is English but, Bamburgh apart, there are no strongholds." I remembered the king's words. What would Gospatric do? Did he know of the king's plans to have him replaced? "I intend to have scouts out to warn us of ambush but I have fought enough times in this land to know that even the most vigilant can be surprised. If I have to I will issue an order that all our men will obey and do instantly. Hesitation in these matters can be fatal."

He frowned and then nodding said, "I will ride as close to you as I can be and it will be my standard bearer and cornicen who signal the orders."

"Of course, My Lord. Perhaps if you send them to me I can make my mind clear. After all there should be no confusion. This campaign offers both of us opportunities does it not? When it is over I shall return to my manor at Eisicewalt and you will have garnered battle honours that will help you in the battles you fight in the future." I was letting him know that I had no ambitions.

He smiled, "You and I shall get on, fitz Malet. I will send them to you."

I had barely reached my tent when the two men at arms arrived. The king's son might prove to be a man I could work with.

"Sir Richard, I am Guy d'Honfleur, Lord William's standard bearer, and this is Roger of Rennes his cornicen."

I studied them. They looked to be younger than their master. They both wore mail hauberks which suggested that their families had money and their swords were good ones.

"Lord William has told you of the arrangements?"

"Yes, My Lord. We will be close to the both of you so that when orders are given we can obey them instantly."

That was not exactly what I had meant and I wanted no misunderstanding. "When I give a command heed it. I will not gainsay the son of King William but I am the military advisor. Do you understand?"

They looked at each other and nodded, Guy said, "Neither of us have been in a battle before, My Lord."

I nodded, "It is noisy and there can be confusion. Your horn and your standard will be the sight and the sound that will, hopefully, bring order. You are important but…" I held their gaze with the pause, "the enemy will try to get at you. You must be able to defend yourselves. You must practise riding without using your hands. I pray that you and your horses are well trained."

The looks they gave me told me that they weren't. "We will both do our best, My Lord."

"And I have buried many men who did their best but found that was not good enough. Stay close to me."

"Yes, My Lord."

Conan and Bergil had been nearby and listening. When the two left they came over and Bergil said, "Have they begun to shave yet?"

"Many of the men led by Lord William are young. Find Edward and Galmr, bring them to my tent. We have much to discuss." As I headed to my tent I reflected that in a perfect world I ought to speak with the other leaders but the problem was that I did not know who they were. These were the knights of the Palatinate and, as such, owed their fealty not only to the king but also to the bishop. I would have to rely on the king's son to command them but while the words would be William's, the orders would be mine.

When my men entered I waved for them to sit wherever they could. "Sit where you are able. We are to be with the men of Durham and the king's son. Within this tent I should tell you that I command but to all those without it will be William who commands."

Conan said, "The Rufus."

I snapped irritably, "Enough of that. He is to be addressed as My Lord."

"Sorry, Sir Richard."

"Until we are close to the Tweed then we travel with the king. Past there we are on our own until we reach the Forth. The king has a cunning plan to trap the Scots with three armies!"

Bergil was a practical man, "And how large is our army?"

"Five hundred or so."

Galmr snorted, "Little more than a warband, My Lord."

"Yet with our men at its heart and that is the key to this conundrum. To that end I want you, Conan, to ride ahead with Ethelred and Elric as our scouts. Their noses and your experience should ensure that we are not surprised." He nodded, "Edward, two men at arms from Lord William's familia will be with me and neither has much experience. You defend them and not me."

"But…"

"If they fall then the warband, as Galmr, calls it, could be destroyed. They are the means by which I will command the army. Lord William has his own familia to guard him but they are young and young men are sometimes reckless." I allowed them time to digest my words. They were all experienced enough to work out their own role.

Galmr said, "Do we ride to war and fight on foot?"

"You do and I shall make it clear that you, Galmr, command the men who fight on foot. They are a ragged collection but I hope that the stiffening of them by you will give me a shield wall that will hold the Scots."

"That means, My Lord, that you will just have me, Aethelstan and Alfred as horsemen."

"I know, Bergil. On the ride north tomorrow, I will have to get to know the other knights. If we have a fight before the army splits I may see their mettle and if not…" They all understood.

The ride north was slow. The king might have made a speedy arrival with horsemen but now he had the fyrd and baggage. I rode with Lord William, the king and Lord Craven but I was not part of their conversation. I tagged along behind and that suited me. I was able to speak to a young knight, Ivo de Vesi and Sir Gilbert Tyson. I knew Sir Gilbert who had been the king's standard bearer when we had defeated Harold Godwinson. He had been given Alnwick as his manor. As I already knew, he had yet to take up the lordship of the manor. He had his familia with him and when this campaign was over, I discovered, then he would build his castle and we would have a worthy knight in place who could defend the River Aln. Ivo was young and had only just been awarded his spurs. He was a younger son and would not inherit the lands in Normandy. He had come with Sir Gilbert for the king's former standard bearer had been in Normandy settling his affairs. He had a small manor there but Alnwick was a much more promising manor.

"Sir Richard, I believe that you have seen my manor."

I nodded, "You have been given a regal gift, Sir Gilbert. There are no defences built by man but nature has imbued the site with natural features." I hesitated, "I do not know what finances you have but if the funds are available then I would build in stone."

He smiled, "I have a young bride and I would have her safe. Before she travels from my home in Normandy I will build strong walls." He looked at Ivo, "And there seems to be much land here for you, young Ivo. From what I have gathered there are few manors yet that the king has given to his men."

Before Ivo could answer I said, "And that is because there are few men left in these parts to farm the land." We were far enough behind the king for us not to be overheard. "The king destroyed this land and the people starved. It may have been necessary but it has made it into a wasteland."

Sir Gilbert was a positive man and he grinned, "That is better then. To start with nothing means we can build for the future."

I liked his attitude but did not envy him the task. The nearest castle to his was Bamburgh and whilst it had a good position it was still just a wooden structure.

Ivo said, "And I am not afraid of hard work."

"Then when we have routed the Scots and I begin to build my castle come and be part of my familia." It was a generous offer from Sir Gilbert.

"But Lord William…"

I smiled, "There will be many others who flock to serve the third son of the king. King William has many titles to bestow and his son will inherit one of them." I did not say that this campaign was to blood his son and he would head south just as soon as it was over and he could get back to Normandy or Lundenwic.

The ride north was a pleasant one. This was the land of the prince bishop and safe. Until we passed the Tyne there would be no danger and even then our numbers would deter any but the King of Scotland himself. I got to know some of the other knights but Gilbert and Ivo were my constant companions. I noticed that most of the knights from Durham kept their distance from me. Perhaps the bishop had spoken to them. I did not care. They would obey my orders for failure to do so would incur the wrath of the king and he had a very short temper.

It was a trouble-free journey for a week and then we parted at Otterburn. The king and his son spoke in private. The king would head for Jedburgh and then take the road for Lauder and the Forth. We would cross the Tweed at the ford to the west of Berwick and head for Dunbar and the Forth. We had the easier journey but the king had the larger army. He had more than twice our number of knights. He would be able to move more quickly than we for he had far more horses than we had and his were better ones. I wondered if he was tempting the Scots who would see an army largely made up of the fyrd. While the king and his son were meeting I sent my six scouts out. Although this was unknown land for all of them they were all good scouts and would soon acclimatise themselves to the terrain. Despite the reluctance of the Durham knights to cooperate, Ethelred and Elric had found information from the fyrd and they said that close by the village of Norham the river could be forded. They would head there.

When the meeting was over and our leader rejoined us I took charge, "My scouts are out already, Lord William. They will find us a camp site."

He just nodded, "Very well." This was mundane stuff and beneath him. I used it to establish that I would give the broader strokes of strategy.

The camp was already struck and we moved out to the north and east. The king would be taking the road that had been built by the Romans. We also used a Roman road but a lesser one and being less well travelled was not as good. In places stones had become dislodged and we had to pay attention to the slightly uneven surface. My two men at arms acted as advanced guards. They rode fifty paces before us and I advised all the knights to keep their long kite shields hung by their guige straps to protect their left legs. I did not chat but kept a good watch on the road ahead.

Conan and his Bretons met us as we approached a hamlet. My men at arms kept watch while we reined in, "We have found the ford, My Lord. Ethelred and Elric are camped there now and ensuring that it will be safe for us. We have scouted the houses ahead and they seem safe. There are just five families there although there are ten houses." He paused and explained, "They have been recently attacked by Scots and Vikings."

The people were pleased to see us, especially when we began to cook our own food and left their livestock and crops unharmed. I think that was one advantage of having so many young knights. They had yet to learn to pillage and plunder.

The king's son was keen to know what to expect and, as we ate, he plied me with questions. "How will they fight us, Sir Richard?"

"Not in the way you might anticipate, My Lord. They have fewer knights and their horses are not as good as ours. They will use ambush and traps. They will try to hamstring our horses."

He looked appalled, "But that is barbaric and goes against all that I was taught."

"At Senlac Hill men like Galmr, housecarls, used their two-handed axes to do the same. There is neither nobility nor honour in battle My Lord. It is kill or be killed. A knight who falls from his horse is easier prey than a mounted man. We will use our horses cautiously."

"I was told that your grandfather was a, what did you call them, housecarl?"

"He was and fought, not for Godwinson but the Earl of Mercia."

"So, you are a mixture of Saxon and Norman." I nodded. "My father regards you as a great leader and yet you are young. You were trained by Taillefer."

"I was."

"Tell me about him."

It was easy to do so and I regaled him with tales of the man who had made me what I was. I kept my eyes on the land as my tongue told the story of the legend that was Taillefer.

The next day Conan and my Bretons rode towards the ford and we headed for the crossing of the Tweed. I knew that we could have travelled up the west bank of the river from Otterburn but the king had insisted that we ensured that the land of Northumbria, that debatable land, was still in our hands.

We were still five miles shy of the river when not only Conan and his Bretons rode in but also Elric. We stopped and they reined in. It was Elric who spoke, "My Lord, there is an ambush at the ford. The Scots are hidden across the water and are in the trees."

He reported to me for that was natural. I turned to Lord William, "As I said last night, My Lord, ambush."

"And that means that when we cross they will hurt our horses!"

I sighed. He was ignoring the fact that our men would be lost too. "If we do what they expect." I turned in my saddle and called, "How many horsemen can swim a river? Raise your hands." My men at arms and the Bretons all raised their arms. About a dozen of the knights from the royal familia also did so. None of the Durham men did. It confirmed what I thought. They were obeying the orders of the bishop. I saw that one of those who had raised his hand was Sir Gilbert. I waved him over and spoke to him and Lord William. "Sir Gilbert, I need you to stay close to Lord William." The king's son frowned, "My Lord, I have a plan to evade the ambush but I need a warrior to be with the horsemen who has battle experience. You do not wish to lose any horses do you?"

"No."

I called, "Galmr." My Varangian came over. "This is my plan. I will take all the men who can swim horses upstream. Galmr, you will command the men on foot. I would have you line the river close to the ford and make a shield wall but remain hidden until the signal. My Lord, you and the knights can line the river behind the men on foot. Ethelred and the archers can be ready to launch arrows." I waved over Roger of Rennes, "You will come with me, Roger of Rennes. I will have two of my men ensure that you cross the river safely." He nodded nervously. I turned to the king's son, "When the horn is sounded once, I want the army to cheer and arrows to be sent. Galmr and the shield wall will take a step forward. You will all wait until the horn sounds three times and when it does so it will be safe for you to attack."

Gilbert and Galmr nodded. Lord William looked at the men who were preparing their horses to cross the river. "There are less than a score of you."

I smiled, "We are mounted and the one direction they will not expect an attack is from their side of the river. Their attention will be on you and causing you as much harm as they can before they melt into the trees. Trust me, My Lord, our appearance will take them by surprise and they will not see the handful of men I lead but the horses and they will hear the horn."

Sir Gilbert said, "It is a good plan and it shows that the king chose well, Sir Richard. It is a bold move."

The king's son nodded.

"Aethelstan and Alfred, guard the cornicen."

"Yes, My Lord."

I saw that Ivo was amongst the horsemen waiting for me. I said, "Are you sure?"

He looked nervous and smiled, "My horse can swim, that I know, and I can cling on for dear life. If I am to impress the son of King William what better way than to accompany you?"

"Good. The river is not wide hereabouts and not as deep as you might expect. Follow me."

I rode flanked by Bergil and Edward. Behind us came the cornicen and his guards then Conan and his Bretons. I would not have the luxury of being able to watch the others cross the river. While the rest had spears I was relying on my swords. We reached the village of Norham. The people there wisely remained indoors. Just before the village a burn flowed from the south to join the river. We paddled across it. The water barely came to the horse's fetlocks. I saw that there was a small island in the river. The distance to it was barely fifty paces.

"We will cross here. I will lead." The command was for Edward and Bergil. The best way to cross a river was for one to find the path and then for the rest to follow. Scout was a good swimmer and I was a confident rider. I urged him into the water. I did not turn for my attention needed to be on the water. It was summer and not winter. The water level was as low as it would ever be and I was thirty paces across before I felt Scout start to swim. Within four or five paces he had found the riverbed and we scrambled up the bank. I waved my arm and, in twos and threes, the rest came across. I walked across the island and saw that the other side of the island was narrower, just thirty odd paces. It was, however, clearly deeper. When the others joined me I walked Scout to the water. Almost as soon as we had entered the swirling waters came up to my boots. He was a powerful swimmer and it was only the middle ten paces where he had to swim but in those ten paces we moved downstream. I reached the other side and dismounted to tighten the girths. I waved the others across. This time Roger of Rennes almost came to grief but Alfred's quick hands grabbed the reins and they survived.

"Tighten your girths and ready your shields." I had done so already and I walked around them as they did the same. "We will not be attacking in a column but a line. I want them to think we are greater in number than we actually are. Roger, ride behind me and listen for my command. Your lips are ready?"

He grinned, "I may struggle in a river, My Lord but I can blow."

"Then mount and follow me."

There was a natural order to the formation of our line. With Bergil, Edward and Conan flanking me the others spread out. The young men of Lord William's familia formed the flanks. I picked my way through the trees. Speed was not important. The Scots would be waiting patiently knowing that an army could not cross a river quickly. They would be intending to hurt us and run. I knew that if they succeeded there would be more ambushes. This skirmish would be as important as any battle. If we won we would eliminate the possibility of more ambushes. I was close to a pine when I saw the first of the Scots. He was a horse guard and that meant that I was close to their horse lines. I held my hand up and the line stopped. I saw that they had but ten horses. There would be more than ten men at the ambush and the ten horsemen would either be knights or men at arms. I drew my sword, having seen enough.

I spoke quietly for my men were all close to me, "Roger, one blast. Alfred then take the horse holder and guard the horses."

"Yes, My Lord." I heard the nervousness in Roger's voice.

"Aye, My Lord," Alfred's, in contrast oozed confidence.

I turned to Roger, "You crossed a river and you can do this. Now blow!"

As he blew I urged Scout on and we headed through the trees. It was not a charge, the thickness of the undergrowth prevented that, but the Scots were clearly not expecting an attack from their side of the river. The backs of their spearmen were to me as I heard a roar from across the river. The arrows made a noise as they descended through the trees. There were screams and shouts. A warrior with a mail coif turned to face me but it was a heartbeat too late and my sword slashed across his shoulder where there was no protection. His spear fell from his hands as Scout bowled him over.

I heard orders shouted in what I assumed was Gaelic. We were among them and as I saw faces turning, I shouted, "Roger, three blasts!" The horn sounded three times and even while I was shouting the command I was bringing my sword down to slice deeply into the skull of a man with a long sword. All around me my horsemen were slashing and stabbing. They were taking advantage of that most fearsome of weapons, surprise.

I heard another roar and knew, without actually seeing, it that it was Galmr who was leading the men across the ford. He would not care that the son of King William was mounted and behind him. He was a warrior and battle was in his blood. He and the men on foot would cross the ford as quickly as any horse. That suited me as I wanted no casualties amongst the precious few knights that I commanded. The Scots were defending now but we had the advantage of height and the spears of the horsemen drove down to skewer men with no armour. When

Galmr and the men on foot fell amongst them then it was all over. The Scots fled.

Lord William and his familia slashed and stabbed at the Scots that they caught. This was their first combat and it could not have been easier. There was a danger that they could be carried away and charge after the fleeing ambushers. I rode to Roger, "Sound the recall." Even though the attack had been swift some of the knights were chasing the Scots through the trees. Whilst they might account for more of the enemy, it also meant that they might be hurt and I wanted none of that.

I dismounted and took my helmet from my head. Edward took the reins. I asked, "Did we lose any men?"

He looked around and said, "None in our attack and young Roger slew his first enemy." I saw that we had taken all the horses and that was unexpected. They had not panicked and fled when we had killed the horse guard. "Have the dead stripped and place the bodies on a pyre."

Lord William headed back to me. His red face was flushed, this time with excitement. "A great victory, Sir Richard." He looked at the arms as they were piled on the ground, "But I see little treasure here. The horses are all bidets and there were no knights."

I lowered my coif and felt the cool air swirl around my head, "And there will not be any until we beard their king. This is the reality of war in the borders, My Lord. We have made a good start and your father will be pleased. If I were you I would send a man to report to him. He will wish to know that his right flank is safe." I was doing what the king had asked. I was mentoring his son.

"A good idea." He turned and rode towards his pueros.

Conan, Bergil and Galmr joined me. Galmr grinned, "There were no knights, My Lord, but there were coins in their purses and the weapons we took, whilst not the best, can be sold to a smith."

I nodded and Bergil said, "Any victory that is this easy is to be applauded."

I was surprised, "We lost none?"

"Some of the Durham fyrd fell but none of ours." It was a sad comment but I understood it. Bergil had trained our men and he wanted no one from Eisicewalt dead. The ghost of Aed haunted us.

Ethelred came over with some animals he had hunted, "And we eat well this night."

Conan added, "And there is Scottish mutton there too."

I shook my head, "That is more likely to be English mutton but you are right we eat well."

Chapter 15

We moved at noon and reached Berwick in the late afternoon. That we were not expected was clear for there were still people in the town and as we rode up to the gates, which were still open, it was obvious that the wooden walls of the citadel would not be defended. Lord William took charge, "Surrender to King William or I shall put every man to the sword."

The few defenders had little choice in the matter. They surrendered and Lord William and his familia enjoyed a night in a hall on a bed. I was resigned to sleeping rough until the campaign was over. Sir Gilbert and his familia joined us as we enjoyed a feast of Ethelred's hunting and left over mutton bones.

"I hope that the rest of the campaign will be as easy."

I had worked out that as we had taken the horses at the ford the survivors had been forced to flee on foot and that meant heading north and west rather than the route we had taken to the northeast. Berwick did not know we were coming. I shrugged, "Until the Scots create more horsemen they will have to rely upon their land to protect them. If we had more horsemen then the campaign would be over. A few judiciously placed castles and mounted knights are the way to control large areas of land."

The son of the king came to speak to us after we had dined, "And where next?"

I had a map I had obtained from Belisarius on my last visit. Much of it was empty but Berwick was marked. I jabbed my finger at a red square to the northwest. “Din Eidyn. It was held by the men of Northumbria until a hundred years ago. It is on the Forth and there is a burgh there.” I shrugged, “I believe it is a wooden one but I am not sure.”

“A burgh, that is like a castle is it not?”

“It is but Belisarius says that in this case the burgh sits on top of a natural rocky feature.”

“And how far away is it?”

“Forty or so miles but we will have to travel along the coast to Dunbar first so it will take three days to reach it. If we rode hard and went directly to it we could be there in a day.”

“But why do we need to go to Dunbar?”

“Because your father, the king, wants the eastern side of this land safe.”

“It will take longer than going directly to Din Eidyn.”

I nodded, “The men on foot determine that. It does not really matter how long it takes as the fleet has yet to arrive with the men who fight on foot. Our little skirmish and the taking of Berwick should ensure that we are not bothered again on the road north.”

“You are confident.”

“Berwick is the only defensible stronghold south of the Forth. Dunbar, so it could be defended but as it is on the coast we cut it off from support and take it without force of arms. A short siege might suffice.”

William went to mount his horse and Sir Gilbert smiled, “But will the son of King William think so?”

He was right and as we headed up the east coast it became increasingly obvious that Lord William wanted more military success. When we neared the castle I saw that it was hardly a fortress. It might have once been and, I dare say could have been so again, but as we approached I saw that it had wooden walls. The road we took and the banners we flew let the defenders know that it was the son of King William who approached.

He turned to me, "Sir Richard, will they fight or will they do as Berwick did and surrender?"

"Hard to say, My Lord. It depends on who is defending the town and castle." He looked at me for illumination. "The land belongs to the Earl of Northumbria, Gospatric."

"But my father has stripped him of his title."

"And this land, My Lord has never been part of England. It was conquered by the Northumbrians and they held it but he still has the right to rule."

We drew closer to the castle. I saw ships entering and leaving the harbour. The king's son reined in, "Could we take the castle?"

I turned to look into the young man's eyes, "We could but it would cost us men to do so. A wooden castle can always be reduced. If nothing else then fire could be used but this castle is not a threat to your father's invasion." I saw him debating with himself. I said, "The last castle I assaulted saw Sir Bruno and myself almost killed. It is not something to be undertaken lightly, My Lord, but it is your decision. Perhaps we can besiege them and hope that they surrender."

"Let us speak to the defenders and see if they will do as Berwick has done and submit to our rule."

When we neared the castle we halted. "What is the procedure, Sir Richard?"

"We remove our helmets, take our standard bearers and ride to hailing distance."

"Will they not try to hit us with arrows?"

"If they do then they are committing a sin. I do not think that Gospatric will risk his soul. Keep your shield close and if I tell you, My Lord, then lift it. In my experience the Scots are poor archers and your shield is well made."

"That will be cold comfort if I am dead."

"I do not think you will die here but keep your horse slightly behind mine."

"Very well." He turned to his standard bearer, "Guy."

I turned, "Alfred, unfurl my banner and come with me." Gilbert nudged his horse next to mine. I said, quietly, "You had better take command. If the defenders prove hostile I do not want his lordship's familia to do something foolish."

He nodded, "Aye, Sir Richard."

I took off my helmet and hung it from my cantle. I nudged Scout and we headed for the castle. It did not bristle with defenders but I saw spearpoints gleaming in the sunlight. "My lord, let us approach."

With Alfred on my left I rode the four hundred paces to the gates. The king's son took my advice and I saw his arm slip through his shield and his hand held it. If I gave a command it could be lifted to cover his unprotected face in a flash. I stopped one hundred and fifty paces from the walls. I could see that the young man was uncertain about what to do. I said, "Let me speak first, My Lord." I cupped my hands and called. "I am Sir Richard fitz Malet and I am here with Prince William, the son of the rightful King of England, William. Who commands here?"

"I am Robert of Dunbar. Earl Gospatric has now left the castle."

It was a simple reply but it told me much. The rebel was not risking apprehension and had fled. He had probably been in one of the ships I had seen leaving the harbour. I turned to the king's son, "My Lord."

He nodded and I watched the confidence grow as he spoke, "We demand your surrender." He paused, "If you do not then we shall reduce your walls and slaughter the garrison."

There was a pause and I saw men debating on the walls. Eventually, Robert of Dunbar said, "And if we surrender?"

"Then the castle becomes ours and you will swear allegiance to King William."

There was more debate and then, as the gates swung open, the castellan shouted, "We agree, enter, My Lord."

We entered the castle and King William gained a fortress in the north at no cost to his army. More importantly, his son was the one who accepted the surrender. We stayed in the castle for two nights enjoying beds and food. Robert of Dunbar was Northumbrian rather than Scottish and did not see a problem in submitting to an English king. The Earl of Northumbria had abandoned his castle and his people. He had no support and whatever the king chose to do would not cause another rebellion. The people were not hurt and we took just the supplies we needed for the short journey along the Forth.

Our journey along the estuary was like a victory march. We had fought one skirmish and taken two castles. Not a knight had been harmed and even the fyrd, wearied no doubt by the long march, seemed in good spirits. They had enjoyed better food in Dunbar than they had expected. As we marched along the road that parallelled the estuary we saw the king's fleet as it edged alongside us. I saw sails ahead and knew that the leading elements had landed already. The king's plan appeared to be working. I knew that his son had not come to any harm. He had survived and he had learned along the way. I was relieved.

We found the ships beached at a place called The Shore. It was within sight of the fortress of Din Eidyn which rose just a mile or so to the south and west of us but we saw no royal standard flying from the battlements. King Malcolm was not within. There were tents close to the river and I saw the standard of Northumbria planted in the ground. Earl Waltheof was there. The cousin of Gospatric, he had rebelled and been pardoned too. Was the king testing him? I wondered at his loyalty.

"We will camp there, Sir Richard. My father's plan appears to be succeeding. Perhaps we should consider taking Scotland."

"Scotland is not worth the effort, My Lord."

He slowed to look at me, "You have mentored me well and guided my hand. For that I am grateful. We have enjoyed great success. I see no reason to stop here. The land close to the Tweed was raw but here the fields are tended and there are men to be taxed. I will speak with my father."

I knew better but I remained silent.

Earl Waltheof was still a Saxon. He wore his hair and dressed just as Harold Godwinson had. He knew how to play the game, however, and he bowed when he greeted Lord William, "I have brought the fleet and the men on foot as I promised your father. How went the journey and the campaign?"

He ignored me as I had expected him to. Lord William turned to me and said, "See to my men for me, Sir Richard. I will go within and speak to the earl."

"Yes, My Lord." I had done what was needed and now I was treated like a servant. I consoled myself with the thought that I had kept the son of the king alive and done as I was ordered. I hoped now that I would be relieved of that burden. Luckily his men had come to respect me, probably more than their leader, and my commands were obeyed instantly. My leaders waited until I had dealt with Lord William's commands and then approached. "Have hovels built close by to the ships. I am unsure of the king's plans but I cannot see that he will bring a fleet here just to let them lie idly by. We have yet to see the royal standard. King Malcolm must be north of the Forth."

Edward asked, "What if King William has defeated him already?"

"Then we would know. Ensure that the men are fed. We are amongst the first here. Aethelstan and Alfred, take some of the younger men and ride to the villages hereabouts. Take animals and food. We need grain for the horses and they grow oats."

Edward looked shocked, "Sir Richard, we do not normally raid."

"Unlike Lord William I do not believe that his father wants Scotland. It is like the thistles that grow hereabouts. It is inedible and painful to hold. We will not harm the people but I need men who can fight the Scots when the day of battle comes. We take from them and feed ourselves. It is the way of war."

Conan nodded, "Sir Richard is correct, Master Edward, war is a painful thing. We cannot be kind for that might weaken our men and would you rather they died?"

Edward saw that we were both right and he nodded. I said, "Take off my mail, Edward. I think that we shall not need it again until the king arrives."

The king arrived two days later from the west. He had taken the citadel of Din Eidyn without a fight and he and his army of knights looked whole. He was in a good mood especially when an excited son greeted him. I stayed in the background with Sir Gilbert and the other older knights while they spoke. Earl Waltheof was also effusive in his welcome. The king said, "Have tables and chairs placed on the shoreline. My knights and I will dine in the open."

As men hurried to obey his orders I chuckled. Sir Gilbert and Ivo were next to me, "What amuses you, Sir Richard?"

"King William never misses an opportunity." I pointed north to the opposite side of the river. The rising smoke from the campfires told us that there were armed men watching us. "He is telling King Malcolm that we rule this side of the river and he is displaying his power. All our knights will be seated. Squires and pueros will be serving them and the enemy will report the size of our fleet and our army. He is winning the battle before it is begun."

The servants sent to find tables and chairs struggled to obey the orders. Every house for miles around was stripped. Our taking of the animals was as nothing compared with the emptying of homes. A trickle of people began to head west. They would confirm to King Malcolm the numbers who were coming to threaten his parlous hold on the crown.

Before the food was served I was sent for. King William and his son awaited me in the huge tent erected for the two of them. King William was looking a little older these days but our victories thus far made his eyes sparkle, "Sir Richard, my son tells me that you have taken two castles and defeated an army sent to hinder you. You are the best of knights."

I knew enough to flatter the son of King William, "The castles were taken by your son, King William. It was he who spoke to them and ensured their surrender."

"Perhaps I should have you work with my two elder sons Richard and Robert. They are like two puppies fighting over the same bone." That he let me know that there was dissension between his sons surprised me. I did not wish that responsibility and I remained silent. "My son will now ride with me. You will continue to lead the knights of Durham."

I nodded, "And where will that be, King William?"

"We cross the Forth using the fleet." He pointed west, "The river is less than a thousand paces wide not far from here. We make a pontoon bridge using the fleet. We can be across in a day. My scouts tell me that there is an army heading from the north." He smiled, "They are travelling to the bridge at Stirling where they hope to stop us. That is a vain hope for we shall head directly north to Perth. The holy place where they appoint their kings, Scone, is close by. We shall strike at the heart of his kingdom and force the king to make peace."

"We could take the land, Father."

The king shook his head, "For what purpose? There is nothing here. At least Wales has gold. All that Scotland has are sheep and the insects that bite. No, my son, we humble the Scots and then you and I return to Normandy to secure our borders with France. We have been away too long." The young man glanced over at me. His father was saying exactly the same thing that I had. It confirmed that I knew what I was talking about.

The feast was noisy. That was deliberate. The king encouraged singing and laughter. The men on foot were assigned the task of protecting our camp. He wanted the Scots to know the size of our army and that we were in good humour. The fleet was still anchored in the river and King Malcolm would have no idea of our plan to cross by a pontoon of ships.

The fleet headed upstream the next day and we broke camp to march the short distance to the crossing point. The king did not order a camp but he had the ships bound together and the wood from nearby houses was used to make a road across the ships. It was my horsemen and the men of my manor, along with the men of Durham, who tested the structure. It was a strange experience. We did not ride our horses but led them. I went first and I insisted that my men walk in single file. The king could go in whatever formation he chose but I wanted no one to fall into the river nor any horses to be hurt. The ships wobbled. They rose and fell alarmingly with the current and the tide. The crews of the ships had sweeps out to keep the vessels as steady as they could but I knew they would be glad when we had all crossed. As soon as we reached the other side we mounted and I led my men to ride towards the fires we had seen burning. The men there had fled and all we found was the detritus of their camps. We swept in a circle back to the landing place and found no opposition. We had caught the Scots unawares but the time it had taken the ships to be tied had shown them our intention. King Malcolm would now know that his army at Stirling was guarding nothing. Messengers would be sent to recall them. They were guarding a bridge we did not need to cross.

As we waited, just a mile from the landing, Edward said, "It will take time to get to the bridge and bring an army to face us. We might be able to take Perth without opposition. This might be like Berwick and Dunbar all over."

I shook my head, "It will take all day and more to land the army. Stirling is just twenty-five miles west of here. King William will not want an enemy to cut us off from the fleet." I waved a hand around the land before us. "The high ground to the north marks the line of march and this flat ground suits our horsemen. He will not hurry. It is better to let an enemy tire himself out marching to battle. It worked with Harold Godwinson. He marched from Stamford Bridge and it cost him his crown and his life."

"King Malcolm is with the Scottish army?"

I shrugged, "I doubt it. King Malcolm seems to me a pragmatic man. We shall see."

When the king arrived less than a quarter of the army had crossed. It was early afternoon. He spoke to the earl and the Lord of Craven as well as me, "We will not be able to land all the army before dark. We camp here. Sir Richard, take the men of Durham and camp half a mile from here. You can be our night guards."

"Of course, King William." It was not an honour but a duty.

We were not the only ones to be charged with a duty. Sir Gilbert was commanded to take a conroi of horsemen and scout out the army to the west of us. We were marching on the road north when Sir Gilbert's scouts returned, a day later. As I was at the head of the camp when the rider rode in and gave me the news, I would be the one to take the messenger to the king.

The king and his son listened as the man at arms made his report, "Sir Gilbert has the enemy army in sight, King William. Their army is heading along the road from Stirling and they are within fifteen miles of us. They are largely men on foot and he said that there are three elements. The largest is made up of Scotsmen. He said that he spied the standard of the Mormaer of Moray." My ears pricked up at the mention of my enemy. "The second largest part of the army is made up of barbarians: Norse and Danes. The smallest component is made up of Saxons."

The king leaned forward eagerly, "Edgar Ætheling?"

The messenger quailed and said, nervously, "Sir Gilbert did not see his banner but he did see the banner of Gospatric."

The king turned to Waltheof, "Your cousin. Perhaps you can rid me of this nuisance, eh?"

"Yes King William."

To me the earl did not sound convincing.

The king looked around. He spied a body of water. "Earl, William, Sir Richard, come with me. The rest remain here until you are summoned."

His ten bodyguards and standard bearer followed us along with his cornicen. We rode down the road. He pointed to the water to our left. "They called them lochs in this part of the world," he said to his son. "We will use that loch to anchor our left. If our enemy tries to move his lumbering men on foot around it we shall ride him down with our horses." It was a lesson in strategy and his son nodded. He wheeled his horse to the right and we came to a thick forest just twenty paces from the road. We could see that on the far side there were streams and bogs. "And here we anchor the right." He turned to estimate the distance. "Just over three quarters of a mile. Sir Richard, fetch the army while my son and I decide upon our dispositions."

I did not mind being a messenger. William was the king's son and his father was building on the work I had already done. I reached the army and rode to the leaders, "We have our battlefield. March the army to the king and spread out between the lake and the forest. The king will decide your positions."

I joined my men, "Alfred, unfurl the banner. The men of Eisicewalt go to war."

Chapter 16

The king's plan was a simple one. We were drawn up so that we had a solid line of men on foot with shields. Some of the men at arms were dismounted and they stiffened the elements of the army that were not as well armoured. He had stakes hacked from the forest and embedded. They would not slow an attacking army that much but they would disrupt its order. The horsemen were placed in three blocks behind the men on foot. We were the threat. The king hoped that the enemy would weaken himself on the shield wall and then, at the decisive moment, he would launch his cavalry, our most potent weapon. I did not like the plan as it put the least prepared in the fore. Few of the infantry had armour. King William was being ruthless. If they were sacrificed then he would not lose any sleep over it so long as Scotland was no longer a threat. I was glad that I was just a lord of the manor. I would have nightmares if I was the one ordering men to be sacrificed. I remembered Aed and his family. At the end of this battle there would be many such families.

What we could not know was how the enemy, and we guessed it was led by the Mormaer of Moray, would be arranged. Sir Gilbert and his conroi rode in and he reported the details to the king. I was close enough to hear his report. "They have three thousand men, King William. He has knights and mounted men. There are fifty knights and a hundred or so light horsemen."

The king waved a dismissive hand, “They will do nothing. The Danes and Vikings?”

“Almost a thousand, King William, and more than half are mailed.”

“The English?”

“Five hundred.”

“Now let us see how they are arrayed. We will camp on our battle positions. Sir Richard you shall command the right. Waltheof, the left. My son and I will command the centre. Once we know how they are disposed we will hold a council of war.”

The enemy began to appear. Their leaders were at the fore and they halted their men as they studied our lines. As all our horsemen were dismounted they would have a distorted view of our force. I saw arms being waved and men were marshalled into lines. After a short time, it became clear that they would be camping and not attacking.

King William sounded the horn and I turned to Bergil, “Take charge. It is a council of war.” Edward followed me as I headed to the king’s tent. He looked to be in a good mood. He waved at me as I entered, “Thanks to Sir Richard here we have an advantage over the enemy.” I had no idea what he meant and it was clear that no one else had either. The king explained, “Thanks to his actions on the Aln the enemy will be expecting a surprise attack this night. They will have extra sentries and that will tire them. When the morning comes we will stand until Terce and then we will mount the horsemen. I want them to think that we plan an attack with our horsemen. We will, instead, advance our men on foot with the horsemen in close support. We have enough archers and slingers to cause them trouble and Sir

Gilbert told me that they have, just behind their camp, an area of boggy ground."

He turned to his former standard bearer who nodded, "When we came back from our scouting expedition one of my men's horses strayed from the road and he sank to his fetlocks. They must have had recent rain on already boggy ground."

The king continued, "With boggy ground behind them we use our weight of men to push them back. Earl Waltheof, you shall have the honour of leading this attack. You can lead the men you brought with you. They will occupy the centre and the left. The men of Durham will form the right."

My heart sank. Waltheof was no leader. "Do you wish me to lead on foot, My Lord?"

He shook his head, "You have a good Varangian with you I believe. This seems a perfect place to use him."

I saw that Earl Waltheof looked even less happy than I did.

"When the moment is right I will sound the charge and the men on foot will open ranks and allow us to charge through. My son and I will lead the attack in the centre, Lord Robert of Craven the left flank and Sir Richard the right."

While his son and the other knights present nodded I was not so sure. Whilst men at arms and trained men would know what to do most of those who would be commanded were the fyrd. What had seemed easy now seemed more difficult. We were dismissed and I headed back to our camp. Lord Craven arrested my progress, "Sir Richard, a word."

"Yes, My Lord."

"You should know that the Bishop of Durham has set his men against you."

"I know, My Lord."

"You know?" He sounded surprised.

"They did not disguise their feelings well but they obey me."

"It may be different tomorrow."

"The men who fight for me are strong leaders. They will hold the line. As for the knights…if I have to charge the Scots with just my oathsworn I will." I smiled, "We swore a blood oath." I held up my palm with the scar upon it.

He shook his head, "I have not heard of such a thing…I just wanted you to know. The king is impressed with you as am I. His son was different when we met again. In a short time, you have achieved much. I would not like to see you fall tomorrow because of another's twisted values."

"And I thank you. It will be an honour to fight with you at any time."

We clasped arms as warriors do. I knew that we would watch out for each other the next day.

I headed back to my camp, deep in my thoughts. "What ails you, My Lord?" Bergil saw the look on my face and knew me well enough to know that there was a problem.

"The attack is to be on foot and Earl Waltheof will lead it."

My other leaders had joined me and Ethelred said, "Perhaps the king wishes to get rid of as many Englishmen as he can."

"Why do you say that, Ethelred?"

"Because Waltheof is about as much use as a one-legged man in an arse kicking contest. He was a young man when we fought at Fulford Gate and was the first to run. He was not even there at Stamford Bridge. He is not a warrior. If he falls then it is no loss to the king and removes another who might be a rebel." My gamekeeper was right, his grey hair covered a sharp mind.

"Galmr, you are to lead the men of Durham."

Ethelred brightened, "Then we have a good chance of victory, My Lord." Ethelred and the Varangians got on well together.

I explained the plan to them. They were not as concerned as I was. Even Bergil seemed happy that my men held the right. "We have a forest to our right and if Waltheof fails, as Ethelred seems to think he will, then we can simply filter into the woods."

I nodded but I knew that would mean we had lost the battle and would mean a long winter campaigning. We needed a quick victory and then we could be home by harvest time. I left Galmr and Ethelred to explain to the men who would fight on foot where their positions would be. I went with my men at arms, Bergil, Edward and my Bretons to the camp of the knights of Durham.

"Gather around so that I may explain the king's orders for the morrow."

Our success thus far meant that they did not come quite as despondently as when I had first issued an order. Indeed, some of the youngers ones were actually smiling.

"We are to remain dismounted until our men begin their attack. We mount and wait for the horn. Then we pass through the ranks of the men before us. That will be easier for us than the king and his son. We will pass through our own men. I have my leaders explaining to the men who will fight on foot what is expected of them. It might be better if you sought out your own men. The quicker that we can pass through their ranks the better." I watched their faces as they decided whether or not they would question me. None did. "If we can win tomorrow then the campaign will be over and you can return to your families. You will no longer have to obey the commands of a Norman bastard. Think on that." I saw the looks on some of their faces and knew that Bishop Walcher had used that insult before.

That night the priests sent by Walcher, Bishop of Durham, came to hear our confessions. Men always fought better knowing that their souls had more chance of reaching heaven that way. I wrote a letter to Ealdgyth. I would leave it in my tent. If I died there were things she needed to know and if I survived then I would destroy the letter. I did not trust others to keep watch and so my men and I took it in turns to watch. We each lost three hours of sleep but the sleep we had was a better one knowing that we were safe.

I rose before dawn having had just two hours sleep following my middle watch. I made water and went to the fire where Conan had organised food for our men. Ethelred was cutting up a squirrel and a pigeon that had been brought down the evening before. With a pot of porridge and a stew made from the animals and greens my men, at least, would have fuller bellies than most. Those who thought hungry men fought better would disapprove of my methods but they worked for me. The smell of food being cooked and the hubbub from the fire woke the rest of my men and soon all my men were up and chattering like magpies. There was banter and there was laughter. My men were but a small part of the five hundred men I would lead but I knew that they were the heart of our part of the line.

When we had eaten and as the king's horn sounded for all men to rise, I went with Edward to arm myself. I had dressed every day in mail on this campaign but preparing for battle was different. I did not normally wear chausses about my legs but this day I would. Next Edward held my padded gambeson. Ealdgyth and her ladies had made me a spare and this one was embroidered with my two stars. I had not yet worn it in battle. I could still smell the rosemary and lavender they had used to keep away the smell of must. The hauberk came next and then the coif. After we pulled on my boots we fastened my two scabbards about my back. Some of the young knights of Durham had spoken of some men they had met who had fought in Italy, wearing linen surcoats over their mail. While I realised this would aid identification of friend or foe I was not certain I would ever travel that road. That done I took my helmet and Edward carried my spear and shield. He laid them before me as he went to fetch Scout.

Having risen first I was the only one of my horsemen ready. Ethelred came over. He would not be using a bow. Instead, he looked like a housecarl. He wore a pot helmet and he had a large round shield such as my grandfather had carried. He had a leather jack but the shoulders were covered in mail links. He also had a coif.

"A good day for a battle My Lord." He sniffed the air, "It will be dry today. A man fights better when it is not raining. It is a fairer combat. Slippery ground means too much luck."

"You are not using your bow today?"

He shook his head, "I spoke with Galmr and his Varangians. We have too few mailed men as it is. I may be a greybeard but there is knowledge hidden beneath this silvery cloud." He tapped his head. "It is better that I join them and we defend Elric and the younger warriors." He hesitated, "I know you will do this, My Lord, but I shall feel better if I hear the words spoken by you. If I fall you will keep an eye on Elric."

I shook my head, "You will not die this day and it was I who took on Elric. I am pleased that you have taken him under your wing and into your heart but know that come what may Elric will be cared for by my wife and I."

His beaming smile coincided with the rising of the sun, "Then bring on our foes, My Lord. Ethelred is prepared to show them how an Englishman can fight."

Edward led our horses towards us. One of these days I would have Uhtred make him a shaffron to protect his head. I hung my shield from the cantle. Edward did the same and then he took my spear to hold it. He had a spare ready. Bergil, Conan and my Bretons, followed by my men at arms, joined us. Like me they were all mailed. Unlike me, the Bretons each had a pair of throwing spears.

Bergil mounted his horse to get a better look at the enemy. "It looks like we are facing the Vikings, My Lord and the English are in the centre."

"Is Edgar's banner there?"

"No, My Lord but I see the white horse."

That was the mark of the Godwinsons and Wessex. That meant the last of the rebels had gathered here to fight against King William. The rebellion was not yet over. This might be the last spark to be dampened.

"So the Scots are on the right?"

"Yes, My Lord and their horsemen are gathered behind the Scottish contingent."

Whoever led the enemy, and I guessed it was the Mormaer of Moray, recognised the danger of the loch. Our horsemen could be around it and attack their rear in a heartbeat. The Scottish horsemen were the antidote to that particular poison.

The king's horn had aroused the camp and there was much hustle and bustle. Galmr came over to speak to me, "We are ready, My Lord. You need not fear for the right flank. We will guard our side as carefully as we did the emperor. If we fail it will be because we are dead."

I nodded. Alfred held my banner. He had a stirrup cup attached to his saddle, Aedgar had made it. It meant he would be able to fight and my banner would still fly. "Watch the banner. I will signal if we need to fall back."

"If that happens, My Lord, it will mean we have lost the battle. Let us pray it does not come to that."

He turned and with his shield across his back headed to the three lines of infantry. The front ones held spears. The second rank had axes and swords and the third was led by young Elric with his slingers and his archers. Young as he was he had impressed the other archers on our journey north. His accuracy and power meant that they happily deferred to him.

Our infantry were three solid lines but, as I led my horsemen to join the men of Durham, the three blocks of horsemen could be clearly seen by the enemy. A few of the younger knights cheered as we neared them. We would wait for the king to mount before we did so. Priests stood before our infantry and we all knelt as we were blessed and Te Deum sung. I heard, drifting across the ground between us, the Scottish and Danish versions as our enemies also sought help from God. Who would he favour?

When the priests retreated silence fell. King William's voice gave the command and the lines of infantry moved forward. Earl Waltheof had two shield bearers before him to protect his body. Lord Craven had one of his men at arms leading his men and Galmr led my men. The king must have had the range marked at night for Waltheof suddenly stopped. It was then I saw the three white stones at his feet. He held up his sword and the lines halted to present spears. Thus far he was impressing me. The Scots were just one hundred and fifty paces from him. He lowered his sword and the arrows and stones flew through the air from the archers behind the infantry. The English and the Vikings raised their shields. Some of the Scots were tardy and as stones and war arrows fell, it was the Scots who suffered casualties. I had an idea before the battle that we had more missile men than the enemy and so it proved. The desultory shower of arrows sent in return clattered against shields and no one was struck. The duel lasted for, perhaps fifteen minutes. I saw a dozen Vikings fall from the men we faced but that was all. I was concentrating on my battle. Edward was watching the king for his signals.

Guy d'Honfleur lowered the standard. One of the shield bearers who had been watching for the signal touched Earl Waltheof's shoulder. He pointed his spear and began to march.

Edward said, "The king and his men are mounting."

"Mount."

As soon as I clambered onto Scout's back I had a better view of the field. I saw that perhaps three dozen of the enemy had fallen but they still outnumbered us. Edward handed me my spear and then took his place behind me with Alfred. It was then I noticed that the men of Craven and my men were ahead of those led by Earl Waltheof. He was moving forward but going more slowly than the men on the flanks. Our line began to bow in the middle. The closer the two lines came to each other the greater the effect of the arrows. Some of our men fell. The enemy's horn sounded and their line moved forward. It did not do to take a charge at the standstill. Perhaps the Mormaer of Moray had identified the problem of the bog. Whatever the reason the two lines came together.

It was the white horse standard that precipitated the almost berserk like charge in the middle. It may have been because they saw the reluctance of Earl Waltheof or it may have been a desire to get at King William, but whatever the reason they ran and struck our line before the two flanks were in contact. Our already buckled line reeled and then the two flanks became engaged. I turned my attention to our battle. The Vikings, I could not tell if they were Norse, Men of the Isles or Danes, were fighting ferociously. Against the fyrd they had little opposition but the stiffening of my men was helping to hold that line. That, allied to the arrows and stones sent by Elric and his archers, ensured that we were holding but only just. I desperately wanted to intervene but our orders were to wait for the horn.

It was as I watched that I saw, to my horror, Ethelred, who was fighting as gamely and bravely as any surrounded by enemies. His age and his stiffness were his undoing. He was speared in the thigh and his shield arm drooped exposing his body. It was then I saw the scarred warrior who had fled from the ambush at Forlan's farm. He now wielded an axe and as another warrior rammed his spear into Ethelred's shoulder Scarred Face swung his axe to split the ancient pot helmet and Ethelred's skull in one blow.

Even above the din and crash of battle I heard Elric's strangled cry of, "No!"

Ethelred's death left a hole but Galmr quickly marshalled his fellow Varangians into the gap and they began to rhythmically swing their axes in what appeared to be long lazy circles. It held the enemy, albeit briefly, but I knew that we could not hold. Earl Waltheof's retreat was now putting pressure on the left side of the men of Durham. There was a danger that the solid line could be broken and if it did so then we were all doomed.

I looked over to King William and saw his lieutenants pointing to the danger. He nodded and spoke to his cornicen. Pre-empting the command I knew was forthcoming I shouted, "Men of Durham, prepare to charge! I was anticipating the order and as I lowered my spear and dug my spurs into Scout the horn sounded. A number of things happened at once.

The right side of Earl Waltheof's line crumbled and men fled, leaving a hole. The men of Durham, realising that they were exposed, turned to their left to present shields to the Danes and rebels who eagerly turned. It meant that, as I led my horsemen, there was a gap and I exploited it. My men and I had started early and with Scout's power and speed we soon formed a wedge. It was unintentional but perfect for such an attack. I skewered a rebel in the side and threw his body from my spear as I pulled back to strike again. The next man to die was a Dane and I managed to spear him in the neck. The warrior I was looking for was Ethelred's killer, the Dane with the scarred face. As more Durham knights joined us so the wedge grew and like a woodsman splitting a log we burst through the Danes and the rebels. One moment they had been on the cusp of victory and the next moment the spears and lances of the knights of Durham and Eisicewalt were in their backs. We were attacking both the English and the Vikings.

The roar from Galmr seemed to put heart into the wavering fyrd and they pushed back at the Vikings. He and his Varangians swung their axes to great effect. I cared not what was going on elsewhere. I was going to kill the Dane who had slain Ethelred. I struck with my spear so many times that I lost count of the wounds I inflicted. All the while Scout was powering towards the heart of the enemy warband and shield wall. When the spear's head finally broke I was within a few paces of the Dane who was whirling his axe in an arc before him. I drew my sword and, as Scout was still moving quickly, gave him the command to jump. His hind legs were powerful and they launched us in the air. His fore hooves smashed into the helmets and skulls of some of the men between the Dane and me. A metal helmet availed them little against his hooves and weight. I slashed with my sword as I was in the air and another warrior fell.

There was a wail and those to the left of me simply turned and fled. The English had broken. I heard Conan shout, "Men of Durham, after them!"

Scout landed on the back of a warrior who had no idea his death would be so swift. I heard his back crack as it was broken. Scarred Face turned and swung his axe. There was a danger that he might hurt my horse and I would not have that. I flipped my sword in the air and holding its tip threw it at the Dane, like a dagger. Taillefer had taught me the trick and it was right that I should use it to save the life of one of Parsifal's heirs. It struck Scarred Face squarely in his forehead and the axe fell from his lifeless hands. I drew a second sword and whirled Scout.

The enemy were fleeing. King William and his knights had hacked the last of the rebels to pieces and were now turning their attention to the Scots. Already the Mormaer of Moray was fleeing as fast as his horse could take him. His oathsworn were mounted and they followed him. He had held his own against the men of Craven but the battle was lost. The fighting was over and from the tiny number of rebels who were fleeing, so was the rebellion, at least here in the north.

The Durham knights were in the distance as, like hunters seeking prey, they chased down the men whom we had broken. The men from Durham who had fought on foot were scavenging from the bodies of the dead but my men were either gathered around or heading towards the body of Ethelred. So far as I could see, as I approached, he was the only casualty we had suffered but he would be a great loss. Elric was cradling the old man's mangled head in his arms and I saw the tears running down his face. He was now a young man rather than a youth but inside he was still almost a boy. He had lost his family and now he had lost the man who had become his new family. I knew just how close Ethelred and the orphan had been. I prayed that he would get over the loss. I dismounted and took off my helmet. Edward took Scout's reins and I knelt.

Elric looked up at me. His eyes were pools, "He should not have been here, My Lord. He should have stayed at home and watched your land."

His words were almost accusatory. I nodded, "But he wanted to come, Elric. He was a warrior. The men with whom he fought at Gate Fulford all died. When I found him he was a shell of a man, the husk of an acorn taken by animals. The man who trained you was given a second chance of life and he took it. Remember him, that is good, but do not waste time in melancholic mourning for he would not want that. You, too, have been granted a second chance of life. Grasp it with both hands. Live your life as Ethelred would wish you to. His soul is but a little way above our heads and I know that he will watch over you."

Galmr put his hand on Elric's shoulder, "He died well, Elric. I did not know him much until we came north but on the road I often spoke to him. He was a warrior. He yearned for this fight. He did not wish to die, no man, except a berserker does, but he died knowing that he was keeping the enemy from you. He fought as he did to protect you."

"Me?"

"Aye," Bergil smiled, "he always watched over you. We talked often, back at Eisicewalt and I know that since you came to our manor you gave him a new lease of life. He saw you as the grandson he never had. Come, we will honour this brave old warrior, here, far from his home. You shall take his sword, not to use, but in remembrance of him."

He was helped to his feet and the body of Ethelred was hefted by the three Varangians and Bergil. I took Ethelred's sword and placed it in Elric's hands. We walked towards a small stand of trees by the little burn that bubbled towards the Forth. The men of the manor used their swords to dig a grave. The turf was first removed and then they dug. The soil was soft and any stones they found as they dug were placed to the side. The Varangians wrapped Ethelred's cloak about his body and laid him in the grave. Elric rammed the old man's sword point first into the earth and then knelt to kiss the old man. He refolded the cloak and then placed the shield over the face and chest of Ethelred of Fulford Gate. The earth was placed over the body and then the stones. Finally, my men marched back and forth over the grave to flatten it before the turf was replaced. We wanted no one, neither animal nor man, to disturb the resting place of an honoured warrior.

That done we stood in a circle around the grave. I took out my sword and held it above me like a cross, "Lord, take this man to your bosom. He was a good man and he died well. Ethelred was the heart of Eisicewalt and leaves a void that will be hard to fill. Know that we shall do so by striving to be as he was. Amen."

"Amen."

No one moved for a while. Edward came close to me and said, in my ear, "Sir Richard, the king is returning."

I nodded, "Bergil, have the men see if there is anything worth taking from the dead."

Elric said, "Archers, let us do as Ethelred would have done and seek shafts and arrows that can be reused." His voice sounded firmer than it had. There was resolution in his eyes and he had purpose once more. He fastened the baldric around his waist and put Ethelred's sword into the scabbard.

I walked flanked by Edward and Bergil. Behind me came the Bretons and then the Varangians. We had been a small number on the battlefield and yet we had acquitted ourselves more than well. When I spoke to the king my head would be held high.

One of my men came over with the sword I had thrown at Scarred Face. I nodded my thanks and slid it into my scabbard. Taillefer's training had paid off once more.

Chapter 17

We camped at the battlefield. The dead were burned but the funeral pyre was placed so that the smell of the burning flesh was taken east, towards the fleeing Scots. It would be a reminder of their defeat. Less than a hundred of the Scots had been killed in the battle and we had lost just forty but there were many others who were wounded. Ours would be healed. The Scottish losses would make it hard to muster another army to face us. The bulk of their losses had been amongst the rebels and the men who came from the isles, Denmark or Norway. We had not lost a single knight.

The king, however, was not in a good mood as he held a council of war. I think part of the reason was that Gospatric had escaped. He had fled early. "Earl Waltheof, this is the first time I have fought alongside you. It seemed to me, from my vantage point behind your lines, that you and your oathsworn did not have your heart in the battle. You fell back too quickly."

The warrior was a little shamefaced. I am still uncertain if he was a coward, a poor warrior or, as he said, a man who was divided, "My Lord, it is hard to fight men alongside whom you have fought in a shield wall."

It was the wrong thing to say and the king almost jumped down his throat as he roared, "You now fight for me! I am the King of England. Edgar is nothing. Your cousin is nothing. When we meet with King

Malcolm, Edgar's exile will be uppermost in my mind."

Sir Gilbert, standing next to me, murmured, "Execution would suit better than exile."

Out of the corner of my mouth I said, "The king does not want a martyr."

King William said, "Your brave behaviour on the battlefield, Sir Richard, does not excuse this interruption."

"I am sorry, My Lord."

"We leave on the morrow and head for Scone. It is clear that is where the Scots are gathering. Earl Waltheof, you can lead the way with your Englishmen and see if you can remove the bad taste of your flight from my mouth."

"Yes, King William."

The road to Scone was marked with the hastily buried bodies of those who had fled the battle. Men had succumbed to their wounds and their comrades had given them a hasty burial. Elric now rode with us. He was no longer needed as a scout. We had taken horses after the battle and my men were well mounted. We were all mounted before but now we had horses for our war gear. I saw Elric looking at the small mounds of earth that we passed. He was thinking that Ethelred's was a better grave. It was unmarked but any one of us could have found it quickly.

No one opposed us but, as we neared Abernethy, just a mile and a half from the Firth of Tay, two Scottish knights approached. King William and his son were well guarded and no one thought that these were assassins but every knight was alert. I was not privy to their conversation but when they turned and headed for the village, the king waved us forward.

"We will make a camp here. The enemy wish to talk."

The tents and standards told us that we had found King Malcolm. As we neared the encampment I looked for the flags of Edgar but I saw none. Nor did I spy any Vikings. There were many Scots but not enough to threaten us. It was clear, from the off, that they were suing for peace and doing so from a position of weakness. Our taking of Berwick, Dunbar and our victories at the skirmish on the Tweed and the Forth had been enough. It was at that moment I realised that I could be home within a month or two.

There were three burns, the Tarduff, Nethy and the Baillo. They formed three sides of our camp. King William was a warrior and he ever had an eye for defence. Our horses had grazing and water and we were safe from an assassin's blade. If the Scottish planned treachery then we could easily forestall it. We had taken animals and food on our way north. The king had the cattle we had taken butchered and cooked. It was a statement. We dined well and the Scots did not. I was invited to dine with the king at the tables his men took from the nearby farms. I was seated next to his son.

The king's son had changed since we had first met. His only real combats had been in the skirmish on the Tweed and the charge against the rebels but both had helped to make him a warrior. Like the other sons of the king, he had been trained in the martial arts but a warrior's real training came in battle. The practised sweeps and slashes of the training ground were nothing compared with the chaos of battle where men's swords, spears and axes could come from any direction. He quizzed me about our part of the battle. The enemy we had fought were a stiffer test than the rebels they had routed and he was anxious to know how we managed to defeat them.

"A mixture, My Lord, of good men with bows and slings, protected by stout warriors with shields and mail."

"You have more men in your small retinue who are mailed than other lords."

"That is deliberate, My Lord. I could have brought more men but I did not wish to risk losing them. We took some mail from the dead and that, when we return to Eisicewalt, will mean I have more men who can be protected in battle. I pay good warriors like Conan and Galmr for professionals are always better than the fyrd. My Bretons and Varangians do not toil in my fields, they practise for war. My line did not buckle as some did because of their stiffening."

I enjoyed the food and the conversation for William was clearly keen to learn all that he could about how to make war.

The next day I was invited, with Earl Waltheof, the Lord of Craven and the king's son to attend the peace talks. The talks were one sided. King William made all the demands. King Malcolm was in no position to question them. I studied the Scottish lords who faced us and realised that one was missing. The Mormaer of Moray was not amongst them. He had fled the field and, presumably, continued his flight north to Moray.

The king listened to King Malcolm who accepted that he had lost and hoped for clemency from King William. King William nodded, “We are in a benign mood, King Malcolm, but we have demands that must be met before any further discussions can take place.”

“Of course.”

“Edgar Ætheling must be sent from this land. He cannot stay on this island nor at your court.”

King Malcolm had married Edgar’s sister and his face showed that he did not like the request but he nodded, “Agreed.”

“Gospatric must be handed over to me for punishment.”

King Malcolm spread his hands, “He did not come from the battlefield. I know not where he is but I will have him apprehended and brought to you if he seeks succour.”

The king nodded, “You will swear allegiance to me and give me fealty.” The king spoke slowly so that King Malcolm was in no doubt, “I am your liege lord.”

There was a pause and King Malcolm nodded.

“Say it.”

“I swear that King William of England is my liege lord.”

“Fetch a Bible. I would have this sworn properly.”

There was a delay as a Bible was brought. I saw the anger on the faces of some of the Scottish lords and wondered if this oath would cause King Malcolm problems. In the short term that would not affect England but if King Malcolm should be removed then it might. When the oath was sworn on the Bible, King William nodded. "And hostages." He pointed at the king's son, Duncan, "your son for one and then others whom I will let you choose." It did not matter who the others were but we all knew that they would be from important members of the king's household. King Malcolm was also given lands in Cumbria. That was clever on the part of King William as it further reinforced his fealty to England.

It took some hours for the treaty to be written and for it to be signed and witnessed. It was late in the afternoon when we returned to our camp. The king said nothing to me but he and his son, along with the Lord of Craven, had their heads together.

The next morning the hostages were brought. They had, of course, servants with them. King Malcolm bade farewell to his son. The twelve-year-old looked to be confused. King William's son, William, showed a kind side to him. As King Malcolm left William went to the youth and spoke to him. The Scottish prince smiled. It was a start. When the Scots left I was summoned by the king.

"Sir Richard, you have served me well and I release you from service. You may return to England. When you reach the fleet tell the fleet commander to sail here to the Tay. We will return to England from Perth."

"Yes, My Lord."

"As a reward for your service you are granted the title of baron."

"Thank you, My Lord." It meant I could now knight others. I also knew that baron meant king's man and I was tied even more closely to King William than before.

We moved more quickly on our return for we were all well mounted with spare horses. Aedgar would be pleased as we had managed to secure a good mare and she could be used for breeding. The company was also stronger. There was no need for Bergil to chastise those who were inattentive or over boisterous. The battle and Ethelred's death had changed them. For the young men from the manor it was the end of an era. They had known Ethelred before I came. They had seen the transformation I had wrought and now that rock had been taken. I knew that each of the warriors would be reflecting on their own mortality. Death could have come to any of them. But for the heroic actions of Galmr and his Varangians then the hole left by Ethelred could have been exploited.

I hailed the nearest ship and was taken aboard. The captain sailed us to the commander of the king's fleet and I gave him his orders.

He was pleased to be leaving the anchorage and he agreed to transport my retinue over the Forth. I was relieved. It was my reputation which had secured us the passage and saved us a long journey back to the battlefield and across the river at the bridge of Stirling. The peace had been signed but who knew what grudges the Scots might harbour? In time all would be forgotten but the raw taste of defeat would still be upon Scottish lips.

It took time to both embark and then disembark men and horses. Fortunately, the crossing was brief. We camped at the village of Leith before leaving the next day for our journey home. Once we passed Durham I contemplated heading for Norton. I dismissed the idea almost as soon as it came to me.

We had too many recently married men who would wish to be with their families. I was amongst that number. I knew that, before autumn, I would have to travel north but the swiftness of the campaign meant we could have the rest of August in Eisicewalt.

What I did do, as we camped at the ruined Roman fort at Persebrig was to mention my plans to my men. “When we have gathered in the harvest I will be taking some of you north to Norton. My manor there needs work.” I paused, “I will also be asking one of you to become my steward and castellan.”

Conan asked, “Is there a castle, My Lord?”

“No, but there is no reason why one should not be built.”

Galmr said, “I have visited that part of the world, My Lord. It is not good farming country.”

“I know, Galmr, but the king gave it to me and I have a duty.”

Edward said, “Remember the bishop, My Lord. He was unhappy that you married Lady Ealdgyth and Norton is his manor.”

“I know and I also know that the danger from the east and the sea wolves is real. I will not command any to take on this task. It is why I will take all of you with me. If none of you choose this burden then I have another in mind.” Ivo de Vesi was keen to have a manor and he might accept the position.

My words had an effect for all were silent for the rest of the evening. As we rode south towards my home I saw my three Varangians speaking together. I knew it would be about the prospect of leaving Eisicewalt. The three were shield brothers and I knew that if one chose the position then the rest would. Of course, they would not make a decision until they had seen Norton. I was unsurprised that my four Bretons kept apart and said nothing to each other. They were different. Conan and Robert were now married and they had wives to consult. I knew that Edward and Bergil were in the same position.

We were seen on the road and like dandelion seeds on the wind news of our imminent arrival reached the manor before we did. The result was a warm welcome with wives and servants all gathered in the yard to greet us.

Aedgar's sons came to take our horses which allowed Edward and Mathilde to be reunited. The young men from the village had all dropped off as we passed their homes and so it was just my familia who were greeted in my yard. It was Ealdgyth who noticed the missing man. After she had hugged and kissed me, ignoring the stink of horse and sweat, she looked around and the beaming smile left her face, "Richard, did Ethelred go directly to his home?" Then she saw a lonely figure. It was Elric who was unfastening Ethelred's sword from his horse. "No!"

I nodded, "He was our only loss but it was a heavy one."

She left me and hurried to Elric. He turned as he saw her approach. She held out her arms and, leaving the sword fastened to the saddle he fell into her arms and sobbed. The sound of his cries made the joy of our reunion vanish like morning mist. Benthe who had been greeting her sons said, "My Lord?"

Alfred said, "Mother, it is Ethelred, he died."

In an instant the happiness and euphoria of our return disappeared. Everyone in the manor had held

Ethelred in the highest regard. There would be a hole that would be hard to fill. Ealdgyth insisted that Elric eat with us. He would sleep in the warrior hall but she was concerned about him. I had married a kind and thoughtful woman. We assiduously avoided talking about the campaign and, instead, focussed on the manor and what had happened since we had left. Animals and babies had been born. Some of the early crops had been harvested and work had begun on a new dwelling for Robert and Maud. They had not complained about living in the warrior hall but seeing Dervilla and Conan in the hall was a reminder of the privacy they did not enjoy.

When she had finished I brought up the thorny question of Norton. “When the crops are largely in I will take my familia to Norton. The king’s campaign has meant I did not get back there as quickly as I would have wished. I promised Algar I would be there by Spring and we are half a year late already.”

She nodded and when I hesitated to continue she asked, “And…I know there is more to come forth. Speak.”

I glanced at Elric but he was far away. I think he was reminiscing about Ethelred.

“We need one of my warriors to manage the manor for me.”

She was a clever young woman and made the connects immediately. “Then Dervilla might leave.”

“She might.” I sighed, “Any one of them could go: Edward, Bergil, Galmr.”

“And Beth has set her sights on Galmr. I am not sure I like this change.”

“It may not be a change.”

"Norton is far from here. Whoever you send would be uprooted from this manor. We are all happy here."

"It might be that none of them choose the task and then I will have to think of another. I have told them all that I will not force any man to leave Eisicewalt."

"You are a good man, Richard."

Elric said, "My Lord, My Lady, I beg to be excused. I am normally abed by this time."

"Of course."

He hesitated, "Sir Richard, now that Ethelred is not here who…"

"Ethelred always saw you as his successor, Elric. As far as I am concerned you are the gamekeeper."

"And does that position include Ethelred's cottage?"

"It does but…"

My wife stood, "You cannot be alone. You need people around you."

"I would take the cottage, My Lord." He smiled, "I will have the spirit of Ethelred with me. I am happy to have the cottage and fear not for me, my lady. Ethelred trained me well and he prepared me for this day. He knew that he had almost run his course and the candle was spluttering. His death came earlier than we thought but it was not unexpected, only the manner in which he was slain. I am stronger than you know. I am made by Ethelred and he was the strongest man I ever knew."

"Then take the cottage."

"I will make the move tomorrow. I will tell the others this night. I would not like them to think I shunned them but I must be my own man."

The next week saw us working but it was as though there had been a shift of some kind. There were arguments and the training saw some accidents that there should not have been. It was mainly the Varangians but the Bretons also clashed. Father Gregory was the one who gave me a hint as to the cause of the problem. I was taking my weekly walk through the village when he arrested me. "I need to have a word, Sir Richard."

Once inside the quiet church I said, "Is there a problem?"

"There may be. I cannot break the sanctity of the confessional but I can direct you to where there may be something that you need to address." He paused and said, "Speak to Galmr."

It suddenly became clear. The heart of all the confrontations and accidents had been Galmr. I saw it now.

When I reached the manor I found him alone in the warrior hall. I decided to be casual, "Galmr, I seek company. Would you walk with me through the woods? Elric is not in his new home and I wish to see how he fares."

"Of course, My Lord." Travelling through woods alone could be dangerous. Men had been accidentally hurt by hunters. We headed along the path that led to the woods. I decided to be blunt. I was not a diplomat, "Galmr, is something troubling you?"

We were almost at the trees and he stopped, "Why do you ask, My Lord?"

"Because the training this week has not gone well and I think that something is on your mind."

He nodded and looked relieved to be able to unburden himself, "There is, My Lord. My shield brothers and I are oathsworn, to each other as well as to you." He hesitated, "I have become smitten by young Beth. I know I am older than she is but she seems to like me."

I was bewildered, "Then all is good and you should be a happy man."

"But if we wed, as we both hope to be, then what of my shield brothers?"

"You are not a monk and neither are they. You are men and men seek female companionship." I smiled, "I am older than Ealdgyth but that has not stood in our way."

"But you are the lord of the manor."

I could not see the problem but then I had never travelled to the east and back. I had not fought for the Byzantine Empire. The bonds between these three would be strong. "Have you spoken to Folki and Haldir?"

He shook his head, "I would not know how to begin."

"They are your oath brothers as well as your family. Just speak what is on your mind and seek their opinion."

"And if they oppose the marriage?"

"Do you think they will?"

"I do not know."

"Whatever happens, Galmr, I need the three of you as warriors. That will not change. I could do with a dozen more like you. Your employment will not cease because you are wed."

When I saw the relief on his face then I understood that I had been part of the problem but he had not known how to broach the matter.

"Then I will speak to them. Thank you, My Lord." He paused, "And I know that you are waiting for an answer so I will give it to you now. I am happy to be the one who runs Norton for you. It will, of course, depend on what we find when we are there. I will not put my new bride into danger. You should know that Beth is also happy for she would have her own home. If Folki and Haldir choose not to come with us then I will understand. I will be disappointed but I will live with that."

Just then Elric ghosted from the trees. He had a couple of magpies hanging from his belt. I was unsure if he had overheard us or not. He had his normal inscrutable expression. The only time I had seen it change had been after Ethelred's death and when Ealdgyth had comforted him.

He tapped the birds, "I do not mind a few magpies, My Lord, but Ethelred always said to keep down their numbers. They can cause havoc amongst other birds. We can add them to the pot."

"Good, we shall return to the hall, eh?"

Chapter 18

Galmr spoke to his brother and cousin. They approved of his choice of bride and, more importantly, supported the idea of his taking on the manor of Norton, if it proved suitable. I was relieved.

Galmr and Beth were betrothed but the wedding would have to wait until we had returned from the north. That was largely the doing of the women of my manor who wanted time to plan the event. They knew that it might be the last time that they saw Beth. Both Ealdgyth and Dervilla felt a certain responsibility towards Beth and they wanted to do right by her.

I left Elric at home. His skills would not be needed. I did, however, take my men at arms, Bretons, Varangians, squire and Bergil. The men left in the village would be more than capable of defending it should danger arrive. The rebellion appeared to be over for the moment. Ely was now secure. The Welsh borders were also in King William's hands and he felt so safe that he and his sons returned to Normandy to stamp their authority on that land.

As I lay with Ealdgyth in our bed I told her my plans, "Algar and Ragnar are both good warriors and leaders but I am not sure that they have the skills needed to protect the people there from danger."

"But you drove the raiders hence the last time you were there."

"As we discovered in Scotland the north is still the place that the men from the icy wastes in the east choose to raid. Bishop Walcher has yet to build a castle and Bamburgh is far to the north. Until King William builds castles then the land will need strong men to protect them. I intend to spend just a month there. In that time we can make Norton defensible and, I hope, have a leader who will choose to stay there. Galmr has indicated he might take it on but it depends upon what we find there."

She was silent for a while and then she said, "You have not been here overmuch, Richard. Is this our future? Will you be called upon to ride and protect others?"

"I will be truthful. I do not know. My life has changed since I met you, for the better, I might add. I need to come to terms with the task appointed to me by the king."

She sighed, "I have chosen this life, Richard, and I will live with the consequences but I would rather you were by my side than facing death and danger far from here." I wondered how that might be achieved.

We knew the journey well and an early start was not necessary. It would be a two-day ride. It would take a day to get to Persebrig and another to get to Norton. We would not use the river for I did not like the men who lived at Stockadeton. I rode Geoffrey for Aedgar wished to breed from both Scout and an ageing Parsifal. We had mares who were ready to be covered and the two of them would ensure good stock. Neither of us were sure how long Taillefer's old horse had left and my horse master and I wanted his strength and seed in as many mares as we could.

I was pleased that Galmr and his shield brothers were more at ease with one another. It taught me that a man should be honest with those alongside whom he fights. Galmr had hidden his thoughts and fears within and that had threatened the integrity of their bond.

I spent more time speaking with Edward as we rode north. Like Galmr he had been wrestling with inner conflict and he chose the ride through the vale of York to unburden himself. "My Lord, now that I am a father I am not sure that it is right for me to be your squire."

"Why?"

"I have no intention of seeking my spurs. My time with you has taught me that I will not choose that road. It is better that you have another who wishes for spurs." He nodded ahead, "Both Aethelstan and Alfred would relish the position."

I knew that they would but that might cause a problem. If I chose one then what would the other think? Both of them were now married. Would my two men arms feel as Edward did? I knew that I was different. I had not had any female entanglement until Ealdgyth. I did not view her as an entanglement but if Taillefer were alive then he would have. He saw the life of a warrior almost as a monkish existence. I was not the same.

"My Lord?"

I had not been aware that I had been silent. I turned to Edward and smiled, "Forgive me, Edward, I was wrapped in my thoughts. Of course you may leave my service. The problem of a squire is a minor one. Both Aethelstan and Alfred can continue to be men at arms and do as you have done. Once we have visited Norton then we will have a winter of peace." A sudden thought struck me, "Is it that you wish the manor of Norton?"

He shook his head, "No, My Lord. I can tell you that now. I have seen it and it holds no appeal. Had you ordered me to take it I would have done so but you wanted a volunteer and that will not be me."

"Then what would you and Mathilde choose for your life?"

"After Aed died his parents lost heart. I have spoken to them and they wish to move to York where they have family. They have told me that there are too many ghosts in the village. Every young man they see become a father is a reminder of what they will not have. I would buy their farm. I have, thanks to you, gold and I would rather they enjoyed it."

"The farm is on my land. If they leave I would give it to you."

"And that is kind but I would feel happier if I gave them gold. Call it weregeld, if you like."

"Then all is well." I looked at him askance, "A farmer?"

He nodded, "A farmer who raises horses too. I have seen the results of Aedgar's work and I think I could do the same. They would not be war horses but men need riding horses too."

As we rode over the Roman Bridge over the Tees I reflected that my life was changing once more. I was used to Edward and he knew my ways. It might be hard to go to war without him behind me.

Approaching Norton from the west meant that the first place we came upon was Rag's Worthy. As soon as we reined in we knew that there was trouble for

Ragnar and his sons, Ragnar and Walter, emerged from hiding and they were armed.

I dismounted, "Trouble, Ragnar?"

"Yes, My Lord." He pointed towards Norton, "Two months since warriors came by boat. They were Vikings. They drove Algar of Belasis and his people from the village and took it over."

"Warriors?"

He shook his head and I saw anger in his eyes, "They call themselves Vikings but they are plunderers. They have recently sent to me here to try to take tribute from us." His eyes flared, "We sent them hence but we go about armed. We have worked here too long to have what we own be taken by others."

I said, "We will stay the night and then, in the morning, I will ride to these men and speak to them. How many are there?"

"They came in just one ship. There are roughly thirty of them. Their drekar is beached on the banks of the Tees. It suffered damage on the voyage here."

I turned to my men, "Dismount. See to the horses and then we will hold a council of war."

His wife Elfrida said, "Our home is too small, My Lord. If you used the barn it would be more comfortable. I will bring food and ale."

Bergil, Conan and Galmr came over to me as the horses were led away. I shook my head, "This was not expected."

Galmr said, "My Lord, two months since is about the time we fought against the Mormaer. Could these be warriors who fled the battle?"

I nodded, "It is quite likely. The journey takes days on a horse but from the Forth to here would take but a day and a night with favourable winds." If I had called in on the way back from Scotland this might have been averted. I had been too eager to get home. The deviation would only have added a few days and…Hindsight was always perfect.

We headed into the barn. We had our coistrels filled and then I spoke, "Ragnar, how many men are there close to here who could fight?"

"There are us three and then there is Ulric who lived at Rus' Worthy. He is old, My Lord." He shook his head. "Just us three."

"Then we cannot count on him. Did Algar lose men in the attack?"

Ragnar grinned, "He spied their ship and took his people away. The drekar had shields along the side and we all know what that means."

"And he is back in his marshes?"

"He is."

I turned to Conan. "When I visit Norton on the morrow I would have you, Conan, ride to the marshes and make contact with Algar. I hope I can persuade these raiders to leave but if not then we shall have to use force to evict them."

Ragnar emptied his beaker, "My Lord, they will not leave quietly. They have homes and there are woods where they can hunt. They have people like me to provide them with food. They will act like warlords. They will not leave peacefully."

"Then we will use force." I looked around at my handful of men. I led ten men. Ragnar had three and two of them were youths. Even if all of Algar's people came we would still be well outnumbered. This would take careful planning. The others all debated our strategy but I was silent as I came up with a plan. I would try to use the law to remove them but if Ragnar was right then there was no reason why they should obey me. I now saw why the manor had been given to me. King William was trying to impose his law on the land. That he had rid himself of those who had lived here was an irrelevance now. While the visit would be a fruitless one I would use it to scout out their defences.

I took, despite the objections from all the others, just my squire and my two men at arms to speak to the raiders. I wanted these men to underestimate us. I did not intend to fight but we went armed and mailed. As we left Rag's Worthy, I warned the three of them, "At the first sign of trouble we turn and run. If they think we are cowards I care not. Keep your eyes open. I need their defences identifying and their numbers ascertaining."

Edward said, "You do not think that they will agree to leave, My Lord?"

I shook my head, "If these are men who fled the battle then there is no reason to think that they will but I have to try. The law is the law and King William has made me Lord of Norton to bring rule and order to this land. They may just be the start. If they can cling on to Norton then they will send for others and the threat will grow. We have to rid the land of this pestilence."

"Yet, My Lord, this land is in the Palatinate. Should the bishop not do this?"

"He should and if we fail then we will ride to Durham and ask for his help."

Alfred said, "But you do not think he will give it to you."

"No, Alfred. The wound is too raw. In the fullness of time the bishop will realise that his dream of setting up the Mormaer of Moray as a threat to King Malcolm was a foolish one. No, for the moment it is we who will have to deal with the problem."

I did not take my banner for I was not sure if the Vikings would regard it as anything other than a trophy. My shield hung over my leg but my squire and men at arms held theirs over their left sides. No one was working the fields around the village. The palisade had only been partly repaired, there was a gate and a hedgehog of trees that ran for forty paces on either side of them. Algar must have made a start but it had not been enough. There was more smoke rising from the homes in the village. This time more than one home was occupied. We were, of course, seen but there was no sound of alarm. Instead the Vikings emerged from the houses with swords, axes and spears. A couple had donned helmets. I counted their numbers as we approached. They all appeared to be men and at a rough count there were twenty-six of them. There would be others watching their ship. Ragnar's assessment had been correct.

I reined in forty paces from the gates which were open. The palisade on either side was the only part which had been repaired. I guessed that this was the work of Algar for the raiders would not have had time to complete as much of the wall. I took off my helmet and hung it from my cantle. I did not know much Norse or Danish and so I spoke in English.

"I am Sir Richard fitz Malet and this is my manor. Who are you?"

The men looked at each other blankly and one said something back to me. This would be more difficult than I had imagined. One of the men turned his head and shouted. Three men emerged from a house. They were all dressed in mail. The others were not. The one who was flanked by the others appeared to be the leader. Certainly the other two were a step behind him. He held a long Danish axe in his right hand. On his head he had a helmet adorned with two small wings. I vaguely remembered such a helmet at the battle where Ethelred had fell. It might mean nothing but, if true, it partly confirmed my belief that these were some of the survivors of the battle.

He reached me and I repeated my words, "I am Sir Richard fitz Malet and this is my manor. Who are you?"

The man laughed and took off his helmet. I saw that he was tattooed about the face and his hair was long and golden, hanging over his shoulders. When he spoke it was in heavily accented English, "You are wrong. This was the manor of Bersi Steanasson. He was given this manor by the father of the true King of England, King Sweyn of Denmark. I am Haraldr Fair Hair and I claim this land for myself and for Denmark."

"And both King Cnut and Bersi Steanasson are dead. This land is no longer Danish, it belongs to King William and he has given me this manor. You are related to this Bersi Steanasson?"

He shook his head, "I know of him. This is mine by right of possession. There were none here when we came and we are taking back what was given to a countryman of ours."

"There were people here but you drove them off." I pointed towards the sea, "I will give you one day to leave this village, take your ship and return to your homeland."

He in turn pointed, not a hand, but his axe at me, "I saw you when the weak-willed Mormaer of Moray fled. Had he had the courage to stay then your head would now be separated from your shoulders. We lost many fine warriors that day and this is weregeld for them. You have three boys with you. Try to take it back and we shall wear your mail and ride your horses."

I nodded, "One day is all that you have and then I will take back my manor and any who are found here will die. Take your ship while you can, Haraldr Fair Hair." I had chosen my words carefully and I saw a frown flicker over his face.

I wheeled my horse around and headed back to Rag's Worthy. The arrow that was sent at me was well aimed but it struck me squarely in the back. It meant that, like the crossbow bolt, it struck my scabbards; I was wearing mail as well as the two scabbards and it was even less effective. I turned and shouted, "You have no honour but I do. I still give you one day." I saw the Dane strike the young bowman who had clearly disobeyed his order. It was a victory for me.

When we neared Rag's Worthy Edward said, "There are many of them, My Lord. Can we drive them hence?"

What he was really asking me was how many of our men would die when we retook it. "What they fear is not our numbers but being stranded here. They do not think we can retake it. However, I do not think this man is a fool and he knows that if I were to raise an army then he could be defeated. His ship is his lifeline, I threatened his ship. He will have more men guarding it now. That means fewer men to fight."

"You have no intention of destroying his ship, Sir Richard?"

"No, Alfred. I want their ship whole so that they can leave this land. When we do attack it will be at night and darkness will mask our numbers. Like the Scots we use the land to aid our attack. They will guard the gate and the wall. We will approach from the river."

We entered the farm. Galmr and his Varangians were with Ragnar. "Well, My Lord?"

"They are Danes, Galmr, and they fought against us." I turned to Ragnar, "They say that they claim the land of Bersi Steanasson."

Ragnar shook his head, "From what I remember of those who lived there, they felt part of England and did not regard themselves as Danish."

"We need Algar and his men. I also need the men of Stockadeton."

Ragnar shook his head, "You will be lucky if they fight. They look after themselves and care not what happens beyond their palisade."

"Then tomorrow I will ride there and see if I can use King William's name to encourage them to take arms." We needed numbers.

Conan returned after dark. He had taken a spare horse and Algar rode with him. The headman of the village dismounted and took my proffered arm, "You returned."

"I said I would."

"Had you come sooner then we would not be living like animals in the marshes."

"That was out of my hands." I shrugged thinking of my mistake, "Perhaps the sisters were spinning. I am here now. Did you suffer any losses when they came?"

"A few scratches, that is all." He looked around, "This is all that you brought? It is not enough."

"You may be right in one respect, Algar of Belasis. We might not have the numbers but what I have brought is quality. Only three of their men were mailed. The men of my familia are all protected by metal links. Ragnar and his sons will fight. That gives us fifteen. Will you and your people fight?"

"We wear no mail but we enjoyed the brief time we lived in houses. We will fight. There are eight of us now who can fight for others came when we invested Norton."

I nodded, "That may be enough but I will ride to Stockadeton tomorrow to enlist as many of their men as I can. Bring all your people here tomorrow. Take a route which goes nowhere near to the Danes."

Ragnar said, "The road that runs through the empty hamlet of Wulfestun is the best way. The forest there is thick and the ghosts of the dead will protect you." There was a story there but this was not the time to hear it.

"And then, Sir Richard?"

"I have given them one day. They will expect us to attack quickly. I intend to make them wait an extra day and then, on the second night, we will attack when they are weary from watching. I want their nerves stretched and for them to fear an attack on their ship. I will go into detail tomorrow. Do you need an escort back to your people?"

He shook his head, "This is my land and I know it well." He clasped my hand. "We have practised with the weapons you left for us. Let us see if we can put them to good use." He sprang on to the back of the horse he had been loaned and galloped off.

The next day I took my Bretons along with my squire and men at arms when I went to Stockadeton. I wanted to make an impression. I also had Alfred unfurl my banner. The last time I had been here my welcome had been lukewarm at best. I would use the authority of the king.

Stockadeton was named for the hedgehog of wood that ran around its perimeter. It was not a large enclosure but that was a good thing. It could be more easily defended. The last time I had been here I had spoken to a priest. This time I would appeal to the men of the town. We rode through the gates and we dismounted. We led our horses to the water trough that stood in the centre of the town. The green or common area lay closer to the well of St John where there was a church. The trough was outside the most substantial house in the town. I hung my helmet from my cantle and waited. A crowd of men and women appeared from the homes and workshops of the town. It was clearly a thriving community but as the land to the north was bare and barren they were a selfish one.

A slightly portly man came towards me. I was wearing spurs and my banner marked me as a Norman knight, "My Lord, what brings you here to our humble town?"

"I am Sir Richard fitz Malet, the lord of Norton and you are?"

"Robert of Stockadeton, the headman." He waved a hand, "I own the workshop that makes tiles and pots." He had money.

"Some Danes have occupied the village of Norton and driven hence the ones who lived there."

The priest appeared. I still did not like him. He said, "The ones who lived there are dead, I buried them. The ones who moved in are incomers."

I turned and fixed him with a stare. My tone changed from the one used to speak to the headman, "And they were there with my permission, Priest. They had no homes and I gave them one. A Christian thing to do, eh?" I turned back to the headman, "I have given these Danes a day to leave but I am not confident that they will do so. I will have to use force. Are there men you could supply to augment my numbers?"

It was almost as though the headman had not heard my last words. "Danes? I did not know they were Danes."

"Have you any men who will fight to drive these invaders from our land?"

"We have learned not to poke the Danes, My Lord. We have strong walls and we are safe."

They would offer no help. "I am King William's representative in these parts. I command you to provide men."

It was the wrong thing to say. The priest chimed in, "Your King William gave this land to the Bishop of Durham. He can order men to fight but not you, Sir Richard."

I whirled and put my face close to his. I dearly wanted to strike him but knew it was the wrong thing to do. “I have known many priests in my life but you are the first one who has crawled from beneath a stone and hissed. Begone from my sight.”

He looked as though he might object until Conan pushed him to the ground. The Breton said, “Slither away!”

The priest was right and we could expect no help from Durham. I decided to appeal to the men of Stockadeton. I turned to face them, “Your priest and your headman lack a backbone. Are there no men in this town who would go to the aid of a neighbour?”

I saw shamefaced men looking at one another. One stepped forward, “I am Ulf son of Walter. My father fought and died at Fulford Gate. I will come with you and offer my sword and shield.”

Another, standing close to him nodded, “And I will come too. I am Tadgh son of Gandalfr and my grandfather was one of the first to live in Norton. He would not like to hear of pirates desecrating the memory of Bersi Steanasson. You have my axe and shield.”

“Then fetch them now.” As they left I turned to the headman, “When I write next to King William and the Bishop of Durham, I will tell them of this place that needs a lord.” I pointed at the house of the headman, “I wonder if Stockadeton has paid taxes.”

I saw the headman pale. “My Lord, we have few warriors and…”

“I can see that the priest you have is a true reflection of the people of Stockadeton. Who knows, King William promised me another manor, perhaps it will be Stockadeton.” I gave him a smile which I hoped would appear like the smile of a wolf about to devour a sheep. It was petty but it had the desired effect.

When the two men returned we left and headed back to Rag's Worthy.

Chapter 19

The two extra men from Stockadeton might make all the difference for they were both warriors. The men with Algar were less likely to be men who had a shield and weapons. I had Ulf go with Conan and Tadgh joined my Varangians. Ragnar and his sons would also fight with the Varangians. Bergil would lead them. By the time Algar and his people arrived Ragnar and Elfrida had made space for the families. I hoped it would not be for long. Ragnar had shown that he was a good man and I would not abuse his hospitality. Survival in the north hung on fine margins. I would ensure that he was rewarded for his efforts. Algar now had more men than when he had been attacked by the slavers. There were eight men and that was important. We needed as many swords as we could get.

I explained my plan. "I will ride with my Bretons to the village tomorrow. That will be the day that I promised them I would return and they will be expecting me. I will ask them to leave and they will refuse. Bergil will take Galmr and his men. They will hide between the village and here. Ulf and Tadgh will be with them. When the Danes send scouts to find our numbers they will be taken by Galmr. I want them to think I just have eight men to support me. When his scouts fail to return they will have to be more vigilant. There is a limit to how attentive a sentry can be. The longer he watches the less he sees. Let them wait and watch all day. We will blacken our faces tomorrow night. Algar, you know the village better than any. I wish to approach from the river and the east. Can that be done?"

"Easily. The ground on that side of the village can be marshy but the undergrowth that grows will afford cover."

"Then you shall lead us that way. Your men wear no mail. They can eliminate the sentries. That done I want some to watch the path to the drekar. If any of those on the ship try to come to the aid of the village they will stop them." He nodded. "Once the alarm is raised then it will be my men who will be at the fore. We are mailed and have trained together. The task of the rest of you will be to protect our backs."

"We are not afraid to fight, Sir Richard."

"I know, Algar, but we are professionals. The men I lead have fought against the Scots and Danes before now. They know how to hew heads and to take blows on shields. I want these raiders removed from my land. If there are any who survive I want them to return to Denmark and tell others that this land is too expensive to take again." They all seemed satisfied with my plan. The faces I looked to for approval were the Bretons, Varangians and Bergil. They nodded.

That night I sat with my familia. I smiled, "A little premature but do any of you wish to be my steward in this land?" I looked at Galmr who had said before we left that he would consider the position. The situation was now different. This was not a peaceful village. Whoever took it on would have to fight to hold it.

Although he had mentioned it before I was surprised when Galmr spoke, I had thought that the dangers we had seen would have made him reluctant to bring Beth here, "This reminds me of the land where I grew up. I have yet to speak to Beth but I think that I should like to live here."

Folki nodded, "But not alone. Haldir and I would come with you. You have taken a wife but our oath of blood remains still."

I looked at Conan, "You would not choose this?"

He laughed, "My Lord, I cannot see Dervilla being parted from Lady Ealdgyth and with due respect to this land, I do not think it would suit her."

I smiled, "I think you are right, Conan." I looked at Edward, Bergil and my men at arms. They shook their heads.

"Then all we have to do is to win back the village."

Bergil said, "And that means defeating a ship's crew of Danes." He smiled at Galmr, "We shall do our best to win a home for you." We had fought enough together to feel a bond of brotherhood that transcended the lands of our birth.

We went at noon the next day to the village. This time I wore my helmet and we carried the banner. The men who were waiting for us saw double the number of men I had taken before and all of us were mailed. The gate was barred. As the palisade was incomplete it would not cause a problem. They had been waiting for us and Haraldr was at the gates. All those we saw were armed and helmed. We reined in one hundred paces from the walls. I knew that my men were counting the ones on the wall and I addressed the Dane. "Your walls are manned. Does that mean you wish to dispute my right to this manor?"

He laughed, "Of course. What can a handful of horsemen do against warriors such as we?"

"The river is mine also and your ship will also be removed."

He shook his head, "Foolish Norman! The ship is anchored midstream and is guarded. I heard your threat. Do your worst. I shall enjoy using your two swords when your head is on my walls."

I shrugged, "I have given you a fair and Christian warning. Whatever happens next is on your head." I stood in my stirrups as though to study the shallow ditch that ran around the half-built palisade. Then I turned Geoffrey's head and I smiled as I saw the nervous look that Haraldr gave the land close to his walls. He feared a sudden attack over a ditch that would not stop horses and a palisade that was incomplete. His nerves would be stretched even further by the time darkness came. We rode down the track to Rag's Worthy. I knew where Bergil and the Varangians waited but I could not see them. When Haraldr's scouts followed us they would have a surprise. We reined in at the farm and an hour later Bergil and the others came with two bodies slung on spears.

Bergil was matter of fact about the corpses, "Ragnar, have you somewhere we can bury these bodies?"

He pointed back up the track. There was a sign with runes upon it, "There at the crossroads. The sign is an ancient one and the runes mark the road to Rus' Worthy. If they are buried with the post in their bodies then their souls will not be free to haunt us."

Algar said, "We will do that."

Bergil dropped two spears, two swords and two seaxes to the ground, "More weapons and two fewer men to fight."

Galmr said, "My brothers and I will return to the path and keep watch."

The Varangians returned at dusk, they were smiling, "The Danes sent more men, My Lord. They came as a warband but when they found no sign of their men nor evidence of a fight they returned to Norton. There were disgruntled voices."

The unknown was our ally. They would wonder what had happened and would still be in the dark about our true numbers. "Good. Then eat and get some rest. There will be no moon tonight and the skies look cloudy. I will rouse you when it is time to follow Algar."

I would not be taking my shield nor my spear. This would be sword work. We ate well for we had brought supplies with us and did not have to take from Elfrida and her family. We had no priest but before we left we each prayed and confessed our sins to God. There was no intermediary but if the priest in Stockadeton was a measure then we were better off without one. We did not take the horses. We would be approaching with the wind behind us and the smell of horses would alert our enemies. In addition, there was a chance that one might whinny and horses would tell the Danes that Normans were coming.

We left well after midnight. I wanted the Danes to have a long watch knowing that it would tire them. We had managed an hour or so of sleep and even when not sleeping we had not had to watch the track for an attack. We followed Algar as he led us through the trees and shrubs to the river. There was a path which ran along the meandering water. The land was boggy in parts but I could see, as I followed in his footsteps, that we were the first to tread this path for some time. Algar halted when he saw the ship in the river. It was anchored but it was low tide and it was slightly canted. I had been told that it had been damaged but it looked repaired now. Perhaps that was our doing. I counted five faces on the ship. There might be more but better to underestimate than over. It meant at least five fewer men in Norton and added to the two slain by Bergil and Galmr, the odds were coming down. We left four of Algar's men to watch the men on the ship. When the path became drier and we began to ascend I drew a sword. I did not think that there would be sentries on this side for, to the Danes, this would be the safer side. I smelled woodsmoke and saw not only a glow but also the sparks of embers from the fire burning in the air. The Danes had built a fire outside a house, the better to keep watch. It was a mistake for their night vision would be spoiled.

When we reached the edge of the village we halted and Algar looked to me. He had done his part and managed to get us close to the village unseen. There had been no sentries for his men to slay. Now it was time for the knight to take command. I had given detailed instructions before we left Rag's Worthy and I used my sword to marshal the men into line. It would be my mailed men who formed the centre. Edward would be behind me and my men at arms would flank me. Conan and his Bretons were on the right and Bergil and the Varangians to my left. Ragnar, his sons and the two men from Stockadeton were to the right of Conan and Algar and the rest of the marsh men would be on the far left. I intended the bulk of the fighting, and the risks, to be done by my familia. I wanted no one from this land to die. We would draw the mailed men to us and those without training and weapons would just have to deal with the more lightly armed enemies.

There was no undergrowth for we were passing over the fields that Algar and his people had planted. Neither leaves nor twigs crackled. My men had weapons drawn and had shields to their fore. I had my two swords. The only ones ahead who would have shields would be those on the walls. The ones by the fire would either be sleeping or, at best, have just a sword or axe in their hands. The first few moments of our attack were vital. The fire they had lit showed that at least half of the men were around the fires. They would not be able to see us as we were approaching from the shadows. The only faces I saw were on the far side of the fire. Looking beyond the men I saw that there were eight men on the wall. Haraldr was one of them. He and his two shield brothers were marked by their mail that glistened in the firelight.

It was the need for one of the Danes to make water that was our undoing. One with his back to us stood and turned. I saw his white face. We were in the shadows and had blackened faces but his sudden turning caught our movement. He could not know how many we were but he gave a shout and I roared, "Charge!"

I saw the Danes rise and grab weapons. Haraldr and the men on the wall, realising that their watch had been in vain hurried to the ladders to descend.

There were only two ladders. It would slow their descent. It meant the mailed men would reach us later than they would have liked. My two men at arms and I were the first to reach the enemy and as I slashed at the middle of the Dane with the need to make water I drew my second blade. It tore through his tunic and into his flesh. Clutching the writhing snakes that tried to pour forth he dropped to his knees. Alfred and Aethelstan had matured as warriors. A year or so ago they might have been daunted by Danes but they were mailed and well armed. They had fought Danes and Vikings before. Their two opponents, neither of whom had either shields or mail, fell and in that brief encounter the fate of Norton was sealed. Three men were down and we almost had parity of numbers. Galmr and his shield brothers were fighting for a home as were the men from the marshes. The left side of our line raced around the fire and began to hack and slash at the Danes. The ones facing Conan and Ragnar did not even pause to fight. They ran and hurtled down the path we had used for the river.

That left the men who had been on the wall but they were, potentially, the most dangerous. I would not underestimate them. "Aethelstan and Alfred, flank Edward." Conan and his Bretons would be able to aid me. The two warriors with Haraldr both held the long Danish axes and the Bretons would be able to deal with them. I knew that Haraldr would come for me. He had a long axe and his shield around his back. He would be confident.

He roared a challenge and ran straight at me. His shield brothers also swung their axes in long loops. It was good that I had given my command to my two men at arms or they might have been caught by the sudden and ferocious attack. I rammed my left-hand sword at the Dane's face and although he caught it with the haft of his axe the speed of my thrust made him take a step back. His two companions had been trying to get at my men at arms but Conan and Robert combined to take one of them out. My men at arms and Edward could deal with the other. As Haraldr had stepped back I was able to swing my right-hand sword at his side. He, too, had quick hands and his axe head sparked as it crashed against my sword. I still had my left-hand sword and even the quickest hands in the world could not move fast enough to stop its swing. It hacked into his side. It was sharp and well made. It cut through mail links and the Dane's gambeson. It came away bloody but the wound would not be a mortal one. It angered him.

"Pretty boy, I shall split you in twain."

Taillefer would have had a witty rejoinder but I knew better. I wasted neither words nor my attention which was on his weapon. He was raising his axe for another swing. As I had thrust with my left hand the strike would come from his right. Anticipating the move I held up my right-hand sword and as it blocked the blow made a cross with my left-hand sword. I easily held the long weapon.

From behind me I heard Edward shout, "Haraldr is the only one left, My Lord. The rest are dead or fled."

"Kill as many as you can before they leave. I want the threat from pirates gone from my land." The words were intended for Haraldr. "Surrender and you shall live!"

"Never!"

"Then die."

I put my head down and whilst pushing with my two swords against his axe brought my head into his face. It was not a butt but it was a strong push and he staggered a little. I swung both swords at the same time and both bit into his sides. I was lucky in that my left-hand sword found the gap in his mail and this time I sawed into flesh and felt the blade grate against bone. He screamed in pain. I had given him the opportunity to surrender and I would have let him go but now it needed to be ended. Even as he tried to raise his axe in a last desperate strike, I lunged with my right hand and drove the sword into his screaming mouth. My hand jarred as I struck the rear of his skull and then the axe fell from his lifeless hands.

I whirled and saw the Danish bodies. "Where are the others?" He and my men at arms were alone.

Edward pointed his bloody sword, "They chased those who fled down the path we used."

"Then after them. They need to know that I live and Haraldr is dead." I sheathed my swords and taking the Dane's axe hacked off his head. I removed his helmet and held his skull by his long golden hair.

I followed the others down the path. It was clear that the tide was on its way in and that dawn was not too far off. The path was now slippery for we had marched up it and now the Danes had run down it. Our speed was not what I would have wished. We found the discarded weapons and helmets by the river. One of those who had fled had been caught by those watching the path and his body lay at an ungainly angle by the path. The ship was still anchored in the river but it was no longer canted. The only way for those who had survived our attack to get to the ship was to swim. Helmets and swords would have drowned them and these men were survivors. They could always get more weapons. They had left anything that might have drowned them on the bank. The men I had left by the river and my pursuing warriors meant they escaped any place that they could. Algar and the ones who had reached the river first were standing and cheering. They had spears and swords raised in the air in triumph. As I neared the river bank the last of those who had fled boarded.

I stood and held the skull of the Dane in the air and I shouted, "Haraldr Fair Hair is dead. If any come back for vengeance they will meet the same fate." I whirled the head in the air and threw it to land half-way between the ship and the shore.

I saw that the sail was being raised and the one at the steering board called out, "It is done. The Sisters have spun. We will not return."

As the first rays from the rising sun rose, the ship was silhouetted as it tacked to turn around and head down the meandering river to the sea. With such a small crew they would be lucky to get home. If they did then they would view that as a gift from God.

I turned, "Come. Let us bring your people to their new home, Algar." He nodded, "Take what weapons you want."

I saw that Ulf and Tadgh both grabbed two discarded helmets. They would now be better warriors. More importantly they would tell the others in Stockadeton of our exploits. It would do us no harm.

We did not return to Rag's Worthy until well after noon. We waited until the dead had been cleared and thrown into the river and taken to the sea on the tide. There they would feed the fishes and neither the land nor the air would be polluted with their bodies. Algar happily accepted Galmr as the one who would command the manor for me. As he said, before we went to collect our horses, he was not a warrior and the attack by the Danes had shown him that Norton needed a warrior as a leader.

We stayed in Norton for a week. We erected a palisade which encircled the village. It took many trees to do so and the felled trees provided kindling for the winter and, when the stumps were removed, land that could be planted with crops. The palisade was necessary. Until Galmr and his men returned they would have to defend the village and a wall was needed. Once it was all done we bade farewell. Galmr and his Varangians would return as soon as he and Beth were wed. I gave the coins we had taken from Haraldr to Ragnar and Algar. It was not a fortune but I wanted them to know that they were valued and that I would share when I was able. We left and headed for Stockadeton. I wanted to get home quickly and we would use the ferry. It would shorten our journey by more than thirty miles. As we rode through the town I saw that the men we passed were shamefaced. Ulf and Tadgh came from their homes to greet us.

"You have shown us, Sir Richard, that cowering behind our walls is not the way men should be. Those were our neighbours and we shunned them." Ulf glowered at the headman. The priest was noticeable by his absence. "I can promise you that things will change here in Stockadeton. There are others who feel as Tadgh and I do. I will visit with Ragnar and Algar for we need to help each other."

Galmr nodded and said, "And when we return I will hold a Sunday wapentake in Norton. If we can learn to fight together then the land will be safer."

"Aye."

I saw nods from some of the other men. It was a start.

Epilogue

While preparations were completed for Galmr's wedding I wrote a letter to the Bishop of Durham and another one addressed to the king. I let them know what I had done and gave suggestions about how things should move forward. I doubted that much good would come from the Durham missive but if I knew the king he would see an opportunity to strengthen the north by appointing a new lord of the manor in Stockadeton. I hoped he chose well.

The wedding was both joyous and sad. It was joyous because both Beth and Galmr were meant to be joined but sad because I was losing three of the finest warriors I had ever encountered and Ealdgyth was losing one of her friends. There were tears. Conan and his Bretons escorted the newly weds and the Varangians back to their new home. We sent a wagon and we now had enough horses to allow Galmr to be mounted and to keep the wagon. They had seen the benefit of being mounted. The horses he took could be used to pull a plough. They could also pull out the tree stumps. Norton would prosper as new fields were added. Benthe and my steward ensured that they had all that they would need for the winter. When they had gone the manor was emptier. We missed the ones who had moved out.

I sat before my fire with my bride. She cuddled close to me on the couch she had bought, "Well, Richard, is that your gallivanting done?"

I smiled, "Ealdgyth, it is but as I know not what is around the corner I cannot promise anything."

She gave me a kiss and took my hand to lead me to our bedchamber, "Then I shall make the most of you while you are here."

Mathilde was well and so was the baby. Edward was relieved to find them so. Many babies did not survive past the first few months. Maud was more than happy at the return of her husband. Conan and his Bretons returned a fortnight later. They had stayed to help make a deeper ditch around the palisade and to make sure that Galmr and Beth were well settled.

"Algar and his people have oats and barley showing. Our boots did not destroy everything and the woods at Wulfestun teem with game. They will not starve this winter and they hope for a good Christmas. They even pulled out some of the tree stumps. By spring, if the frosts do not come early, they can plough and sow."

We had a fine celebration too and the difference between this Christmas and the last one was that we had many more who were wed. The feast that Christmas was a rich one and as both Dervilla and Ealdgyth found that they were with child, it was as though we had the greatest gift of all. We had endured the storm and survived. Life was good.

The End

Glossary

Alclud - Auckland (Bishop Auckland)
Alvertune - Northallerton
Bidet - another name for a nag or poorer quality horse
Bluberhūsum - Blubberhouses
Caestre - Chester
Cernemude - Charmouth (Dorset)
Chevauchée - a medieval raid normally led by knights
Cingheuuella - Chigwell
Coistrel - a wooden or leather drinking cup that could be carried on a belt.
Din Eidyn - Edinburgh
Donjon - keep (keep was not used until the 14th century)
Douvres - Dover
Dornwaraceaster - Dorchester
Eisicewalt - Easingwold
Faleston - Falstone
Haliwerfolc - The men of the saint (Cuthbert)
Hog bog - a place close to a farm where pigs and fowl could be kept
Jazerant - a padded light coat worn over a mail hauberk
Ledecestre - Leicester
Lincylene - Lincoln
Ljoðahús - Lewis
Maersea - River Mersey
Manchet - the best bread made with wheat flour
Northwic - Norwich
Persebrig - Piercebridge
Pueros - young warriors not yet ready to be a knight
Raveled or yeoman's bread - coarse bread made with wholemeal flour with bran
Remesgat - Ramsgate
Snotingham - Nottingham
Socce - socks also light shoes worn by actors/mummers

Tresche - Thirsk
Ulfketill - Elvington
Ventail - a detachable mail mask
Wallington - A hamlet near to Morpeth
Wallintun - Warrington
Wulfestun - Wolviston
Yeckham - Acomb

Canonical Hours

Matins (nighttime)
Lauds (early morning)
Prime (first hour of daylight)
Terce (third hour)
Sext (noon)
Nones (ninth hour)
Vespers (sunset evening)
Compline (end of the day)

Classes of hawk

This is the list of the hunting birds and the class of people who could fly them. It is taken from the 15th-century Book of St Albans.

Emperor: eagle, vulture, merlin
King: gyrfalcon
Prince: gentle falcon: a female peregrine falcon
Duke: falcon of the loch
Earl: peregrine falcon
Baron: buzzard
Knight: Saker Falcon
Squire: Lanner Falcon
Lady: merlin
Young man: hobby
Yeoman: goshawk
Knave: kestrel
Poor man: male falcon
Priest: sparrowhawk
Holy water clerk: sparrowhawk

Historical Background

A Danish wife was one where a couple married by common consent without a religious ceremony. It was a common practice at the time. It enabled lords to have more than one wife and for those lower down the social scale to be married.

The notion of fire arrows heated in a forge comes from the siege of Brionne in 1092 when Robert Duke of Normandy used the idea. I suspect he would have heard it from his father Duke William. Apologies for allowing my hero to take the credit.

Taillefer is a wonderful character for a novelist. He flashed, a little like Haley's Comet before the battle, briefly across the sky. His only recorded reference was that he asked the duke if he could start the battle. The duke allowed it. Taillefer rode his horse before the English army, showing off riding tricks. Then he juggled with swords, sang a song and challenged any of the English who cared to try to fight him. One housecarl did so and was promptly slain by the skilful Norman. Growing cocky he then rode too close to the companions of the dead housecarl and he was surrounded and he and his horse were butchered. I thoroughly enjoyed making up a backstory for him!

The various battles I describe are, in the main, historical ones but I have added others. The details of the battles are my fiction. I always aim to tell a good story but the historical figures I describe all played their parts. I weave my webs around real people but make up characters to bring them to life.

The Danish invasion and the taking of York were the trigger for King William's revenge. All the Normans in York were slaughtered with the exception of William Malet, his wife and sons. The Danes did leave. They went to the Humber and raided the lands around there. King William paid the Danes to leave. The harrying of the north only lasted a few months and I find it hard to believe that his relatively small army could have destroyed all that was attributed to them. People fled and hid. The Normans took their animals and it was starvation that killed most of the people. It allowed the king to put in place his own knights so that rebellion would not rear its head again.

The English nobles did themselves no favours by changing sides so often. King William is often portrayed as ruthless yet he forgave Gospatric, Morcar and Eadwine not once but twice. It seems to me that he did all in his power to incorporate the English aristocracy into his new kingdom.

Many people wonder why in England we still speak English and not Norman-French. The answer is a simple one. The Norman ladies hired English wet nurses and nannies. They taught the young nobles English for they could not speak Norman.

Hereward was a rebel but his position in English history comes from a piece of fiction written in the middle of the nineteenth century by Reverend Charles Kingsley. The novel shows the power of fiction for he took a relatively unknown man and made him into a sort of Robin Hood character. The truth was that he sacked a cathedral and joined the Danes in their rebellion. His end is as mysterious as his life. What is known that when Ely was retaken then the rebellion in the Fens petered out. Hereward disappears from history.

The taking of the Morcar is well documented. Eadwine is a little murkier. The exact date of his death is not universally agreed upon nor the manor of his death. Some said he was betrayed to the Normans and others that his own men slew him. English rebels did support King Malcolm and after the Scottish king had married Edgar's sister, Margaret, he became more aggressive towards England.

In his defence King William did forgive both Gospatric and Waltheof many times. In the end one would be executed the other die in exile.

This is a piece of fiction and there are some events that are made up by me. Obviously the Ealdgyth story line is one. King William did invade Scotland but I made up the skirmish on the Tweed and the battle by the loch. The Peace and Treaty of Abernethy were very real and I have written the effects accurately. This was the beginning of a long dispute between England and Scotland. Edward 1st almost resolved it but failed. It would last until King James VIth of Scotland became King James 1st of England and even after that time there was rebellion, 1745 marks the end of a war that began in 1072.

The next books will be the story of how the Normans took Saxon England and changed it forever. The series will end before the Anarchy series starts.

Companions of Duke William:

1) Robert de Beaumont, later 1st Earl of Leicester

(2) Eustace, Count of Boulogne, a.k.a. Eustace II
(3) William, Count of Évreux
(4) Geoffrey, Count of Mortagne and Lord of Nogent, later Count of Perche
(5) William fitz Osbern, later 1st Earl of Hereford
(6) Aimeri, Viscount of Thouars a.k.a. Aimery IV
(7) Walter Giffard, Lord of Longueville
(8) Hugh de Montfort, Lord of Montfort-sur-Risle
(9) Ralph de Tosny, Lord of Conches a.k.a. Raoul II
(10) Hugh de Grandmesnil
(11) William de Warenne, later 1st Earl of Surrey
(12) William Malet, Lord of Graville
(13) Odo, Bishop of Bayeux, later Earl of Kent
(14) Turstin fitz Rolf a.k.a. Turstin fitz Rou and Turstin le Blanc
(15) Engenulf de Laigle
These are the names of the knights we know who followed Duke William to England. There were others as these were the only fifteen whose names were recorded; I have made the others up.

Books used in the research

- The Norman Achievement - Richard Cassady
- Norman Knight - Gravett and Hook
- Hastings 1066 - Gravett
- The Norman Conquest of the North - Kappelle
- Norman Stone Castles (2) - Gravett and Hook
- A Short History of the Norman Conquest of England - Edward Augustus Freeman
- The Tower of London - A L Rowse
- The Tower of London - Lapp and Parnell
- The Adventure of English - Melvyn Bragg

Griff Hosker October 2024

Other books by Griff Hosker

If you enjoyed reading this book, then why not read another one by the author?

Ancient History

Roman Rebellion
(The Roman Republic100 BC-60 BC)

Legionary

The Sword of Cartimandua Series
(Germania and Britannia 50 A.D. – 128 A.D.)

Ulpius Felix- Roman Warrior (prequel)
The Sword of Cartimandua
The Horse Warriors
Invasion Caledonia
Roman Retreat
Revolt of the Red Witch
Druid's Gold
Trajan's Hunters
The Last Frontier
Hero of Rome
Roman Hawk
Roman Treachery
Roman Wall
Roman Courage

The Wolf Brethren series
(Britain in the late 6th Century)

Rebellion

Saxon Dawn
Saxon Revenge
Saxon England
Saxon Blood
Saxon Slayer
Saxon Slaughter
Saxon Bane
Saxon Fall: Rise of the Warlord
Saxon Throne
Saxon Sword

Medieval History

The Dragon Heart Series

Viking Slave *
Viking Warrior *
Viking Jarl *
Viking Kingdom *
Viking Wolf *
Viking War*
Viking Sword
Viking Wrath
Viking Raid
Viking Legend
Viking Vengeance
Viking Dragon
Viking Treasure
Viking Enemy
Viking Witch
Viking Blood
Viking Weregeld
Viking Storm
Viking Warband
Viking Shadow

Rebellion

Viking Legacy
Viking Clan
Viking Bravery

The Norman Genesis Series
Hrolf the Viking *
Horseman *
The Battle for a Home *
Revenge of the Franks *
The Land of the Northmen
Ragnvald Hrolfsson
Brothers in Blood
Lord of Rouen
Drekar in the Seine
Duke of Normandy
The Duke and the King

Danelaw
(England and Denmark in the 11th Century)

Dragon Sword *
Oathsword *
Bloodsword *
Danish Sword*
The Sword of Cnut

Norseman
Norse Warrior

New World Series
Blood on the Blade *
Across the Seas *
The Savage Wilderness *

Rebellion

The Bear and the Wolf *
Erik The Navigator *
Erik's Clan *
The Last Viking*

The Vengeance Trail *

The Conquest Series
(Normandy and England 1050-1100)

Hastings*
Conquest
Rebellion

The Aelfraed Series
(Britain and Byzantium 1050 A.D. - 1085 A.D.)

Housecarl *
Outlaw *
Varangian *

The Reconquista Chronicles
(Spain in the 11th Century)

Castilian Knight *
El Campeador *
The Lord of Valencia *

The Anarchy Series
(England 1120-1180)

English Knight *
Knight of the Empress *
Northern Knight *

Rebellion

Baron of the North *
Earl *
King Henry's Champion *
The King is Dead *
Warlord of the North*
Enemy at the Gate*
The Fallen Crown*
Warlord's War*
Kingmaker*
Henry II
Crusader
The Welsh Marches
Irish War
Poisonous Plots
The Princes' Revolt
Earl Marshal
The Perfect Knight

Border Knight
(1182-1300)

Sword for Hire *
Return of the Knight *
Baron's War *
Magna Carta *
Welsh Wars *
Henry III *
The Bloody Border *
Baron's Crusade*
Sentinel of the North*
War in the West*
Debt of Honour
The Blood of the Warlord
The Fettered King

Rebellion

de Montfort's Crown
The Ripples of Rebellion

Sir John Hawkwood Series

(France and Italy 1339- 1387)

Crécy: The Age of the Archer *
Man At Arms *
The White Company *
Leader of Men *
Tuscan Warlord *
Condottiere*
Legacy

Lord Edward's Archer

Lord Edward's Archer *
King in Waiting *
An Archer's Crusade *
Targets of Treachery *
The Great Cause *
Wallace's War *
The Hunt*
The Prince and the Archer

Struggle for a Crown

(1360- 1485)

Blood on the Crown *
To Murder a King *
The Throne *
King Henry IV *
The Road to Agincourt *
St Crispin's Day *
The Battle for France *

Rebellion

The Last Knight *
Queen's Knight *
The Knight's Tale*

Tales from the Sword I

(*Short stories from the Medieval period)*

Tudor Warrior series
(England and Scotland in the late 15th and early 16th century)

Tudor Warrior *
Tudor Spy *
Flodden*

Conquistador
(England and America in the 16th Century)

Conquistador *
The English Adventurer *

English Mercenary
(The 30 Years War and the English Civil War)

Horse and Pistol*
Captain of Horse

Modern History

East India Saga
East Indiaman

Rebellion

The Napoleonic Horseman Series

Chasseur à Cheval
Napoleon's Guard
British Light Dragoon
Soldier Spy
1808: The Road to Coruña
Talavera
The Lines of Torres Vedras
Bloody Badajoz
The Road to France
Waterloo

The Lucky Jack American Civil War series

Rebel Raiders
Confederate Rangers
The Road to Gettysburg

Soldier of the Queen series

Soldier of the Queen*
Redcoat's Rifle*
Omdurman*
Desert War

The British Ace Series

(World War 1)

1914
1915 Fokker Scourge
1916 Angels over the Somme
1917 Eagles Fall
1918 We will remember them
From Arctic Snow to Desert Sand
Wings over Persia

Rebellion

Combined Operations series

(1940-1951)

Commando *
Raider *
Behind Enemy Lines
Dieppe
Toehold in Europe
Sword Beach
Breakout
The Battle for Antwerp
King Tiger
Beyond the Rhine
Korea
Korean Winter

Tales from the Sword II

(Short stories from the Modern period)

Books marked thus *, are also available in the audio format.

For more information on all of the books then please visit the author's website at www.griffhosker.com where there is a link to contact him or visit his Facebook page: Griff Hosker at Sword Books or follow him on Twitter: @HoskerGriff or Sword (@swordbooksltd)

If you wish to be on the mailing list then contact the author through his website.: Griff Hosker at Sword Books

Made in the USA
Las Vegas, NV
29 April 2025

21509523R00198